In the Way of All Flesh

Caitlin Alise Donovan

Young Adult Books
by Regal Crest

ISBN 978-1-61929-420-2

First Printing 2019

9 8 7 6 5 4 3 2 1

Cover design by AcornGraphics

Published by:

Regal Crest Enterprises

Find us on the World Wide Web at
http://www.regalcrest.biz

Published in the United States of America

Acknowledgments

There are so many people behind the scenes who support an author when she is writing a book. Fully expressing the depth of my gratitude to everyone who gave a word of encouragement when I needed it would be a book unto itself. But I will do my utmost to give you all the credit you deserve in this short space.

The first person who should be acknowledged is my mother, Janene Donovan, who is always my greatest ally and was my constant shoulder to cry on throughout this whole process. I may not have been able to write even the first word of this without a mother 100% supportive of my dreams behind me. I dedicated this book to her because she is the strongest and warmest person I know. I wouldn't be who I am today without her. I feel a bit awkward about the lack of mothers in this book because of that (though there are some good future moms), but I did model the positive traits of Manee's father — such as his kindness, dedication and willingness to stand up for his daughter — after her.

I'm also blessed with a dad who inquires about my writing and lets me pursue my dreams, so I thank him as well. The rest of my family is also lovely. Thanks to Jean, Bond, Michael, Kelly, Bella, Jonah and Fia especially for your constant enthusiasm and for throwing a great publication celebration. You're all stars.

I'd be remiss not to thank my teachers and classmates from both UNCA and Queens University in Charlotte. I wrote this book while completing my Bachelors and then my Masters in Fine Arts. The advice and encouragement I received from both educators and my peers at the workshops greatly shaped this book. Fred Leebron in particular offered me a lot of support, but so did many others. I deeply appreciate all of you.

I'd also like to thank my sensitivity reader, J. The feedback was invaluable.

Many thanks to all my friends both in the flesh (hah) and online who offered me constant motivation and support. There were lots of times I felt like giving up, especially during the long slog of searching for a publisher. But you guys never gave up on me and that's what kept me going. It means the world to me. Thanks especially to Will for answering my questions and giving great feedback.

Finally, thank you to everyone at Regal Crest who made this book possible: my editors, Mary Hettel and Micheala Lynn; the graphic designer responsible for the lovely cover, Ann McMan, and the woman in charge of it all, Cathy Bryerose. I'm grateful to you for giving me a chance and letting me finally get this story out there.

Dedication

To my mother, who showed me how to love and live.

Part One

Chapter One

THE BACK OF my neck prickles. Stephanie Pierce is watching me again. I'm used to people hounding me, but it usually doesn't go on for this long. Stephanie has been bothering me since the beginning of the school year, and I wish she would hurry up and get bored with it already. It's hot enough in the stuffy, cramped classroom without this girl's burning gaze making it worse.

Our ninth-grade teacher, Charlotte, coughs and nervously runs her fingers through her limp blonde hair. Her hand starts to creep toward the cigarettes she keeps in her pocket.

"I'm going to go get some papers. Everyone, keep working on your study guides," Charlotte says before slipping out the door.

The students immediately erupt into chatter. I jerk my chair around to face Stephanie. This girl is so beautiful that just looking at her makes my heart pound faster. Her perfectly arched brows and high cheekbones give her every glance this sharp, smart edge. She exudes confidence in a way that I envy. Her dark hair fans out in wild waves, giving the impression that it's whipping fearlessly in the wind, even though the air is perfectly still. Her skin is a warm, rich brown, and her full, rosy lips are curved into a playful smile as she watches me with her chin cupped in her hands.

"Why are you so interested in me?" I hiss.

Stephanie shrugs. "I think you're cute."

I groan. That is such an obvious lie. My looks couldn't contrast more with Stephanie's sunny beauty. I'm plain and chubby. My only notable feature is the stringy black hair that covers my face like a shroud. "Whatever. I know you're just fascinated by the freak show. Soon enough, you'll get bored and move on."

Stephanie's expression softens. "Sounds like you learned that from experience." Then her mischievous smile is back and sharper than ever. "But *my* experience has taught me how to pick out people who stay truly interesting, even when they're not new or exciting anymore."

She's just making me more and more irritated. "How can you tell who's interesting?"

Stephanie leans close, her voice dropping to a whisper. "It's easy. They're the people who try to stay out of the way and hide how interesting they are."

My breath catches in my throat as I stare directly into Stephanie's eyes, which are her most striking feature. The brown and black in them pulses and flickers like the earth about to crack. Sometimes, I swear there are strange lights dancing at the edges of her irises. No matter how hard I try, I can never look away.

"Yeah, well," I finally manage to mumble. "You might find I have good reason to hide how interesting I am." I draw myself up, giving Stephanie the darkest glare I can muster. "The last person who looked too deep pretty much drowned."

Stephanie freezes in her seat, not even breathing.

And then she bursts out laughing.

I slump as Stephanie clutches her sides and rocks back and forth, nearly overturning her chair. Her laughter echoes throughout the room, and our classmates stop their conversations and turn to stare.

"God," Stephanie says, wiping tears from her eyes. "You're even cuter when you try to be scary."

I blush. "Shut up," I mumble, looking at my lap. I hate the feeling of everyone staring at me; the heat is already suffocating enough. I wipe my face and wince as sweat dribbles down into the spaces between my fingers. My gloves are completely soaked.

Stephanie is still chortling. "Seriously, as if a tiny little girl like you could ever hurt anyone!" She moves to hit me on the arm, and I yelp in response, nearly falling from my desk in my attempt to avoid her.

"Christ, seriously! Would you cut it the hell out, Stephanie?" Callie Moore snarls from her desk a few seats beyond me. She's leaning back in her chair with her thick legs crossed. Her black braid twitches as she looks at us through hooded eyes. "I hope she gives you her syphilis or whatever she has."

"Like she could! We're not even having sex!" Stephanie scoffs. "Syphilis *is* only if you have sex, right?" she mutters at me out of the side of her mouth.

I just sink into my oversized turtleneck and wish I could sweat myself to death.

"Anyway!" Stephanie focuses on Callie again. "Manee doesn't have a disease, so just shut up, Callie!"

"Then why the hell would she dress like a mummy?" Callie rolls her words out slowly and clearly, as if Stephanie is a dangerous animal she needs to calm. They're punctuated by the earsplitting screech of chair legs scraping against cheap linoleum as she turns her chair around to face us directly.

"Stephanie, don't," I say quickly, but there's no stopping this girl.

"Manee is cursed!"

Callie laughs uproariously and so does half the class. I'm going to pass out from embarrassment. I *knew* I never should have said that to Stephanie; it had just slipped out back when we first met.

"What are you smoking?" Callie snorts.

"She's crazy," says one of the boys watching us, but it's stated in an indulgent, almost affectionate manner. I get treated like an untouchable for keeping to myself and dressing strangely, but because Stephanie is pretty and sociable, her over-the-top antics are viewed as "quirky" rather than annoying. The world isn't fair.

"It's true!" Stephanie says, jumping up from her seat. "Don't think you're wiser just 'cause you're older than me, Callie. You're the one who's scared to go near her!"

Callie's face darkens and she gets up from her seat, knocking her chair to the floor as she draws herself up to her full height. "You think I'm scared?"

I tense. Callie is the biggest girl in our class thanks to being held back two years, and right now she looms like a mountain—no, a volcano about to erupt.

"You think you're so damn cute," Callie scoffs, tossing her braid. "But you're a stupid little twit. She's given you some cracked-out story because you'll eat it up. I'll show you her curse is nothing more than fungus flesh."

Callie takes a step toward me.

"No!" I jump up, nearly overturning my desk in my effort to get away. I look around the room desperately. Where is Charlotte, why does she have to smoke so damn much?

All the kids in the classroom are getting up and moving closer to see the confrontation better. They converge on me, forming human walls, eyes all round with curiosity. I'm in the back row so I'm easy to corner. Now I can't make a break for it without risking contact. Fighting means contact too.

My eyes dart from side to side until they fall on Stephanie, who's still standing at her desk, biting her lip and looking unsure about what to do.

'You said you were my friend. Prove it. Friends help each other!' I want to shout this, but my voice has died. I can only communicate with beseeching eyes.

"You don't need to freak out. We're not gonna think less of you for seeing it. You always go off by yourself anyway, why do you care what we think?" Callie takes another ominous step forward as I back up against the wall. "You just wanna feel sorry for yourself."

Stephanie's eyes shift between the two of us. I press flat as I can, trying to make myself one with the wall. I wish I could just melt into it, remain there forever, suspended and safe in the space between.

Finally, Stephanie shoves her desk aside, putting herself between Callie and me, her hand on the large girl's shoulder. "C'mon, leave her alone."

Callie shakes her off. "You want to see more than anyone, Stephanie, so shove off."

"Come on," Stephanie says again, but the protest is weak. There's something sharp and coldly curious in her eyes as she looks over at me, like a scientist watching an experiment unfold. Her hand drops to her side, and she just stands there, staring.

I give up on her and run for it, ducking under Callie's raised arm. To Stephanie's credit, she moves aside to make an opening for me, but it's too little too late. Callie grabs my wrist mid-step, forcing my sleeve up before I can react. Her meaty hand claps down on my trembling arm.

"There's nothing there! So what, you just didn't want to touch us? You think you're better, is that it? How does it feel to be touched by scum, then?" Callie growls, squeezing tightly.

I can only stare hopelessly into her dark, furious eyes as the familiar pulling sensation begins. It's like my brain is a spaceship floating in the starry expanse inside my skull, only now the ship's window had been broken and the pressure was so great everything is being sucked out into the atmosphere.

Every time it happens, there's this vague sense of the person who touched me enveloping me, like I've got to pass through their shadow on the way to their fate. Callie's is excruciating. I'm suffocating; my brain is heavy and dull in my head. My flesh wriggles on my bones and I hate it. I want to rip it all off and be unrecognizable.

Then it's over. I'm no longer inside Callie's brain but in Callie's future. Her near future, apparently. My stomach buckles. The Callie in front of me doesn't look any older than the Callie I know now.

She's sitting at a bus stop, hunched over and clutching a

duffle bag to her chest. It's near a busy intersection, and cars are rushing past at lightning speed. A gloomy gray sky makes the entire street look sad. The pavement is cracked and dotted with puddles from a recent rainstorm. A black car whizzes through one of the puddles near Callie, drenching her, but she doesn't react at all. She just keeps staring at the pavement, looking more like a crumpled rag doll than a person. I'd always seen this girl as a hulk, an advancing giant, but now everything about her seems small, like she's shrinking in on herself.

I don't really have a physical form during these visions, if that's what you want to call them. I can't feel my body or anything. I can only see and think. It's like that weird feeling I get in dreams sometimes, where I'm a consciousness floating around without a body, simply witnessing events. I sometimes imagine myself as eyeballs floating in the air, but those eyeballs would have to be invisible since nobody ever sees me during these things. I can't blink or look away either. The only thing I'm capable of doing is shifting my point of view, which I do now, moving my perspective closer to Callie.

Callie's eyes are not like I've ever seen them. Instead of being narrowed in anger or alight with malicious laughter, they are dull and empty, the color of decaying tree bark. There are deep shadows under them. Her cheeks are raw and chapped looking. It's clear she's been crying hard recently, but now even tears have abandoned her. Between that and the duffle bag, she's probably running away from home or something.

A car horn honks loudly. Callie's head jerks up and she stares down the street. A spasm of fear crosses her face, and she stands up, still clutching her bag. Her eyes dart back and forth and then, without warning, she dashes directly into traffic.

I want to scream at her to stop, but I have no voice. The street erupts with the screeching of brakes being slammed down and the loud blares of horns as Callie weaves through the intersection. Most of the cars on the road quickly skid to a stop. But one doesn't. A large red SUV hurtles forward, right at the girl in the middle of the street.

When Callie sees what's coming, she freezes in her tracks. The blood drains from her face. Her skin turns the color of sour milk.

Get out of the way! Get out of the way! I try to shout at her with all my might, but of course it's utterly futile.

As two tons of screaming metal speeds toward her, Callie's body relaxes. She stands there, closes her eyes, and lets it happen.

I want so desperately to close my eyes as well, but, as always, I can't. No matter how hard I beg for this vision to turn off, nothing will happen. I am helpless. I have to watch as the car smashes into Callie. Watch as Callie's body folds like wet laundry. Watch as she hits the ground with a sickening crack. Watch as the tire rolls over her chest like it's running over a speed bump. Hear her bones shatter, the sound ringing through the air like gunshots.

The car finally screeches to a halt, but it is far, far too late. Callie lies flat on the ground, her chest completely caved in, jagged bits of bone sticking out. Blood bubbles out of her nose and mouth, and her eyes swell, the skin around them turning shiny and purple. Her empty gaze shifts slightly until her eyes are boring right through me. I feel certain that Callie sees me watching now and sees me not as a comfort but as the Grim Reaper, the loss of all hope, the final phantom sent to torment her.

As people gather around, Callie struggles to breathe through the shattered cavity that is now her chest. All that comes out is a strangled rasping moan, high and piercing, like a muffled scream, or a dog keening. It grows softer and softer until at last, she goes completely silent, eyes still and unseeing.

And finally, I am pulled back to the present.

Callie's eyes are no longer still and unseeing, but narrowed and frantic.

"What the hell!" She shoves me away. "What did you do to me? God, I feel dizzy!"

I run. I run as fast as my trembling legs can carry me, plowing right by Stephanie. I fling the classroom door open and sprint through the parking lot, cupping my hands in front of my mouth as I heave. I barely manage to make it to the abandoned playground before everything in my stomach empties out all over the mulch.

Chapter Two

"MANEE? OH, JEEZ."

I didn't hear Stephanie come after me. I wipe my burning mouth and don't open my eyes, hoping that if I keep still and ignore her, Stephanie will just go away. But then Callie's purpled eyes and keening cry flashes in the darkness behind my eyelids, and I cough up bile from hitherto unexplored depths of my stomach.

My body shakes so badly I fall to my knees. I'm so busy hacking I barely notice when Stephanie pulls back my hair, ensuring my stringy black mop doesn't get plastered with any more regurgitated food. It only really registers when I'm finally unable to vomit anymore and Stephanie lets go. It takes a few seconds before I can bring myself to look behind me. Stephanie is gone.

I bow my head. What was I expecting? Of course she left, this is repulsive.

But then Stephanie reappears with some wet paper towels from the school bathroom. She kneels next to me and puts a hand on my shoulder. She dabs at my mouth and hair with the towel, cleaning up the sick. Her touch is hesitant and gentle, two words I never would have associated with Stephanie before. I feel the warm weight of her hand even through my shirt.

"You shouldn't touch me," I murmur. The words feel heavy as they leave my lips. I jerk away from Stephanie before skin-to-skin contact is made, leaving her hand with the rag hanging in midair. "Besides," I say, hugging my shuddering body. "You didn't help me before. Why now?"

"I tried," Stephanie begins, then she stops herself. "No, you're right. I didn't really try. I wanted to see. And that was wrong. I just didn't think it would be this hard on you."

I'm surprised at the bluntness of the statement. Is she being real? I don't know what to think. As she stares at the ground, I turn away and try to cover up my vomit with the surrounding mulch.

"I'm so sorry," Stephanie says hesitantly. "I'll leave if you want me to."

I just keep digging up mulch with my fingers. I'm honestly not sure what I want.

"Do you want to talk about what happened?"

There it is. I bite back a bitter laugh. Of course that's what she really wants to know. I stop my digging and look directly at the girl crouched next to me. She cringes. I must be giving her a piercing look. Well, it's good for her to feel what it's like being on the receiving end for once.

Something inside me is ready to burst, like an invisible hand has clamped down on some organ, making it swell bigger and bigger until it's finally ready to explode and spew everywhere. I run my fingers agitatedly through my vomit-plastered hair.

"You really want to know?" I snap, glaring furiously at the ground. "Do you *really*?"

Stephanie is silent. The rusted-out swings behind her creak faintly in the wind. I let out a small, hysterical giggle, scraping my nails against my forehead.

"Okay, then here it is! The big scoop!" I croak. "What happened was that I saw her die, thanks to you. That's what I see when I touch people! Their deaths. So there you go! There's the dirt you were looking for! Now you don't have to bother pretending to be my friend. Go ahead and tell the whole class the hot gossip! I'm sure that'll get you in with the cool kids like you want!"

I'm breathing hard by the end of the rant and as soon as the words leave my mouth, I realize what a crushing mistake it is. Stephanie will spread this through the class, and it's sure to get back to a teacher. I'll be sent to the psych ward again. But maybe it's for the best. I mean, look at me. Maybe that really is where I belong. At least if I'm sent away, that means I won't be here when *that* happens to Callie. I shut my eyes and the balloon of rage inside me deflates. I'm just so tired.

"Callie must have died pretty horribly, then," Stephanie says softly.

I grit my teeth, squeezing my eyes shut even tighter. Why is she still here?

"Yeah, she sure did."

"Do you think there's any way we can help her?"

My eyes snap open. Stephanie's gaze is distant and her mouth is pursed in a fretful sort of way.

"Are you for real?" I growl. "You believe me?"

"Well, it kinda fits with how upset you are and Callie feeling something weird when she touched you, so, yeah, I guess I do." Stephanie tilts her head. "What, no one's ever believed you before?"

"Only a girl in a mental institution," I say with suspicion.

Stephanie laughs. "My brother's always telling me I belong in one of those, so I guess that explains it."

I don't buy this. I'm not sure what Stephanie has to gain from continuing to talk to me like this, but there's no way I've found another Jocelyn.

"I mean, even if you are lying, I'd feel really bad if Callie ended up dying because I didn't believe you." Stephanie taps her chin thoughtfully. "So what do you think we should do to help her?"

The little cluster of nerves at the base my skull aches. I rub the spot. "Look, I don't know what kind of game you're playing here, but there's nothing we can do to help. It would only make things worse, trust me. She doesn't even want our help. She wants to run away and she probably also wants to die."

"I see, so she runs away from home and gets herself killed," Stephanie looks up at the sky and sighs mournfully. "Ahhh, she does seem like that type."

"What?" I say, forgetting everything else for a minute in my confusion. "No, she doesn't!"

"Well, she always seems pretty unhappy to me." Stephanie bites her lip.

"What? The way she lords over everyone?"

"Haven't you heard bullies take it out on others because they hate themselves?"

"Yeah, but no one actually believes that," I snort.

"I mean, she was held back and everything."

I'm getting pretty sick of Stephanie acting like she has everything figured out. I force myself into a standing position, ignoring my dizziness, and look down at the girl crouching in the dirt. "Well, trust me, trying to stop her will do more harm than good. She's going to run away from home and she's going to die and nothing will stop that. You can't change someone's fate."

"You know that for a fact?" Stephanie asks.

"Yes, I do!" I cry, my cheeks burning. It's not fair this girl can just take everything in stride while I'm falling apart at the seams. "Look, I tried to save my grandmother when I saw what was going to happen to her. I tried to tell them all. But they thought I was making it up. I told her to take care of her heart so she didn't have to have any surgery. That reminded my grandma to visit the doctor for a checkup. And you know what? That doctor found an 'urgent problem.' They did an emergency operation and she died. She was allergic to the anesthesia! All you do when you try to change things is speed up someone's death." I spit the last part out and wait for the impact on Stephanie.

Stephanie continues to rub her chin, carefully mulling it over. Finally, she focuses on me again, her expression serious. "Well, not to be insensitive, but it sounds like your grandmother was screwed either way, so I wouldn't really go off that one time. I think we can help Callie. If we don't, her death's on our heads, y'know?"

I gape at her. Not to be insensitive? Here, I stupidly told this girl things I've never told anybody, not even therapists, and this is what I get. Of course.

"I said something wrong there, didn't I?" Stephanie scrambles to her feet and puts her hands up like someone surrendering. "Sorry, I do that a lot!"

I shake my head numbly. "It's fine." I kick some more dirt over my vomit. "Thanks for helping me. I think I need to go home now. Not really feeling that great, you know?"

I turn and start the walk back to the brown-brick office park our crappy little charter school shares with some roofing business.

"I really did want to make you feel better!" Stephanie calls after me.

I keep walking but turn my head slightly to see behind me. She's shouting with her hands cupped over her mouth. When she realizes I'm not going to stop, her arms fall to her sides.

I can't help but feel a twinge of pity, so I call back, "I do feel better, it's okay," in a flat sort of voice.

In a way that's true. It's as if someone has scraped my insides raw, but at least I'm not shaking anymore. I still feel the weight of Stephanie's warm hand on my shoulder. It was nice. For a while. But it wasn't meant to last. It never is.

Chapter Three

THE ONLY PROBLEM with going home early is that my dad has to pick me up, and that means being pelted with a million questions.

"Did you have an episode?" He prods as soon as we get into the car. "Should we call your therapist?"

"No!" I assure him quickly. I'd only recently gotten him to stop insisting on therapy. "It's just a bug or something, I started feeling dizzy and throwing up out of nowhere."

"You're probably overheated from wearing all those layers." He sighs as we cruise down the highway. "I wish you'd stop."

I've got to change the direction of this conversation quickly. "Overheating makes someone throw up?"

"Maybe it does. You don't know! You're not a scientist!" Dad says petulantly. I'm often told I get my immaturity from him.

"Neither are you!"

"That's for sure," he laughs, tugging on the Looney Tunes-patterned tie around his neck. Then he frowns, his eyes losing their usual playful twinkle. "And that means I should probably take you to a doctor to figure out why you're feeling sick. Are you sure it's not a fever?"

He reaches over to feel my forehead, but I jerk away from his touch. He freezes and we just look at each other for a second. He can't hide the hurt in his eyes. I refuse to hide the fear in mine.

He pulls his hand back. "Sorry," he says, in a slightly strained voice. "I forgot."

We spend the rest of the ride home in awkward silence.

As soon as we arrive, I rush upstairs. There's always something comforting about being in my own room. The kids at school might be surprised if they ever found out that gloomy Manee Srikwan papers her walls with pictures of superheroes, from Sailor Moon to Superman, but I really do love a flashy fighter for justice. I kick aside some manga and comics strewn on the floor, settle down on my fluffy bedspread, and pull my huge stuffed cat close to my chest. I breathe into its soft, fake fur and try not to think about anything that happened today.

Peace and quiet doesn't last long. Dad pops in soon to ply me with food. Ten minutes later, he's asking me to put a thermometer in my mouth. I tell him he should get back to work, but of course he doesn't listen. "Not while my daughter is sick!"

I only get some relief when my sister comes home and inevitably demands attention with whatever drama she's embroiled in today. I listen to her stomp around and rant about some obnoxious boy in her high school's charity club, who only causes trouble for dear Ms. Carnahan, that club advisor she so adores.

I lie back and let Mai's lamentations wash over me. There's something almost comforting about hearing my sister's problems. It would be so nice to live in a world where my biggest issue is classmates being annoying about their crush on the hot teacher.

But I'm stuck in my world. And in my world, the issue with my obnoxious classmates is one of them is well on her way to becoming a pile of gore on the pavement.

I've been avoiding the thought, but it's lying in wait like a thumbtack buried in my brain, ready to make me stumble on its sharp point.

Callie is going to die. She is going to die horribly. And it's going to happen soon.

I curl up into a ball, trying to bundle up in my body heat, but still I'm freezing cold. What if it's this year? God, it probably will be.

I wonder how Stephanie will deal when it happens. I don't buy that she really believes me. Stephanie is the kind of person who's eager to be the hero on some grand adventure. It's all just a fantasy to her. I supplied her with a cool quest, a game of "Save Callie," and she's ready to win. She's not ready for the crushing reality.

But when Callie dies, Stephanie will see how helpless we all really are. She'll lose that dancing light in her eyes and her warm, confident smile will fade. The girl who boldly offered me her hand and beamed at the idea of being cursed will be gone for good.

I want to say it will serve her right, that it will be a wake-up call she needs to hear, but instead the thought makes my chest ache. When Stephanie flashes that daring, toothy grin and says anything is possible, you almost believe it. I don't want to see her lose that. I don't want to see Stephanie become like me.

I PLEAD SICK the next day, saying that I'm still nauseous. The museum won't let my father miss any more work, so he reluctantly allows me to stay home alone.

I spend the day immersed in cheesy manga, anime, and superhero stuff. It's the best way to get my mind off things. My favorite stories are the kind where a good heart and the power of teamwork can accomplish anything, where people who fight each other eventually see the light and become best friends. In these stories, death is a short vacation and the good guys always come back. It's the beautiful world Jocelyn and I wanted, crystallized on page and screen. It's nice taking day trips in that world and forgetting the rules of the real one.

I often draw the characters from these stories. I try reproducing panels from the comics I read once in a while, though I can't resist adding my own flourishes. I realize suddenly with a jolt of embarrassment that the hero I'm drawing, the one who brings back the dead, looks a lot like me. I crumple up the paper, disgusted at myself. I'm thinking too much like Stephanie now. I can't go completely forgetting reality like that.

The doorbell rings. Pulling on my gloves, I clomp down the stairs and cut through the living room to get to the front door. I peer through the peephole and jump back when I see who's on the other side. In my shock, I rip the door open without thinking.

"How the hell did you get here?" I exclaim at Stephanie.

"Looked you up," she says cheerfully. She's carrying a box of cookies. "I just wanted to apologize. Can I come in?"

I want to say no, but I can't bring myself to just slam the door in her face.

"Your cookies can," I settle on, stepping to the side so Stephanie can enter. "Oh, um, you have to take off your —"

Stephanie kicks off her shoes before I can even finish my sentence and marches in. She immediately makes herself at home, plopping down on the living room couch and setting the cookies on the coffee table. She surveys her surroundings with an appraising eye. The room is neat and bright thanks to Mai and Dad's conscientious care. Two squashy armchairs sit across from the coffee table, and the mantelpiece and walls are bedecked with happy pictures of our family. There are a few colorful paintings Dad had gotten as gifts from the museum too. The brightness of it all distracts guests from our cheap furniture and how old the TV in the corner is.

"It's a really nice place," Stephanie offers.

"Thanks." I wobble at the doorway, unsure of what to do. "Uh, do you want anything to drink?"

"That's okay," Stephanie says. "I just wanted to talk to you. I feel really bad. I've been going over what I said and I feel like I just sort of barged in and that's why you were mad. I didn't mean to say that if people die it's your fault or anything."

"That's not what I'm really upset about." I walk over to one of the squashy chairs and sit down. Clasping my hands in front of me, I force myself to look Stephanie in the eye. It pisses me off that her eyes are the same general shape and color as my own. I hate seeing something so reminiscent of myself on such a pretty person. It's like the world wants to tell me, "Hey, it's not like your individual features are heinous, it's just the composition that's a mess." I shake it off.

"I'm worried you think this is a game. You don't understand it's real. If you try to save Callie and she dies, and I know that she will, I don't think you'll take it well."

Stephanie is silent for a minute, looking down at her feet. Then she looks up and I'm taken aback by how much her eyes have changed. There's none of that familiar light and cheer in them. It's like the candle inside her was blown out.

"I'd get through it," Stephanie mutters. "It wouldn't be a new experience for me, not being able to save someone."

I stare Stephanie, unsure of what to do with that. "Then why?"

"Because I have to try," she says. "I mean don't you think that's better than doing nothing?"

Her voice wavers slightly. She wilts, as if something heavy is bearing down on her and she's about to break. This isn't at all the Stephanie that I'm used to. It kind of hurts to look at her.

I'm gripped with a sudden fear that the confident, happy Stephanie is gone forever, that I've somehow killed her smile already. I have to say something, anything, to bring her back.

"Fine. Fine, we can try. If that's what you really want, we'll give it a shot." The words tumble out of my mouth.

The effect is glorious. The sun shines out of Stephanie and I'm bathed in it. I suddenly appreciate the sparkle in Stephanie's brown eyes and the cute little dimple on the side of her mouth.

"Thank you! Thank you. I promise I'll take full responsibility," she says in a tremulous voice.

"Sure," I mumble. Stephanie is so beautiful right now it's distracting. "Uh, what exactly is your plan here?"

"Well," Stephanie says, clasping her hands over her heart. "We'll be her friend, of course!"

I can't help but wonder if this girl really does live in the world of cheesy action heroes who make friends with their opponents after beating them up. "She kind of hates us, so that might be difficult."

"People always say about a runaway or suicide, 'If only we knew, we could have been there for her.' Well, we do know." Stephanie drums her fingers on her knee. "I know an adult who might be able to help us out, but we need to become friends with Callie if we want to convince them to meet up." Stephanie pumps her fist. "We'll be there for her. Starting tomorrow."

Where on earth does she get all this energy? It makes my head spin. But I can't help but smile back at her. "Okay, okay. I can try."

"Awesome!" Stephanie says as she tears open the box of cookies. She hoists a chocolate-chip cookie into the air. "A cookie toast! To our new partnership!"

I take a cookie hesitantly, and at Stephanie's urging, bump it against the one she's holding.

"So, where's the family?" Stephanie says as she demolishes the snack, spraying crumbs everywhere.

"Dad's at work and I think my sister's at her charity club thing," I say with a shrug.

"They leave you home alone?"

"Not much choice sometimes, Dad's the only parent. Your parents don't ever leave you alone?"

"They do; my brother doesn't," Stephanie says shortly. Then she jumps up and walks over to the mantelpiece to examine it. She notices the little Buddha statue. "You're Buddhist?"

"Not really. But Dad is. That's actually from Thailand; my grandparents brought it when they moved over here."

Stephanie looks over her shoulder and grins at me. "You're half-Thai, then? I thought you might be! Me too."

"Really?" I say, my eyes going wide.

"Yep, we're both *luk kreung*," Stephanie says, using the Thai term for "mixed-race." "Though I have *phiu dam* and you don't."

I don't understand the last term. My face heats up. "I never really got to be super fluent because Dad speaks it way less than English. Mai did because she's really smart."

Stephanie laughs. "I'm not really fluent. My mom doesn't spend much time with me, so not much chance to learn. I just like to show off the few words I do know. *Phiu dam* basically means dark skin. I picked up on *that* when I was pretty dang young, thanks to certain relatives and their whispering." She rolls her eyes. "My mom ditching the guy she was 'supposed' to stay with for a black man is still a hot topic. But enough about that. I take it you're part white?"

"Yeah, my mom's white," I say, my heart pounding with excitement. "This is so cool! I've never met another half-Thai kid outside my family. It's like we're connected!"

"Yeah," Stephanie says slowly, twirling a lock of her hair around her finger as she leans against the wall. "I guess. Hey, um, what happened to your mom?"

She sure is blunt. I rub the back of my neck awkwardly. "She, well, she ran off a few years ago." I give a totally fake little laugh. "I mean, at least she's not dead. She won't die until she's in her sixties in this hospital where she's with a man who's not Dad."

"Wow," Stephanie says with a frown. "That's pretty rough. So you've seen the deaths of all your family?"

"Yeah. It's old age for both my sister and Dad, fortunately."

"You mentioned a mental institution. Did your family send you there because they didn't believe you?"

For someone who's unwilling to go into her own tragic backstory, Stephanie sure has no problem prying into mine.

"It's complicated," I say tersely.

Stephanie smiles apologetically. "Sorry, I was being too personal, wasn't I?"

I give her an exaggerated sigh. "I really should tell you to shut up. I don't know why I keep opening up to a weirdo like you."

Stephanie flashes her white teeth again, almost blinding me. "I guess it's like you said. We must be connected somehow."

Chapter Four

JUST AS PROMISED, Stephanie and I put "Operation: Save Callie" into action the day I come back to school. We find Callie working on her math homework at a table in the library during free period. She's hunched over the worksheet with sweat gleaming on her face.

"H-hi," I greet her. Callie turns around in her seat. When she sees us approaching the table, she scoots away like she's afraid of catching our cooties.

"You okay there?" Stephanie asks.

"I don't want you to touch me again!" Callie points at me with a shaking finger.

You're the one who touched me, you pig, I want to say, but instead I force out, "I won't," through gritted teeth.

"Manee just wanted to see if you were doing all right," Stephanie says.

"Yeah, I know you got a shock or something when you touched me, and I'm sorry. It's a, uh, special medical condition. That's why I wear the gloves and stuff." I normally wouldn't tell such a stupid-sounding lie, but Callie isn't very bright, so she'll probably buy it.

I suppose wrong. Callie snorts and rolls her eyes. "Yeah right, freak. I know you did whatever it was on purpose. You feel so guilty you can't even look at me."

I wince at that one. It's true, I am finding it difficult to meet Callie's eyes. Every time I look, all I see are swollen, dead ones.

"She's shy, you know that," Stephanie says, crossing her arms. "Look, we want to make it up to you." She looks at me pointedly.

"We can help you with that," I mumble, pointing at Callie's work.

Callie's face darkens. "You making fun of me? I don't need any help."

"Well, you kinda seem less than halfway done with that," Stephanie says, squinting at the paper. "And math class is in thirty minutes."

"It's none of your business!" Callie says gruffly. But Stephanie's words make her glance over at the clock, and her eyes fill with panic. "Okay, well, maybe just this once. Since you owe me."

Stephanie hands over her math homework and Callie begins hurriedly copying.

"I forget about assignments all the time too," I offer awkwardly.

"Don't assume I'm stupid like you. I did it as soon as she assigned it, it's just I couldn't spare more than three hours, okay, so it ran a little overtime," Callie grumbles as she scribbles furiously.

Three hours? The assignment had only taken me an hour and I'm terrible at math. I exchange a quizzical look with Stephanie.

"Done!" Callie slams down her paper with a smirk. She bounds up from the table, clutching her sheet, and zips out of the library without so much as a goodbye.

"Well, at least that went by quick," I say.

"It was just a first step. She'll be wanting us to help her from now on," Stephanie says confidently. Then she frowns. "I wonder if that really took her three hours."

"She was probably exaggerating." I shrug. "Or not really trying." I pick up Stephanie's homework sheet. "Erp. Some of these answers are different from mine."

"Really?" Stephanie asks, tilting her head. "Huh. How good are you at math?"

"Not very. I generally get 'C's if I work at it. You?"

"I get 'A's."

"Ah." I cringe. "I guess we know who's wrong, then."

Stephanie grins. "I don't mind explaining some stuff to you if you want."

"I can already see your head swelling up like a balloon," I groan, but I take out my paper.

JUST AS STEPHANIE predicted, Callie continues to accept our help. We meet in the library almost every day. It isn't much of a change for me. I've spent most of my lunch periods there even before this. I've always loved libraries. I imagine I'm in a cottage made of books whenever I'm in one. But our school's library is more like a collapsing cave than a warm home: there are barely any books and the whole room sort of sags in on itself. Hardly anyone bothers coming in here.

Callie seems to like it, though, which is a surprise. Sometimes when Stephanie and I come in, she's already here and thumbing through a book she got off the shelf. She always quickly shoves it away when we sit down though.

"Why don't you check one out?" Stephanie suggests once.

Callie snorts. "I don't have time for that. Books take me forever and everything's too busy at my house."

It isn't clear what exactly is going on at Callie's house, but it is clear she gets hardly any homework done there. This might be partly because of how slow she is. Whatever the subject is, Callie does her work at a snail's pace, chewing on her tongue as she reads things several times, often crossing out and erasing words and numbers over and over.

But she rarely asks me and Stephanie to do the work for her. She'll shove a math paper at Stephanie or an English paper at me and demand "Explain!" gruffly, jabbing her finger at a particular part. Stephanie always obliges, patiently outlining each step in clear, simple language; I end up listening and taking notes way more than I do in actual class. Even Callie can't help but be impressed. "You're a lot better than our stupid-ass teacher at least," she mumbles once.

Callie and I don't really connect as much though, except for when I get excited and start ranting.

"So really, I think Charlotte's wrong in saying *Lord of the Flies* is a tale about what people do when society's rules are removed, it's really specifically about what white, rich British boys do, so in my essay I wrote, what?" I trail off, blushing. Callie is looking down at the table at me and smiling slightly.

"Nothing. Just never heard you talk so much before." Callie doesn't meet my eyes, but her smile remains. "You're an even bigger dork than I imagined."

"Isn't she, though?" Stephanie says, circling her fingers around her eyes in a mime of nerd glasses. "It's so great."

I expect Callie to protest, say she meant it as an insult, but instead she just snorts and leans back in her chair. I am flummoxed. When exactly did Callie stop hating me? When did we start talking to each other like normal people? It just kind of happened. Weird.

The weirdness continues a few days later. I glance over at Callie during one of our sessions. She's glaring down at her eraser-marked worksheet, chewing angrily at the end of her pencil. I barely believe it, but I think I see the glimmer of tears in her eyes.

Callie catches me looking and snarls, "What?"

"N-nothing!" I squeak, nearly falling back in my seat. "Sorry!"

"I could do this if I had more time, you know!" Callie throws down her pencil forcefully. "I could get into this stuff and be just as nerdy as you two freaks! It just takes so damn long! And I think studying like this is helping but it's just not enough."

Callie breathes heavily for a few more seconds and then the anger seems to drain away. She slumps in her seat, looking mournful. It's the most vulnerable I've ever seen her. I don't know what to say. But Stephanie pounces on it immediately. She leans forward, her eyes glinting.

"Then how about we get together outside of class too? My parents are friends with this high school teacher's aide, Ava Carnahan. I've asked her before if it would be okay to bring some friends to study. She could give us a quiet place to work and even help us out."

The name Carnahan sparks something in my memory. "Huh, I think my sister mentioned a woman named Carnahan was the head of her charity club." Also, she basically wants to be adopted by her.

"Small world! My brother's also in that club, actually."

"A teacher?" Callie narrows her eyes suspiciously. "Is she good?"

"She's the person who taught *me* math," Stephanie says proudly.

"Huh." Callie thinks for a second, then shrugs. "Okay then. I got nothing to lose."

"Nice!" Stephanie claps her hands together excitedly. "The three of us are going to study in style! I can't wait."

"Yeah!" I say automatically. It's startling to hear that agreement and realize I mean it. Somehow, I've come to like our little study sessions. It's weird as hell, but true.

MS. CARNAHAN'S NEIGHBORHOOD turns out to be a far nicer neighborhood than I'm used to. Where I live isn't a dump or anything, but it's dingy. There are potholes on the road and the buildings are cramped and mismatched. There isn't much space for backyards or any of that. This neighborhood is all along a spotless little road, full of pristine gardens and neatly trimmed hedges. The houses match: they're all white and boxy and almost shimmer in the sun. They're evenly spaced too, with big sprawling yards.

One house is perched atop a grassy hill with a winding gravel driveway. Though it is far away, I can see it has a large front porch, complete with a swing.

As we get off the bus, Stephanie jerks her head toward it. "'S where I live."

"Damn, Pierce," Callie whistles. "What are your parents, oil kings or something?"

"It's actually cement and chemical stuff. Mom inherited the branch our family owns over here and she and dad both manage it. Keeps them pretty busy."

"Wow. What's a rich bitch like you doing going to our crappy little school?"

I was wondering the same thing, minus the profanity.

Stephanie shrugs vaguely. "It was more my speed. Didn't wanna go to my brother's school."

She offers no further explanation, instead pointing to a house farther down the road. It stands out from the others, a ton of wind chimes decorating the porch and colorful rocks laid out in the yard.

"That's Ms. Carnahan's place."

When we knock at the door, a tall woman with olive skin and silky, shiny brown-black hair that falls to her shoulders answers. A wide smile spreads across her lips as she looks down at us, her clear bright eyes sparkling behind large tinted glasses.

"Hi, I'm Ava Carnahan, Stephanie's sometimes-babysitter," she says, beckoning us in.

Callie only grunts, but when she gets inside she inhales deeply and grins. There's a heavenly scent of chocolate chips in the air.

"I-I'm Manee. Th-thanks for having me," I stammer. My face is on fire. I wasn't expecting a teacher to be quite so beautiful.

Ms. Carnahan stares at me, her brow furrowed.

I freeze under her gaze. Do I have something on my face? Or is she just ogling my weird clothes?

"You wouldn't happen to be related to Mai Srikwan, would you?"

"Oh!" I inwardly sigh with relief. "Y-yeah. She's my sister; she talks about you a lot."

"I thought so! You look so alike. You both have those beautiful eyes."

Heat erupts so intensely in my face I'm in danger of boiling myself. For as long as I can remember, I've wished I looked like Mai; she's cute and slender and I'm blah and doughy. Mai's got an adorable little pixie nose whereas mine is comparable to a pug's. This is the first time I've ever been told my sister and I share a single pretty trait. "Thank you," I whisper.

"Anyway, go ahead and take a seat!"

Ms. Carnahan's house is just as colorful and tidy inside as it is outside. Silk hangings and calming landscapes pepper the walls, and a low little coffee table is set out for us in the living room, surrounded by beanbag seats.

"I'm going to grab some drinks. Does anyone want anything?"

Callie and Stephanie both request Coke. I mumble about not needing anything, unable to look at Ms. Carnahan directly. Stephanie notices this and rolls her eyes. "Manee will take some green tea, it's her favorite. She always brings it to school."

Pleasure surges through me. Stephanie really doesn't miss a thing.

"Jeez, you're controlling," Callie mutters as Ms. Carnahan leaves. "Let the girl speak for herself."

"'S fine. That's just how she is," I say, trying to hide how happy I am. I sink into the beanbag, my body relaxing. Callie is not quite as content. She keeps shifting around, swearing under her breath and jerking herself up each time the beanbag tries to claim her.

After serving our drinks, Ms. Carnahan settles down next to us, and the study session begins. It doesn't take long for Callie to start visibly struggling. Soon, sweat pops up on her face and she's licking her lips so often they're quickly inflaming. She keeps erasing, again and again, one time so violently the page tears.

Ms. Carnahan watches her with concern. "Can I take a look?"

Callie hands it over.

Ms. Carnahan's lips purse as she examines the paper. She puts it down slowly and turns to face Callie. "Callie, it was good that you came to me. I think we should definitely have you tested for a learning disability."

Her words drop like a bombshell. Callie's face goes pale. "W-what? Why would we do that?"

"It would just be the best way to determine exactly what the issue here is."

Callie's eyes dart around. "Th-there's nothing wrong with me. I'm not a freak!"

"Of course you're not. This would just be to get you the help you need," Ms. Carnahan says soothingly. "If we contact your parents, we can get it set up."

"No!" Callie jumps up, nearly overturning the table. Her face is gray now. "Do *not* call my parents! Where is this even coming from?"

Ms. Carnahan holds her hands up in a calming gesture, confusion clouding her face. "I—I thought this was why you came, though. Stephanie said all of you were concerned."

"You what!?" Callie rounds on Stephanie. She's gone from gray to fire-engine red. Stephanie glances away awkwardly. "You go behind my back and without even saying anything? What kind of sick joke is this? Were you just looking down on me this whole time, thinking I was some re—" Her voice cracks and she can't go on. Her arms hang limply at her sides and her eyes are dull and empty. My chest tightens. In those eyes, I see the shadow of that Callie who waited at that bus stop, drained and broken, who just stood there like a zombie as the car slammed into her and shattered every bone. I jump up in a panic, reaching out for Callie like I'm about to pull her from the street. But she jerks away.

"I'm out of here." Callie grabs her backpack and stomps for the door, but Ms. Carnahan runs after her and grabs her by the arm. "Wait! Callie, I know how this feels!"

Callie tries to wrench herself from Ms. Carnahan's grip. "No, you don't!"

"I do! I also have a learning disorder!"

Callie stops in her tracks, blinking in confusion. "You? But you're a teacher."

"We can do anything we put our minds to." Ms. Carnahan lets go of Callie's arm and puts a hand on her shoulder. "Look, we don't have to do a test or contact your parents or any of that if you don't want to. But let me tutor you and help you study. Let's just try it out for a bit."

Callie stands there for a moment, breathing heavily. "Y-you really promise you won't tell my parents?"

"I promise. I didn't tell my own parents at first when I was younger either. My sister gave me the help and support I needed until I was ready. I can do that for you."

She chews on her lip. "O-okay. I'll stay. But only because I can't get held back again." Her eyes flick down. "Or else."

For the rest of the visit, Callie doesn't acknowledge me or Stephanie. She studies with Ms. Carnahan, taking notes and listening intently to her suggestions. When she leaves, she doesn't say goodbye. It makes me want to melt into a puddle of shame. But Stephanie doesn't seem to feel the same way. Whenever I looked at her, there's a small smile of triumph on her face.

Chapter Five

AFTER CALLIE LEAVES, Ms. Carnahan gives Stephanie a hard look. "Stephanie, you should have been honest with Callie. You really upset her." Her eyes flick over to me and she shakes her head. "We'll talk more about this later." Her cell phone buzzes on the table. "Ah, I have to take this," she says after glancing at it. "Be right back."

As soon as Ms. Carnahan exits the living room, Stephanie's grin returns.

"You shouldn't look so happy," I hiss. "Why didn't you just tell her you were going to get Ms. Carnahan to test her?"

"Because she would never have come if I had," Stephanie hisses back. "She wouldn't have believed Ava understood. She was all convinced she was the only one who had this weird thing messing her up, but now she sees she's not alone."

"I guess." I look down at my gloved hand. Not alone, huh? Wonder what that feels like?

"You might not be the only one either," Stephanie says, leaning forward.

I duck my head. I hate how Stephanie can read me so easily. "I—I wasn't thinking about that."

"Really?" Stephanie cups her chin in her hand. "Haven't you ever wondered if there might be others?"

"I don't think there are. I looked around on the internet when I first got my powers, didn't find anything. It was kind of a relief, honestly."

Stephanie raises her eyebrows. "It was?"

"Yeah." I pull down my sleeve, covering up a bit of exposed wrist. "It'd make me sad to know other people had to deal with this."

"Oh." Stephanie flops back in her beanbag, looking disappointed.

I look away. I lied just now. My reasons for relief are far more selfish. I'm afraid if there are other people who have visions, they'll tell me things I don't want to hear. I still hold out hope the visions will just go away someday, and I don't want anyone to come along and tell me they're permanent or that they'll get even worse somehow. What terrifies me above all is learning that I make people's deaths come sooner when I touch them or something like that. It's true Dad and Mai have a fairly long life ahead, but all my other visions were pretty rough. It could be that if I'm scared or stressed when I touch someone, I make them die horribly and horribly soon. Callie's just one example.

In the end, it's just better not to know.

The doorbell rings, interrupting my dark thoughts. Ms. Carnahan reenters the room and answers it.

"Thanks for taking care of my sister!" Mai comes in, grinning ear to ear.

"She was a great houseguest," Ms. Carnahan says warmly. It gives me a shiver of pleasure. Mai looks surprised, but she quickly smooths that over and takes one of Ms. Carnahan's cookies. "Mmm," she moans, "you make the best food."

Stephanie steps forward and introduces herself to Mai. Her eyebrows shoot up. "Wow, you're definitely Tony's sister. You look a lot alike."

"I pull it off better, though," Stephanie says and offers her hand to shake.

Mai laughs and takes it.

Before I go out the door, Stephanie catches me by the sleeve. "Ava's wrong, y'know. You don't look like your sister."

My breath catches in my throat.

"You're way cuter." Stephanie winks.

My heart swells. It's an obvious lie, but I adore Stephanie for telling it.

Steph chuckles and waves me out the door. "See you tomorrow."

As Mai drives back home, she's also smiling. "Your friend seems really nice. I'm glad you finally made one."

I ignore the sting of that last statement. "Yeah, she's cool."

"And I'm glad she introduced you to Ms. Carnahan. She's a great teacher. She'll be a good influence on you.'

There it is, that ever-present condescension. I grind my teeth and glare out the window.

"I'll be happy to pick you up from all your little sessions, you know."

I goggle at Mai, frustration forgotten. "What, really?" *But you hate doing things for me,* I want to say.

It wasn't always that way. When we were children, we were practically joined at the hip. Whenever Mom sighed about how she didn't know where she went wrong with me, it was Mai who held me as I cried and told me I was fine the way I was. It was Mai who read picture books to me while I sat on her lap. It was

Mai who carried me along the trail during one of those grueling hikes with Mom and she even defended me when Mom berated me for being so weak and slow.

That all changed after the mental hospital. Mai broke away and we became strangers. In some ways, she's still the girl I've always known. She still secretly loves pigtailed braids and sundresses and pop music. But she's also someone who can barely stand to look at me anymore.

"Yeah," Mai says lightly. "I like that you're doing this. Plus, it's always nice to see Ms. Carnahan. I can have her all to myself to talk to about club stuff. No Tony getting in the way."

"Well, okay. Thanks," I mumble.

Mai looks directly at me for once, and smiles. "No problem."

For the first time in a long time, we feel like sisters again.

STEPHANIE AND I sit glumly in the library. I stare at the spot on the faded blue carpet. It seems to get bigger every month, and I can't figure out how. I wonder whether I can see it spreading if I squint hard enough. It's like some gelatinous creature is living under the rug and seeping through.

"Looks like Callie's not coming." Stephanie finally breaks the silence. "We should go look for her."

I tug at my hair nervously. "Don't you think maybe we should just leave her alone for a while? I mean, it was us interfering that hurt her in the first place." *Stephanie* interfering, to be super specific.

"We're only trying to help. Look, it's more me she's mad at, so if you find her, you shouldn't have much of a problem talking her down." Steph gives me her gentle grin. "I know you can do it. I'll check inside, you take outside."

With that, she jumps up and strides out of the library. I watch her hair bounce with each step she takes. "I am pathetically easy to boss around," I mutter. Allowing myself one final huff of annoyance, I get up from the table and shamble off to track Callie down.

I check the playground first. It's filled with kids eating lunch, but Callie isn't among them. That leaves the parking lot. From where I am, it doesn't look like Callie is there either, but the far side is blocked from view by the parked cars and jutting building, so I can't be sure. I make my way up the sidewalk. A few feet closer and Callie comes into view. She's sitting at the very end of the sidewalk, right near the entrance to the lot, staring at the ground with her head bowed.

I approach her cautiously. Callie lifts her head and jumps up like a startled rabbit the second she sees me. She immediately runs across the parking lot, right into the path of a car turning in from the street.

My stomach buckles. The sickening crack of Callie's ribs shattering echoes in my ears and the image of her body shredding grotesquely flashes through my mind. I run forward, screaming "watch out!" But my frantic feet betray me and I trip spectacularly. I hit the concrete hard, knees and elbows first, but barely feel anything. I jerk my head up immediately, eyes searching for Callie.

Callie skidded to a stop just in time. The car rolls by her, the driver shouting that she should be more careful. Callie ignores him, staring at me in pure confusion.

"Oh, thank God," I breathe, a heady relief filling me.

"Are you okay?" Callie moves tentatively in my direction, still utterly bewildered.

I wince. My knees and elbows sting. Pain has returned to me in a rush, and so has reason. Callie couldn't have become street pizza here. She's supposed to die at an intersection. Also, that car was going, like, two miles an hour. I just totally freaked out for no reason. I force myself into a sitting position. My sweatpants are ripped at the knees and a bloody mess is visible through the tears. My gloves and shirtsleeves are shredded too. Just great.

Callie comes to a stop in front of me, eyes flicking down to my scraped forearms. "Jesus. I don't get you at all."

"What's not to get? I'm a human disaster," I snort. I flick away some gravel embedded in my elbow. My heart is still beating a million miles a minute, and now I'm getting berated by Callie on top of it.

"No. Well, yeah, but that's not what I meant. Why are you acting like you care about me so much all of the sudden? Out of nowhere you and Stephanie just start like, watching out for me, and I don't get it."

I open my mouth and then close it. My knee-jerk response was, "It's not personal, I just don't want to see anyone die." But now I realize that isn't really true. I can't stop thinking of how horribly fragile Callie looked in the vision, a shivering wisp, small, insignificant, unsupported. I see flashes of that little wisp sometimes when I look too closely at Callie. And I feel a strange pull when I do.

I hesitate and sigh. "It's going to sound bizarre, but you

know how when we touched, you said you felt something? Well, I felt something too. I felt like you were alone. And I'm pretty familiar with that feeling so, I don't know. It's like I understand you now. And because I understand, it makes me want to help."

Callie blinks at me. Then she guffaws. "Ha! You don't understand me. If you did, you wouldn't have pulled that shit with Ms. Carnahan. Treating me like some freak."

"When did I ever say we think you're a freak?" I snap, heat rising in my face. "Jesus! You're the one who calls me a freak all the time! But you can't take a little heat?"

Callie's eyebrows shoot up. "Even a little bitch can bite, huh?" She tilts her head. "I guess you're right. You're way more of a freak than me, with whatever your deal is."

I do my level best to ignore the insults. "Look, Steph shouldn't have gone behind your back to Ms. Carnahan. But why does it freak you out so much? The idea of having a disorder or whatever?"

"You wouldn't get it."

"Try me," I snap.

Callie raises her eyebrows again, but she looks weirdly pleased over my aggression. "Fine. My parents already see me as a huge disappointment. If they find out there's something actually wrong with me, I don't even want to think about it." Callie frowns, tugging on her ponytail. "I have to be normal for them. I have to be."

And just like that, Callie is that wisp again. Just a fragment of a person. I wonder if this is how I look to others too.

"I have to pretend I'm normal too," I say softly. "My dad sent me to a mental hospital once."

Callie grins wickedly. "Wow, that's hardcore. Can't exactly say I blame him, though."

I grind my teeth. "I should have known better to confide in you. Forget it." I push off the ground. I really want to jump up and leave in a huffy flounce, but my wounded knees ruin that plan. I let out an involuntary hiss of pain and wobble dangerously.

Callie grabs me by the arm, steadying me. Her fingertip brushes my skin through the rip in my sleeve. I get a shock and only barely stop myself from pulling away. Callie realizes what she's doing and lets go.

"Sorry," she mumbles.

"It's okay."

"It didn't feel weird that time." Callie examines her hand

thoughtfully. Then it falls to her side and she bites her lip. "Look, I really am sorry. About before too, when I forced you. I don't know what your deal is with the touching thing and I don't want to know, but I shouldn't have."

Callie's ears are turning red and she is looking everywhere but at me.

I'm hotter under the collar myself. "Thanks," I manage to say. "I'm sorry about the thing with Ms. Carnahan."

"I don't need anyone's pity, okay? Hanging out or whatever, it's fine, but I don't need *help*." Callie scuffs her shoe on the ground.

I hesitate. "I thought that's what friends do, though. Help each other out."

Callie screws up her face. "But it's always just you two helping me. Makes me feel weird, like I owe you something."

"Well, then," I think about it carefully. "If you want to help us, maybe you can shield us at dodgeball or something. Or like, pretend to injure me so I can get out of gym class completely." I shrug.

A genuine smile crosses Callie's face. "Hmm, not a bad idea. Can I actually hit you, to make it look extra real?"

"And now I'm filled with regret," I groan. I start to limp toward the nurse's office, only to have Callie offer me an arm to lean on.

"Helping each other, right?" she says gruffly.

I stare at her for a second and then take it. "Yeah. Thanks." *Maybe this can work, after all*, I think to myself as I hobble off with Callie at my side.

Chapter Six

IN THE WEEKS following the conversation in the parking lot, Callie, Stephanie and I settle into a comfortable routine. Callie enthusiastically makes good on her promise to "accidentally injure" both of us during P.E. periods, allowing us to sit out. It's blessing for exercise-phobes like us.

"Whatever you said to her in the parking lot that day, you really got to her," Stephanie whispers to me as we sit on the side of the playground. We're watching Callie rampage down the makeshift basketball court. Everyone's too afraid to get near her, so she dunks basket after basket, much to the P.E. teacher's consternation. "You totally turned her from foe to friend."

I blush and mumble, "Not really," but something's definitely changed between Callie and me. She even defends me from other students now. My classmates have this game where they'll hover for a few seconds with their fingers perilously near my face and breathe down my neck all menacingly. I've learned to just keep still and ignore them, since they're afraid to actually touch me. But these days, whenever someone starts up that game, Callie will turn and glare at them. This freezes most people in their tracks, and they're certain to run back to their seats if Callie actually gets up and walks toward them.

"You don't have to do that," I whisper once when Callie passes my desk.

"Do what? I'm getting some water," Callie grunts.

I smile to myself. I can't believe it, but I'm actually glad Stephanie prodded me into doing this whole thing with Callie.

We visit Ava Carnahan's house twice a week for study sessions now. Sometimes we even stay for dinner. Callie always wolfs down anything Ms. Carnahan cooks like she's starving, her cheeks pink and shiny and full.

Ms. Carnahan shines even more happily in response. "My sister had a big appetite. It's like she's with me right now."

It actually makes me jealous how much Ms. Carnahan favors Callie. She's always looking at her fondly and comparing her to her sister, who, from what I can gather, is both very beloved and very dead. It gets grating sometimes. Still, I'm willing to put up with it for Callie's sake.

It's during one of those study sessions at Ms. Carnahan's that

I finally meet Stephanie's mysterious brother, Tony. The doorbell rings and when Ms. Carnahan answered it, there he is, holding a plate of chocolate-chip cookies covered in Saran Wrap. He's a lot lighter skinned than Stephanie, but I can still instantly tell they're related. He shares his sister's attractive face, full lips, and high cheekbones. Steph groans at the sight of him.

"Tony! Hello there," Ms. Carnahan says warmly.

"Hi," Tony responds, a smile spreading across his flushed face. I can practically see hearts in his eyes. "I, uh, made you these," he mumbles, holding out the plate. "From that recipe you told me about. I wanted to see what you'd think, as the expert."

"Oh, I'd love to try some!" Ms. Carnahan chirps. "Come on in! Your sister and her friends are already here." She gestures to the living room behind her, where Stephanie, Callie and I are sitting, our homework spread out before us.

As soon as Tony sees Stephanie, the smile drops off his face. "*Half*-sister," he says.

"I don't know why you're so insistent about that, it isn't really all that important of a distinction." Ms. Carnahan rolls her eyes as she takes the cookies from Tony. "I'm going to get some plates, okay? Let's all be nice and have a snack together."

She leaves. Tony walks over, looking at Callie and me skeptically. "Friends, huh?" He drops down to his knees and hisses at Stephanie. "You'd better not be getting Ava involved in any of your bullshit."

"Well, now that you mention it, I was going to ask her to do a blood sacrifice for me. We have the goat ready and everything!" Stephanie hisses back. She's shaking.

Tony's face turns shadowy. "I'm serious. You know she's delicate. If you fuck around with her, I'll make you *pay*."

"Your beloved Ava is a grown woman, she doesn't need a white knight!"

"What's going on here?" Callie interrupts them, her voice loud over the whispers. "Why do you think Stephanie's going to do something to her?"

Tony starts to say something, but then Ms. Carnahan comes in with a stack of plates. "Is everything all right?"

Tony instantly forces a smile and says, "Yeah! Yeah, we're all good."

Stephanie and Tony don't say anything to each other for the rest of visit, but a tense atmosphere remains regardless. I desperately want to ask Stephanie what's going on.

So does Callie, apparently. As soon as we meet up the next

morning around Stephanie's desk, she asks, "What was that all about with your brother?"

"*Half*-brother," Stephanie says in snide imitation. "And a whole asshat. He's always treated me like shit. And in case you didn't notice, he has a huge crush on Ava, so he felt obligated to do some ridiculous posturing."

"But why does he treat you like that?"

"He's my brother. It's his job. Your sister gets on your case too, right?"

She's got me there. Callie doesn't seem to buy it, though. But before she can say anything else, we're approached by our teacher, Charlotte.

"Callie, I'm going to need you to come to the office with me," she said grimly.

Callie's eyes widen. "Am I in trouble for something?"

"Just come with me," Charlotte said, her face like stone.

Callie obliges, her mouth tightening nervously.

I share her nerves. "What do you think that's about?" I whisper at Stephanie.

"I'm not sure but I don't have a good feeling," Stephanie mumbles.

It seems like an age before Charlotte comes back. When she does, it's without Callie. She launches into our morning English lesson without even a glance at Stephanie and me.

I can't concentrate all through class. I keep glancing at the door, hoping Callie will come in, but she never does.

When class ends, Charlotte calls Steph and me up front.

"I just wanted to let both of you know that we've taken care of the bullying issue with Callie," she says, not really looking at us as she puts some papers in her desk drawer. "I wish you'd have come to me about it, but fortunately your classmates were looking out for you. I don't want to cut into your class time, but we should meet after school and discuss how to handle these situations in the future."

My heart plummets down to my gut. "Bullying issue? Wh-what?"

"I think there might be a misunderstanding." Stephanie's voice is unusually polite. She's staring at Charlotte super intensely, though.

Charlotte gives us a pitying look. "You don't have to pretend. We know she's been repeatedly injuring you in gym class. Classmates have come forward and told about how she attacked you and how she's constantly shadowing you during class. And we're not stupid. We've noticed this all coincides with the improvement in her schoolwork. When someone threatens you into letting them cheat, you need to report it."

"You've got it all wrong!" I cry frantically. "We're friends! We've been seeing a tutor together and—and she hasn't been injuring us, we were faking it."

"It's all right," Charlotte says in what she probably thinks is a gentle voice, but just comes off as condescending. "There's no need to cover up for her. You're safe now." She checks her watch. "I've got to get to a meeting." She picks up her binder.

"Ma'am," Stephanie says softly. "If you would just let us contact our tutor, we could prove what we are saying."

"We can talk about all this after school," Charlotte says distractedly. "Just meet me here, all right?" She steps around us, and marches for the door.

"Wait!" I start after her, but Stephanie grabs my sleeve. "It won't do any good. We can deal with her later. The important thing right now is to find Callie before she does anything stupid."

"Right," I breathe. We both rush out to the parking lot. Callie is standing on the sidewalk, slumped against the brick building that holds the principal's office. My heart sinks when I see that her face is red and her eyes are shiny.

"Callie!" I call, my voice strained. Stephanie and I run toward her. She looks up as we approach, then looks down again.

"My parents are coming to pick me up," she says in a croaky voice. "They're suspending me. They might even decide to expel me." She rubs her eyes, which are starting to swell up from the crying. "Y-you told them I was bullying you?"

"No!" I say vehemently. "We didn't want any of this to happen, you've got to believe us, it was just the teachers making stupid assumptions!"

"I don't know what to believe anymore," Callie mumbles.

"We're going to clear this up." Stephanie pulls out her phone. "We'll call Ava and she'll come talk to them and tell them how she's helping you!"

"Tell everyone how I'm wrong in the head?" Callie gives a rough, ugly laugh. "That might be even worse than this."

"Callie, please!"

"Look, it's too late to fix it. Whatever happens, whatever you guys say, my parents are going to blame me. It's going to be my fault, that's how it always is." Callie's voice breaks and her face sags. It's like she's aging before my eyes, her flesh and bones crumbling to dust. "It's just fate. I'm the big, mean, dumb ugly one with no future. I can't escape it."

She bows her head, letting her tears drip onto the sidewalk like falling rain.

"You're not ugly or dumb," I begin.

"There's no such thing as fate, Callie, you need to fight!" Stephanie talks over me.

"Just go away!" Callie explodes, slamming her fist into the brick wall behind her. "God, shut up! Why would you even care? You don't. Just admit you don't! You'd be better off without me!"

Before we can respond, the receptionist comes out of the office. "What's going on?" She glares at Steph and me. "Shouldn't you two be in class?"

Stephanie immediately goes into that weirdly polite mode. "I'm sorry," she says, looking at the receptionist very directly. "We aren't skipping class. We were just—"

"We need to speak to the principal!" I talk over her frantically.

"She's not available right now, you'll have to come back later. *You* need to come inside," the receptionist snaps at Callie. Callie obeys her, not looking at Stephanie or me. "Are you going back to class or do I need to escort you?"

"Again, I'm sorry. We'll return to class right away." Stephanie beckons for me to follow her. I have no choice but to do so.

"How could you just give in like that? Now what are we going to do?" I ask Stephanie in panicky whisper.

"Don't worry," Stephanie says. Her voice is hard and determination is etched in her face. It's a complete turnaround from the shrinking violet of a second ago. "I'm going to get Ava over here and we'll fix this."

I nod. But Callie's words keep echoing in her head: *It's fate.*

Ms. Carnahan doesn't pick up, but Stephanie assures me she'll answer at lunch. We return to class and sit through it in silence. I can't take my eyes off Callie's empty seat. It's the longest class has ever felt, like every second spins slowly, cuffing me about the face as it goes.

During lunch break, we finally get ahold of Ms. Carnahan. Stephanie gives me a too-wide grin when she finishes the phone call. "She's going to call the office and explain. She has Callie's number too, so she can check on her. She even says she'll pick us up after school and we can go see her."

I manage a weak smile. "Good." But I'm still sick to my stomach.

"It's going to be okay," Stephanie repeats, forcefully this time, like she's demanding it be true.

At the end of school day, both of us bolt out immediately. It takes a while for Ms. Carnahan to arrive. Stephanie paces back and forth the whole time. I squeeze my arms around myself, wishing my psychic powers were actually useful. What I wouldn't give to be able to communicate with Callie telepathically or at least track her location. Finally, Ms. Carnahan's little red Honda pulls up.

She thrusts open the door, her face pale.

"I called Callie's parents. They can't find her. She ran off. Do you two have any idea where she might have gone?"

Stephanie and I exchange terrified looks.

"Callie was at a bus stop," I squeak.

"A crowded intersection; it's probably one within walking distance of her house," Stephanie continues, her eyebrows drawn together in concentration.

"I've driven her home, she lives on Emery Road," Ms. Carnahan says quickly. "You think she's at a bus stop near an intersection? There are a couple we can check."

Stephanie nods, immediately flinging open the car door and jumping in. But I can't move. There's something I can't shake off. A horrible certainty that getting in that car is only going to make things worse, that everything we do will just hurt Callie more at this point.

"Manee!" Stephanie says sharply. "Get in! You're not going to see anything bad, I promise."

A lump rises in my throat. I gulp hard, looking into Stephanie's eyes, wide and wild with desperation. I force myself past all the warnings blasting in my brain and jump in the car.

"Let's drive."

And drive Ms. Carnahan does, at a reckless, breakneck speed I would never have thought her capable of. My nausea has nothing to do with all the twists and turns, though. I look over at Stephanie. Her face is perfectly blank and her eyes are empty. She's like a machine gearing up for its next automation.

In contrast, Ms. Carnahan is the least calm I've ever seen her. Even though she doesn't know anything about the vision, one look at her tells me she still fears the worst. Her face is bloodless and her eyes focus on the road with an intensity that borders on scary.

The instant we turn into the street leading to the intersection, I just know it's the right place. The street is gray and nondescript with no particular markings, but the chill I feel is unmistakable. It will happen here. I grip the handle to the door so hard my knuckles go white.

Stephanie seems to understand what I'm thinking with a glance. She rolls down the window and cranes her neck, gazing down the busy road as we join its traffic. The bus station comes into view. A large figure is hunched on the bench.

Relief floods me. Callie is still at the station. She hasn't seen whatever it is that will make her run out into the road.

Then I realize it, just as Ms. Carnahan spots Callie. "There she is!" she cries.

"Wait, don't!" I scream, but I'm too late.

Ms. Carnahan hits the horn, drowning me out. Callie's head jerks up and she locks eyes with me for a second. She leaps up and runs.

I slam my eyes shut but I can't block out Ms. Carnahan's terrible scream.

Chapter Seven

I WONDER IF everything inside me died alongside Callie. That's how it feels, anyway, as I sit on Stephanie's porch hours later. I'm just an empty carcass now. I can only listen numbly as Ms. Carnahan cries. There's been no break in her tears since the accident. It's a wonder she hasn't dehydrated already.

Stephanie keeps pacing back and forth across the porch, her eyes hard and glittering like diamonds. Through it all, there have been no tears, no unsteadiness, no screams from her. She just seems angry.

Ms. Carnahan's sobs grow louder and louder. Tony has his arm around her and is rubbing her back in slow circles. She's muttering to herself now, over and over like a mantra. "It's all my fault, it's all my fault."

"It's not!" Tony cries, taking her by the shoulders and shaking her. "Why would you think that?"

She shakes her head and whimpers. "It is. It is. I honked the horn, I scared her, I distracted the driver in front of me. My fault, my fault."

"No. It's *not*. I know whose fault it really is," Tony growls, his eyes flashing. He stares down his sister like a bull preparing to charge. "You did this, didn't you?" He says in an oddly quiet voice. "You're pulling this shit again. And you dragged her into it even though I warned you not to!"

Stephanie stops pacing and faces Tony. "Yes," she tells him in a flat and emotionless voice. "It was my fault."

Tony's eyes glitter with tears now too. "What the fuck is wrong with you? You just have to destroy everyone I care about, don't you? Look what you've done to her!" He takes a step toward Stephanie, looking ready to rip her apart.

"Stop," Ms. Carnahan says. Tony freezes in his tracks. Ms. Carnahan gets to her feet. She looks so small. The blanket draped around her is swallowing her. Her expression is vacant. "It's not her fault. Let's go inside for a minute, Tony."

Ms. Carnahan doesn't stay to listen to Tony's protest and heads for the door. Reluctantly, he follows her. Before entering the house, he looks at me over his shoulder and says, "You'd better be careful around her, or you'll be next." He slams the door behind him to punctuate the statement.

Now it's just Stephanie and me on this empty porch with nothing but silence between us.

"What was he talking about? What'd he mean?" I ask. My voice feels raw and scratchy.

"Nothing," Stephanie mutters, a shadow passing over her face. She sits down on the stoop beside me. "How are you doing?"

That's all it takes to open my floodgates. I cry big, ugly sobs that tear at my throat on the way out. It's like I'm vomiting tears.

Stephanie comforts me much like Tony comforted Ms. Carnahan, muttering, "It's not your fault," over and over.

"But I should never have done this! We couldn't save her, we just made things worse!"

"Yeah, I know," Stephanie says heavily. "I really screwed it up. I'm sorry. Sorry I put you through all that."

I shake my head. "It was my choice."

"I didn't try hard enough, I let her slip away." Stephanie squeezes the bridge of her nose. "But this won't happen again. Next time I won't make these mistakes. Next time I'll do whatever it takes."

The words hang in the air and for the life of me, I just can't understand them. Maybe I heard wrong. "Next time?"

"Next time we have to stop someone's death. I'll do absolutely everything I can, even if I have to devote every waking minute to it."

Stephanie's eyes are bright and blazing. I don't see a light inside them anymore—I see a wildfire. I edge away from her. "Stephanie, what was your brother talking about when he said you destroy people?"

Stephanie wobbles at this like I've shoved her or something. Her lips press together. "Oh, that."

"This, or something worse, has happened before, hasn't it," I say flatly.

Her whole body tenses. She looks down at her lap, her face bloodless.

"Tell me."

She opens her mouth, then closes it. She bows her head. Her curtain of hair covers her face.

"You're not going to tell me? Even after all we've been through, even though I told you everything, even though I told you my deepest secrets?" My voice breaks and I put my head in my hands. God, I'm stupid. Here I'd been so worried about destroying Stephanie's innocence, but maybe she never had any to begin with. Callie's death doesn't even seem to matter to her. All she can think about is her next chance to repeat this, like it's a fun little science experiment.

I should have known. Everything about Stephanie was too good to be true from the start. I allowed myself to be swept away by this beautiful brilliant girl, allowed myself to imagine there was something between us, that Stephanie genuinely wanted to help me and Callie. But it was probably just a game to her from the very beginning. Callie and I were nothing more than interesting playthings, toys for her to break.

I'm so sorry, Callie. You deserved so much better.

"Okay," I finally say, not looking at Stephanie. "I get it now. You'll have to find someone else to play around with, Stephanie."

I get up slowly because it feels like if I'm not careful, I'll collapse under the weight of it all. I focus all my energy on taking that first, heavy step forward. No matter how hard it is, I have to tear myself away from her.

But something catches on my sleeve, forcing me to stop.

It takes a second to realize it's Stephanie's hand. I turn. Stephanie lifts her head at last, her curtain of hair falling away. The face that's revealed sends a jolt through me. Sweat is dribbling like tears down Stephanie's forehead and cheeks. Her skin is so tight around her face, she seems about to rip open. Something's trying to burst through her.

"Fine. I-I'll tell you," Stephanie's mouth trembles with each word. "I'll tell you what Tony meant. I—I really don't want to, but I'll do it, okay? Please don't leave me too. I couldn't take it."

I hesitate. I can at least hear her out, I guess. "All right." I sit back down.

"Okay," Stephanie mutters, wiping her face with her sleeve. "This is my first time ever telling the whole thing, so it might be a little bumpy." She scrubs her eyes with her knuckles, takes a deep breath, and sits up straight. She doesn't look at me, instead staring straight ahead. Her hands shake in her lap, so she knots them into fists.

"Here's what happened. W-when I was eight, my brother had two friends. Matt and Andrew. Well, I guess Matt was my friend too. My brother never liked me much, even back then, but Matt, he would always let me play with them, even when Tony complained."

Stephanie smiles softly at the memory, her posture relaxing.

"Matt would always play really, uh, roughly by the school stairs with Andrew. I knew it was dangerous. I knew he could fall. But it made Andrew mad when I said anything so I stopped bringing it up." She bows her head wearily. "And then it happened. Matt died right in front of me."

My breath catches.

"Yeah," Stephanie says with a sick little smile. "He fell down the stairs and broke his neck. I was watching. I saw it coming. I saw that he was going to fall. I could have grabbed him but I was a coward. I was afraid I'd fall too. So I did nothing. And he died."

We sit in silence for a second. I watch pink slowly tinge the sky as the sun sinks down, down, down. I'm light-headed and little sick. It's like I'm sitting next to a person with an open wound and I don't know how to heal it. Or even how to deal with the sight of it.

"You were a kid, Stephanie. It wasn't your fault. Actually, it was way more Andrew's fault."

"Andrew didn't know any better. I did. That's why I told everyone I did it. It was never really the same with my brother after that," Stephanie says, eyes closed, shoulders tense. "He's never forgiven me. He thinks I did it on purpose."

"What?" I squawk. "You really just let everyone think it was you?"

"I did eventually explain that I didn't actually push him. But Tony didn't believe me. And Andrew wasn't going to admit he had a part in it. He said it was me. It might as well have been."

I don't know what to say.

Stephanie's lips quiver. "I really thought that I could save someone this time." She wipes her eyes. "I really do want to help people, I do. That's why I went up to you. You looked so alone. And then I realized we were the same."

"The same?"

Stephanie flushes, twiddling her thumbs. "We both blame ourselves for not stopping the deaths we saw coming. I wanted to prove to you that we could get it right. I failed, but still." The muscles in her jaw tighten. "I feel like I owe it to Matt to keep trying." Her eyes burn once more. "There just has to be a way. There has to be!"

I stare in awe at the girl in front of me. Now it's clear where that blazing wildfire in her comes from. It's a flame she desperately keeps burning just to get through the darkness around her, a flame I let go out in myself long ago. It rages so brightly I can't meet eyes with it. I duck my head.

"I wish I was as strong as you," I mutter. "But I'm too afraid of it happening again."

Stephanie slumps listlessly. "No, I wish I was more like you. I wish I could cry. That I could mourn her or something. I don't know what happened to that part of me. Maybe my brother is right. Maybe I am a monster."

I wrestle with myself as the air grows heavy with the approaching night. I know it must have been hard for Stephanie to share this.

"We can be monsters together, then," I finally make myself say. "My mother always thought I was one. That's why, when I first got the visions, I tried to just bury it all deep inside me. But then, Grandma happened and I knew it was real. And I'd seen that Mom was gonna be with someone other than Dad when she died. I thought maybe I could stop it. So I tried to be good, to make her want to stay. But everything I did just seemed to make her more and more revolted to be around me. One day, she just took off." I blow a lock of hair away from my face. "I think she always knew something was wrong; that's why she never liked me."

"There's nothing wrong with you," Stephanie interrupts, glaring.

"Then why do I keep losing people? I just don't ever want to see anything like what happened with Callie again."

Stephanie groans. "Okay, fine, I get it. I won't force you into anything like this anymore."

I brush my hair aside, peering at Stephanie. "Really, for real?"

"Yeah." Stephanie hugs her knees to her chest. "I've lost some people too. And I don't want to lose you."

"Me too. You're the first friend I've had since," I pause. "Since a long time ago."

"Callie was your friend for a bit there," Steph says gently.

Just hearing her name stings. "Unfortunately for her." I wipe my eyes. "Let's go inside and check on Ms. Carnahan. I should call my Dad too, he's probably worried."

I get up, but my legs are still too shaky to support my weight. I wobble, but Stephanie catches my arm before I can fall.

"Thanks," I mutter. I remember a similar situation with Callie and want to collapse all over again. "God, I'm a mess."

"It's okay," Stephanie says as she helps me into the house. "We'll get through it together."

Chapter Eight

DEALING WITH MY family after Callie's death is just as difficult as expected. Dad basically pulls up every "dealing with trauma" resource he can get his hands on and showers me with frantic advice. What's worse, he insists I should go back to therapy.

"No, I don't need to. I barely knew her," I lie through my teeth. "We studied together just once. And I didn't see anything. I closed my eyes when it happened and I stayed in the car. Really, I'm okay."

It takes several more hours and tons of fake cheerfulness, but Dad finally relents. Mai, however, is not so easily pacified. She knocks on my door later that night. I don't answer, but she lets herself in anyway. She shuts the door behind her and leans back against it.

I ignore her as best I can. I'm stretched out on my bed, trying and failing to read a comic.

"I just wanted to say I'm sorry this happened. Also, I'm worried," Mai admits, her eyes fastened to the floor. "Ava's a mess over all this. I know all of you studied together a lot. Why are you lying to Dad?"

I carefully close my comic, torn. This is the first time my sister has gone out of her way to talk or offer me any sort of comfort in quite a while. A part of me wants to seize this chance and try to rebuild our relationship. But another part doesn't want to share the truth about Callie with anybody, especially a sister I barely know anymore. I feel if I start talking, it'll be like a cork has been pulled on an upside-down bottle: everything will spill out of me and I won't be able to stop it. What if I say something about the visions? I'll be sent back to the hospital before I can blink.

So instead I say, "The truth is I didn't even like Callie. I just didn't want to tell Dad that because it sounded bad. I only hung out with her because Stephanie made me. So yeah, I'm really not that upset."

The harsh words sting my throat. I sound like such an asshole. I can tell from Mai's slightly curled lip that she agrees with me on that.

"I see. Okay. I won't bother you, then." She turns sharply on her heel and leaves, slamming the door behind her.

She hates me more than ever now. I should have come up with a less despicable lie.

I sink face down into my bed, resting my forehead on my comic. I kind of wish it wasn't a lie. Things would be so much easier. Maybe if I repeat it over and over, it will become true.

"I didn't like her at all. She was mean and rude and a bully and she just ran off without listening to us, so why should I care? W-why do I?" Tears fall on the comic, reducing Wonder Woman's face to a splotchy mess. "Why did it have to be this way?"

Of course, there is no answer.

SCHOOL IS EVEN more stressful than home. Everyone seems to know the details of Callie's death somehow, including how Stephanie and I were there. Nobody approaches me about it, but I feel them staring all the time. I see fear in their faces. If I walk near any of them, they run away.

My only solace is that I can still look over at Stephanie during class. She gives me a sad little smile each time.

"Don't let them get to you," she says when homeroom ends and we gather at our cubbies.

"I'm used to being stared at," I tell her. "But I don't like people being scared of me. They think I killed her somehow."

Stephanie looks stricken. "That's not true!"

"I know they've asked you all about it." I saw Stephanie yelling at a few of them to leave me alone. "But no one wants to go near me or ask me anything. I get it. If I was in their position, I'd suspect me over you or anyone else too. And hey, in a way, they're kinda right."

"Don't start with that!" Stephanie snaps.

I shrug and pull a turtleneck out of my cubby.

"Are you going to change into that?" Stephanie asks. "It's not cold out."

"I need to make extra sure I don't touch anyone after what happened." I fan myself. Sweat is starting to bead on my skin already. "Dad's started nagging me about overheating though, so I gotta be sneaky about it."

Stephanie bites her lip.

A few days later, Stephanie meets me by my cubby and thrusts a large white box into my hands.

"Open this at home. And I demand you use it."

With that, she swivels around, leaving me standing there, my expression probably suiting someone who's been handed a live chicken more than someone who's gotten a gift.

I'm almost scared to open it. I wait until I get home in case it's something weird. I place it in front of me on my bed and spend what feels like an hour staring at it. Finally, I rip the top off like I'm ripping off a Band-Aid.

It's a long-sleeved shirt, gloves, a kerchief, veil and stockings, all made out of the sheerest material I've ever seen. It's transparent, and the cloth is barely there, a silky whisper.

It takes me a second to understand why I've received it. I look down at the sweat-soaked gloves I wear now. My heavy clothes are hardest to handle when it's hot out. It's like I'm moving through steam that surrounds me and inflames every part of my body.

But this stuff will cover me up without giving me heatstroke. I can wear it over and under normal clothes and it will feel light and breezy. It's so sheer that people might not even notice I'm wearing it right away. I tug at it. Pretty sturdy material too.

Where did Steph even find such things? Did she make them herself? I reach for the note.

> Everything with Callie was my idea. It really wasn't your fault. You do deserve to be happy. Take it from me and take this.

I hold the gauze up. I'm a bit different from the norm because when I hear the word "veil" it's usually black mourning veils that pop into my head, like the ones the old folks wore at my grandmother's funeral. Since that day, I've thought of veils as something that shield you from the world and hide your grief and tears. As my sister would say, "Typical gloomy-guts logic."

But this white gauzy stuff reminds me of a wedding veil. A sheer piece of cloth that connects you to someone, instead of cutting you off from them. I bury my face in the silky stuff and cry.

Part Two

One Year Later

Chapter Nine

"OH MY GOD, just lay into him!" Steph yells, pumping her fists at the TV. "Everyone knows this whole 'I don't want to fight you' crap never works, I want to see pummeling!"

"There's a lot more to this kind of stuff than pummeling," I say as I sip my soda, cross-legged on the couch next to Stephanie. I watch the heroine take a painful kick to the gut from her brainwashed friend. "This is a tormented person lashing out. She feels partially responsible too: she was so wrapped up in herself she had no idea what he was going through. She doesn't want to add to the hurt."

"Only you could get a feelings attack about this kind of movie." Stephanie rolls her eyes but she smiles fondly. "Sometimes the best therapy is a good beating."

"My God, I hope you never go into counseling," I mutter as the heroine attempts a cool-down hug on her friend, who struggles against her embrace.

"Why not! I've had tons of practice with you!" Stephanie sticks her tongue out at me.

"If we're choosing your career based on our relationship, you should be some sort of boot-camp instructor," I snort as the boy throws off the heroine with an angry growl, pile-driving her into the dirt.

"I'm just trying to toughen you up! Hey, I think we need our own friend-to-friend fight!" Steph pounces on me, going for a gentler version of the wrestling move being used in the movie. "Try to escape my wrath!"

My skin tingles and my heart pounds as Stephanie's writhing body crushes against mine. I feel the heat of her body through the thin film of her sleeve, her curly hair brushing my face.

"Steph, Steph, please! You need to stop! No skin contact, remember!"

Stephanie jerks away. She sits back with a sigh and twirls a lock of hair while I try to compose myself. She smelled faintly of lavender, and it still tickles my nose. I can't figure out if the scent came from her hair or her skin.

"I wouldn't mind," Stephanie says, snapping me out of my reverie.

"What?"

"Contact. I wouldn't mind."Steph's eyes dart anywhere but at me.

"Steph, I'd see your death," I remind her.

Stephanie shrugs. "Yeah, but then it would be over and we could be normal with each other. Touch, y'know."

She brushes the tip of her hair against her lips.

My face goes hot again.

Stephanie continues, "Besides, I think I know how it's going to happen. I sort of want to know whether you'll see what I see for myself."

A chill shoots through me. "You think you know how you'll die? How?"

Steph makes a *tsk* noise, causing her hair to unravel from around her finger. "I'll tell you if you touch me."

I draw back. "No. I can't believe we're having this conversation. Seeing your death would be terrible for me. You know that!"

"Oh come on," Stephanie laughs quietly, lowering her eyes. "You get mad at me a lot! Don't tell me you've never imagined how great it would be to see me dead sometimes."

Her words sting like a slap. I curl my shaking hands into fists in my lap.

Finally, Steph looks at me again, and her eyes go soft. "I'm sorry. I went too far again, didn't I? I'm so stupid."

I'm fighting down a lump in my throat the size of a snowball. "And you get on me for being negative."

"I'm a hypocrite," Steph admits. "Me and my mouth." She strokes my silken sleeve. "I didn't mean it. I just, it's weird, I never thought I'd say this to anyone, much less, well, I don't want there to be anything getting between us."

We're interrupted by Dad coming into the living room from the kitchen. He's wearing the frown to end all frowns. My chest tightens. What's going on?

"What's up, Mr. S.?" Stephanie says with alarm as he rubs his forehead.

"Oh." His hand slides down. "Well, I'm not sure if I should be the one to deliver this news to Stephanie, but you're going to find out sooner or later."

He sits in the chair across from the couch we're on. He leans forward, his expression grave.

"Mai called to tell me that Ms. Carnahan lost her job today."

Both Stephanie and I exclaim in surprise. "She what?"

Dad nods solemnly. "Her behavior has been erratic lately.

She's missed quite a few days. She's broken down sobbing a few times while teaching and well, apparently she came in drunk and said she'd had enough. Mai saw it all, unfortunately. It wasn't pretty."

My gut ties itself in a knot. I knew Ms. Carnahan hadn't been doing well ever since what happened with Callie. But I hadn't thought it would get this bad.

"God," Stephanie moans, putting her head in her hands.

"I'm sorry, Stephanie. But this is just one of those things," Dad says gently. "It's nobody's fault. I'm sure she'll get through it; she has a lot of people who care about her. It'll be fine."

"You really think she'll be okay?" Uncertainty gnaws at me.

"I do," Dad reassures us. "But your sister is really shaken up over this, so we need to be sensitive to her tonight. We should treat her nicely." He looks pointedly at me as he says this, and I'm offended by the silent reprimand. Mai is the one who was always not nice *first*.

"Fine," I mumble.

"Are you okay, Stephanie?"

"Yeah." Stephanie takes her head out of her hands and gives an unconvincing smile. "Thanks for telling me, Mr. S."

"You're welcome." His smile is equally unconvincing, but he appears to be at a loss how to comfort Stephanie. Then his face lights up and he snaps his fingers. "That reminds me! I got something for both of you!"

"What?" I ask suspiciously. Dad's gifts tend to be embarrassing.

"Just wait," he says, bustling out of the room.

He comes back in carrying two books. They're pretty hefty. He kneels down to hand one to me and one to Stephanie. I take mine cautiously. On the cover, it reads *Dealing with Grief and Depression: The Road to Recovery*. There's a picture of two colorful hands piecing a broken heart back together.

"Dad," I groan. "Another one? You got me something like this a year ago too."

"That one was about dealing with immediate tragedy. This is about long-term healing. There's lots of things in this that might be helpful, like a recovery journal." He sighs. "I know it's been a while, but I also know what happened to that girl was hard on you. And I don't want you two going down the same road Ms. Carnahan's going down. I want you to be able to talk about it and ask for help."

I peer over at Stephanie, afraid this is humiliating for her. But on the contrary, her eyes are shining as she examines the book. "I can't believe you thought to get one for me too."

"Of course I did!" He straightens up, looking affronted at the very idea he wouldn't. "You're practically part of the family at this point. I'm as worried about you as I am for Manee."

Stephanie's eyelids flutter. I wonder briefly if she's blinking back tears, but the next moment she's jumped to her feet, dry-eyed and boisterous as ever. She hugs Dad with all her might. "Thanks so much."

Dad beams so hard after receiving that hug from Stephanie that I get a slight pang in my chest. I can't remember the last time I'd made him that happy.

"Well, I'd better get cooking. Stephanie, are you staying for dinner tonight? I've got a new recipe. And if you want, we can pick up where we left off with our last lesson."

"I wish I could," Stephanie says heavily. "But it would be the third time this week and my parents will probably think I'm off performing necromancy or something."

Dad's eyebrows contract. "What's necromancy?"

"Nothing you'd be interested in hearing about," I tell him hastily.

He purses his lips, edging on a pout. "Fine, fine. But Stephanie, I can call your parents and let them know nothing bad is going on."

Steph's thousand-watt smile flickers. "They're very busy, so you probably wouldn't be able to get hold of them. But thanks for always offering."

"Keep going like that and he's going to adopt you any day now," I joke weakly after Dad leaves the living room. "You'll be his favorite daughter for sure."

"That sounds like a dream come true," Stephanie sighs, collapsing back onto the couch. "I could eat good food every day! I could learn Thai every day and become amazing at it! It would be the perfect life with the perfect dad."

"You only think that because you don't have to deal with how overprotective he is." I pull my purse off the floor and show Stephanie a black bottle inside. "He gave me pepper spray a while back, if you can believe it. I told him I'd get in trouble if the school found it, but he told me they can just call him and that my safety is the most important thing."

"That. Is. So. Cool!" Stephanie is practically sparkling. "I wish he'd give me some!"

"You would," I groan. Then I bite my lip. "Do your parents

really think you're doing necromancy?"

"If it's bad, they think I do it," Steph shrugs. "I might be the favored child with your dad, but I am definitely not with them. Tony won't even acknowledge my dad as family, but Pops will still take him over me any day."

"Well." My heart starts to pound faster. "Maybe if I came over and finally, y'know, met them, I could explain that you're not getting up to anything bad." Heat returns to my face. I almost can't believe my own boldness.

Stephanie raises an eyebrow. "You could, but don't you think visiting Ava's more of a priority for us right now?"

"Oh." My heart sinks. As horrible as it is to admit, I almost forgot about Ms. Carnahan just now. Just the thought of going back to her house makes me wince. I hate being places where Callie used to be. I asked Dad to transfer schools just to escape her ghost. And the few times I've talked to Ms. Carnahan since Callie died have not been pleasant, to say the least. "Are you sure she even wants to see us, though?"

Stephanie runs her fingers across the cover of the grief journal. "Maybe not. But I feel like I have to do something." She picks up the journal and starts flipping through it. "I wonder if Ava has one of these. Or if I should get her one. God, I know what happened really messed her up, but I had no idea it'd get *this* bad."

"Yeah, I didn't think it would either," I mumble. "I wish we," I don't need to finish the sentence. I know we both feel the same. The mess with Ava Carnahan is something we made together.

Stephanie gives her sad little smile. "No matter how much you wish and torture yourself over it, it's not going to change what happened."

"I know that."

Stephanie's mouth tightens slightly. "Do you ever regret telling me?"

"What?"

"You know. Because it ended up like it did."

It takes me a second to figure it out. All things considered, I should regret it. But.

I smile at Stephanie. "Not really. I just wish it hadn't led to everything that happened afterward."

"Yeah. That makes sense. Funny how things can get out of control so quickly." She shakes her head. Then she closes the grief journal with a snap and slaps it down on the table. "Well, no use dwelling. Let's just finish up our movie."

"Are you sure?" I feel like there's more to say, but I also can't deny a part of me just wants to forget about all this.

"I just want to turn my brain off for a bit. Nothing like a good distraction."

A distraction does sound nice. I look at the screen and groan. "It's already at the credits. We talked through the entire end."

"No big deal, just rewind."

"I'll spoil it for myself," I lament. "Even scene selection lets you see stuff."

"Okay, you big baby, close your eyes and I'll find our place," Stephanie laughs.

I'm glad the laugh doesn't sound forced. "Thanks, I just hate spoilers."

"Says the girl with psychic powers."

"That's why I hate them! I can get the ultimate spoiler if I'm not careful!"

Stephanie's mouth curls with amusement. I kick back, trying to forget all about my guilt and fear and, just for this moment, enjoy being next to my friend. In all the excitement, I forget that Stephanie never finished what she was going to say earlier.

Chapter Ten

AFTER STEPHANIE'S DEPARTURE, I have nothing to do besides dread my sister coming home. As I take my gloves and veil off, I wonder what I can possibly even say to Mai. I have to say *something*. Mai loves Ms. Carnahan with all her heart and no matter how you look at it, it's partly my fault things turned out like this for her.

After what seems like hours, I hear the sound of gravel crunching as Mai's car rolls in. Dad hears it too and dashes to the front door. As soon as Mai comes in, she's scooped up into a hug. She slumps into Dad's embrace, closing her eyes.

I approach hesitantly, wringing my hands. "I'm sorry, Mai."

"Thanks," Mai mutters without bothering to look at me.

This stings, as petty as that is. "I really mean it. Tell me if there's anything I can do." I inject as much strength into my voice as I can.

Mai detaches from Dad and finally looks at me. A pang hits me when I see she's struggling not to cry. She's so utterly raw and vulnerable, all her grief written on her face. She twitches her hand, inviting me to come join the hug.

I take a shaky step forward, slowly raising my arms. But when I'm close enough to feel the heat from Mai's body, a wave of panic crashes into me. Every death I've ever seen flashes in my mind: Callie's broken chest and swollen eyes, my mother wasting away in the hospital bed, Jocelyn's body curled on the floor, my grandmother seizing up, and the life draining from Mai's own papery face in a distant future. Something blocks my throat. It doesn't make any sense. I've already seen their deaths; I have nothing to fear. But still my body revolts. I take a step back and the noose loosens a bit. I suck in air hungrily.

"Manee?" Dad's eyes are wide with concern.

Mai's expression has no trace of worry, however. Her nostrils flare and her tears seem to boil in her eyes. "Typical. You can never be there for anyone. Not even Ms. Carnahan! I know you haven't tried to help her at all!"

"I did try," I grunt, looking down at the floor. I don't want to go into detail about exactly how those visits to Ms. Carnahan's house went. "It's just hard for me to get close to people; you know that."

"Because of the 'visions?' I thought you told the hospital people and Dad you were cured. Was that a lie?"

I don't answer her. I just glare at the carpet with my fists clenched by my sides.

"That's *enough*," Dad cuts in. "Ms. Carnahan's situation is not your sister's responsibility. She *is* trying her best to help. Don't take things out on her." He has that rarely heard authoritative edge to his voice.

"Sorry, I forgot," Mai says, wiping her eyes, her lips pressed together in a bitter smirk. "Gotta be gentle with Manee. Her feelings always come first."

"Mai," Dad says softly.

"I'm fine. It's fine. I know it isn't her fault. I'm gonna go up to my room, okay? I'm pretty tired."

Without a glance back, Mai rushes up the steps.

"I'll bring dinner up in a few minutes," Dad calls after her. He attempts to give me a reassuring smile. "Don't worry. I'll talk to her."

"It doesn't matter," I mumble. I trudge back to the couch and sink into the cushions. Why did I even bother?

A small sigh makes me look up. Dad leans heavily against the wall, looking at the ceiling. There's a strange dullness in his eyes and the lines around his face seem deeper. I'm used to thinking of Dad as a big, anxious kid but he looks very old right now.

I squirm uncomfortably. This is my fault. I've once again denied him what he wants more than anything, for us to be able to touch again like a normal family.

But I just can't do it.

It isn't like I see his death every time he touches me. The visions are a one-time thing for each person, but sometimes when he reaches for me, I can't help but remember. I remember that someday my father's solid, smooth hand is going to turn gnarled and bony, that it will claw at his chest for a few seconds, and then finally go limp as his eyes close.

In some ways it's lucky. His death is the best one a daughter could hope for a parent: peaceful and late in life. It should be more comforting than traumatic. Still, my skin crawls every time I think about it.

But that's not the real reason I haven't touched him in years. The reason is I promised him I wouldn't.

I didn't have full-blown visions when I touched people until I was around eleven. They coincided with my period, a double whammy of puberty hell. However, as far back as I can remember, touching people gave me an unpleasant feeing, like I'd just dreamed something scary and forgotten about it. I'd get dizzy too. It just got stronger and stronger as I got older.

My mother always seemed to know there was something "off" about me. Whenever I tried to explain to her about the feelings I got, she'd sigh and look so sad. So I stopped talking about it, even as it got worse and worse.

Then Mom walked out on us, shortly after I caused Grandma's death. When she left, I shut down. I couldn't eat, couldn't move, couldn't talk. I couldn't leave the house. It felt like any action I took, no matter how small, would cause something else terrible to happen. If I just stayed hidden away, I couldn't wreck anything else. I wouldn't bother anyone ever again.

That wasn't true in practice, though. Of course my breakdown bothered my dad. He coaxed me outside eventually, wanting me to take baby steps back into the world. It was supposed to be nothing, a literal walk in the park.

But all it took to make me fall apart completely was a passerby almost brushing against me. I can't remember what happened very clearly, maybe I just don't want to. Apparently, I ran somewhere and hid myself away. All I recall is feeling like I'd stopped breathing. I was sure I was dying and thought, "Finally, it's my turn." I remember the sound of someone crying and choking at the same time. I remember knowing it was me, but not being able to stop it or understand it. Dad found me eventually and I guess I must have told him everything through my sobs, about the visions, about how I couldn't ever touch anyone again, about how it was all my fault.

I was taken to the hospital for observation. The doctors didn't believe me about the visions, of course. They said it was just how I "rationalized my own desire to cut myself off from people in the wake of my trauma." I begged Dad to believe me.

"Even if I did, it wouldn't matter. You can't go on like this. I want you to feel happy again. I want you to be able to go outside. I want you to touch people. At this rate, I'm scared you'll hurt yourself, or disappear forever. I couldn't take that."

I promised that I wouldn't, that I'd try harder, that I'd do anything at all if only he wouldn't lock me away with a bunch of strangers, if only he wouldn't have me poked and prodded by endless people. But he didn't listen. Under the doctor's advice, I was sent to a children's mental hospital.

It was terrifying at first, not because anything about the

people there was particularly scary, but because there were so many. So many deaths I could potentially see. And even there, the other kids thought I was weird. The hospital was mostly filled with kids who were so depressed that they needed to be under constant observation. My "delusions" didn't fit in.

"I think they sent her to the wrong place," I heard one kid whisper during group therapy. "She needs to be locked up tight."

The only one who didn't whisper was a girl named, Jocelyn. She made the hospital bearable for me. She believed in me completely. I had never felt so close to anyone. When the doctors encouraged me to try touching people again, Jocelyn volunteered to be the first test subject. She was really curious to see how she would die.

The answer to that was something that haunts me to this day. I tried so hard to warn her. I pleaded with her through tears, but Jocelyn refused to believe it.

"You're a liar after all," she told me coldly. That was the last time we ever talked.

The day I got discharged, I stood there silently as my father filled out the final paperwork with the receptionist. Mai kept close to the door, looking around nervously as if she expected the crazies to jump out of nowhere and attack her with foaming mouths.

Finally, we were allowed to leave. I wanted to burst out the double doors but I just followed my family quietly out into the parking lot. As soon as we were outside, my father turned to face me. I noted the dark circles under his eyes and the way his chin trembled slightly. He regarded me as if I was a strange, mysterious creature he didn't know how to approach.

It was understandable. Every day when he'd visited me at the hospital, I'd simply sit there like a doll, refusing to speak.

"Manee," he began, shifting awkwardly from side to side.

"It's okay," I said with a wide smile and glassy eyes. "You know, I had to touch a bunch of people in there. So I'm used to it now! I can even touch you."

I held my arms out, and he approached me, hands shaking, hardly daring to believe.

I shoved him. Hard.

"There. I've proved I can do it. That's the last time I'll ever touch you."

I left him standing off balance and marched past my flabbergasted sister to the family car.

Mai never forgave me for that. "Do you even know how

much sending you to that hospital wrecked him?" she hissed at me later.

Maybe that was true. But I couldn't bring myself to care. I'd begged him not to send me away, but he'd done it anyway. I still have nightmares about all of it. The worst part is, I can't even make him understand what it is I've been through, with Jocelyn, with any of it. If I tell him, he won't believe me. That hurts more than anything. So I cling to the promise because it feels like the only piece of power I have anymore, the only protection, the only control.

But as I gaze at my dad's tired face here and now, I'm terribly sad I'm not the kind of daughter who can give him a comforting hug, the kind of daughter Stephanie would gladly be. Slowly I get up from the couch.

"Um, I'd like to help you with dinner, actually."

He smiles faintly at me. "That would be nice, thanks."

We chop vegetables side by side that night, and after a while, the silence between us changes from tense to comfortable. Then Dad starts in on stories of how he and my grandfather once cooked together like this for the family's short-lived attempt at a restaurant. *Bpoo* lost interest, like he did with so many of his "projects," but dad never forgot the joy of cooking.

Rather than reminding him I've heard all this before, I keep quiet and listen. It isn't much, but it's enough to bring a little light back in him. I'm glad I can at least do that, if nothing else.

Chapter Eleven

WHEN I SEND Steph some texts complaining about my argument with Mai that night and don't receive the usual automatic response, I figure she must have gone to sleep early. But I feel real concern the next morning when I board the bus and Stephanie isn't there waiting with a seat saved like usual. I sit down next to a kid that smells like weed who's nodding off with his cheek pressed against the window. I turn as far away from him as I can, chewing on a stray strand of my hair as I stare down at my phone. Is Stephanie out sick or something? But if she is, she should have texted me about it. After all, she texts every time she stubs her toe or argues with her brother.

Her *brother*. "Shit!" I yelp.

The kid next to me wakes up with a jolt and glares at me.

I ignore him, cursing myself. How could I forget Tony? True, I haven't seen him since the night Callie died and Stephanie always avoids talking about him beyond the occasional mention. But I still clearly remember the fierce way he glared at Stephanie back then as he put his arms around Ms. Carnahan. That alone tells me how badly he has to be taking the news about her. Here I've been complaining to Stephanie about my sister being crabby over Ms. Carnahan, while Tony must be giving her all kinds of hell. No wonder she isn't responding. She must be so disgusted at me for sending her all these whiny messages but not even bothering to ask about Tony. I quickly punch in a text:

```
shit i'm sorry I forgot about tony u must be
mad. is he giving you a hard time? PLEASE
ANSWER!!!
```

I stare at the phone throughout the bus ride, but still no response. When I arrive at homeroom, Stephanie's seat is empty. I sit down beside the unoccupied desk, feeling unmoored. Homeroom is the only place that feels like my old school at all. The teacher distractedly fiddles with his phone and doesn't care whether we sleep through the whole twenty minutes. And Stephanie's always in the seat next to me, ready to lean over whenever I threaten to nod off myself. It made me so happy when Stephanie insisted on transferring here with me. I could always count on her to whisper some dirty joke to send a shock through my system, waking me up better than any morning coffee.

Or at least that's usually the case. Homeroom's almost over now but still no Stephanie.

I glare down at my phone. Where is she? Did Tony do something to her? Like *what?* Driving her out to the middle of a swamp and abandoning her there?

I knead my forehead with my knuckles, attempting to massage my brain back into a rationally thinking organ. I know I'm overreacting. But no matter what meds they give me, there's that well of anxiety inside that will never completely dry up. After everything that's happened, all I've lost, it's hard not to worry all the time that I'm an inch away from losing Stephanie too.

The bell rings. I slowly get up from my seat, phone still clutched in my hand as everyone files out of the classroom. Still nothing. My teacher gives me a raised eyebrow from his desk. I sigh, grab my backpack, and head out. Trying to weave through crowded hallways is the thing I have the most difficulty with in this new school. And now it's even harder since I can't stop glancing at my phone every five feet. Just when I'm about to give up and put it away in my purse, it buzzes loudly.

I hurriedly swipe to the text Stephanie's written with a crying emoji:

```
Sry just got here had to head str8 to calc!
didn't mean to worry you just got held up! cu at
lunch <3
```

Relief floods me. She's okay. And doesn't seem mad. The tension drains from my muscles and I drop my phone back in my purse as I enter my art history class.

Lunchtime rolls around, and when I find Steph waiting in our usual meeting spot just outside the cafeteria, I run to her as fast as my feet will carry me. "Stephanie!"

"Whoa, maybe you should simmer down! It's like I'm a hero returning from battle or something," Stephanie says with a grin.

"Yeah, well, I thought something was wrong! I sent you so many texts but you took so long to get back to me!" I huff.

"Ah, yeah." Steph's smile turns soft. "Sorry 'bout that."

"What happened?"

"Nothing much." Stephanie shrugs as we walk into the cafeteria together. "Like I said, just got held up."

She looks away as she says this. Avoiding eye contact, that's always a sign something's up with Stephanie.

We grab our trays and stand in line. My neck prickles in discomfort at how close the boy in front of me is. I back up slightly and bump against the stainless steel counter. I try to shake it off and focus on talking to Stephanie.

"Was it Tony that held you up?"

"Yeah," Steph says evenly, staring down the long counter at the vats brimming with artificial-smelling food. "We just had a small argument."

"About Ms. Carnahan?" I ask hesitantly as the line inches forward.

A shadow falls over Stephanie's face. "Yeah."

"Have you talked to her?"

"I stopped by her place last night. She's not super responsive, to say the least. It's like talking to a completely different person." She glances over her shoulder at me. "Kind of wish you'd been there with me."

Now it's my turn to look away. "Sorry," I mumble as a lunch lady dumps a lump of mashed potatoes on my tray. "Maybe you can get Ms. Carnahan to talk to Tony for you? Explain it's not your fault?"

"It didn't really seem like the right time to ask her for something like that."

"But if Tony's giving you a bad time!"

"Look, like I said, we just got distracted arguing!" Stephanie snaps, snatching up one of the Jello Cups laid out at the end of the counter. "I missed the bus and had to get a cab."

I'm pretty skeptical about this explanation. "Really? Cuz whenever you're around your brother it always seems to me like you can't wait to get away from him. I can't see you staying with him by choice."

"Why are you so hyped up about this? Are you thinking he's going to murder me or something?" Stephanie rolls her eyes as we approach the cash register. "Actually, it might be a good idea to check for that. You should use your powers on me."

"Shut up," I mumble as I hand the bored cashier a few dollars. He drops the change on my tray without even glancing up at me. Steph pays too, and then we make our way to our usual table in the corner of the room.

After we sit down, I take out my wallet to put the change away and Stephanie asks, "What's that?" She points to a crumpled note sticking out of it.

"Ah," I groan, "it's something the sub in art history gave me. He caught me doodling in class today and invited me to some art group. It was weird and embarrassing."

"Whaaaaaaat?" Stephanie drops her fork and leans forward excitedly. "That's great! 'Bout time someone was smart enough to recognize your talent. Have I ever met this guy?"

"I dunno, maybe you've seen him. Tall black guy with short hair, mid-twenties, high cheekbones, wears a tie."

"Ohhhh, yeah, I've seen him. He's hot," Steph sighs dreamily.

"I guess," I say, unable to keep an edge of annoyance out of my tone. "If you like that sort of thing."

"No worries, I like *all* sorts of things," Stephanie smirks. "Lemme see that note."

I hand it over and Stephanie examines it, her eyes lighting up. "Wow, a meeting tonight! See, I'm always telling you you've got things going for you. If you put yourself out there more, you'd have gotten an offer like this sooner."

"I don't *want* offers," I mutter as I press my fork flat against my potatoes, squeezing the powdery white mush through the tines.

"Why? I thought you wanted to be an artist. Networking with other artists and getting noticed is how your career gets started."

"Ugh!" I wrinkle my nose. "I don't care about stuff like that."

"I mean, it's not just that. You can meet people."

"And why would I want to do that?"

"To find people like you! They could be a lot closer than you think." Stephanie pauses for a second and then clears her throat. "I mean, those sensitive artist types are always talking about having weird visions. You can relate."

"That's the last thing I want to relate to someone about," I snort.

Stephanie frowns. "Okay but, still, new experiences are good. And wouldn't you like to have something to do rather than just go straight home for once?"

"What?" I'm about to say that I want nothing more than to go straight home, but then I notice that Stephanie is unusually focused on her peas, picking at them awkwardly. I get it instantly: Stephanie's the one who doesn't want to go straight home. Is the tension with Tony really that bad?

"Fine," I sigh. "Let's go to the art club together."

"Really?" Stephanie's eyes widen.

"Sure," I mutter grimly. "It'll be a great opportunity to figure out my tolerance for pain."

So, at the end of the school day, we make our way to the room noted on Mr. Barnes's card. We run into the man himself on the way. Stephanie immediately turns into that weird deferential person she becomes around most adults she doesn't know, thanking him politely for letting us into the club and never taking her eyes off him. I trudge behind her and Mr. Barnes as he leads us down the stairs and to the east wing, a part of the school best known for having a perpetually out-of-order bathroom.

My heart pounds irritatingly loudly. What am I going to find in the clubroom? I keep picturing a bunch of black-clad hipsters in berets painting at fancy easels with their noses up in the air. Oh God, what if there are models? What if we have to draw a nude model?

Thankfully, I'm spared this. Instead, we're shown into a dimly lit classroom full of empty desks. There's only two other students, and they sit near the middle of the room, sketching on loose-leaf paper, their only supplies a worn-out looking paint set, some crayons, and a box of colored pencils placed between them.

"We've still got a bit of growing to do as a group." Barnes's laugh sounds forced. "But maybe you can help us with that. Come, meet your new friends!" He shoves some desks aside and swings a couple around so that Stephanie and I can sit facing the other two. Then, giving us an encouraging nod, he sits at his own desk off to the side.

Stephanie and I greet our new "friends" and give our names, though my voice comes out small and shaky. A bubbly white girl with a nose piercing and big pink sweater introduces herself as Emma.

"I recognize you!" she chirps at Stephanie. "We have a Lit class together, right?"

There's skinny black kid with a shaved head and red t-shirt as well, but he barely looks up from his art to greet us, muttering vaguely that his name is Jackson. Whatever he's sketching is a mess. He keeps erasing it and starting over again, so the paper's a giant smudge.

Pencil in hand, I look down at the blank page and sweat. How am I supposed to draw surrounded by people like this? I glance over at Stephanie and she gifts me her gentle smile. I relax.

"Y'know, I've never heard your name before. Mo-ney?" It takes a second for me to realize Emma's addressing me. She's scrutinizing me like I'm some rare animal. "Is it like, you were named after cash, or is it spelled different but just sounds the same?"

I bite back a sigh. "No, it's—"

"You're pronouncing it wrong," Stephanie snaps before I can finish. "It's *Mah*-nee. And the *nee* is more stressed. And of course it's not spelled like money. Jeez."

Stephanie stares Emma down like she's preparing to challenge her to a duel. I'm torn. It's nice not having to give lessons on pronouncing my name for once. I'm happy to have her take this one, but her interrupting me to do it is annoying.

"Well, I've never heard of it before," Emma says, cheerfully oblivious to Stephanie's annoyance. "What's it spelled like then?"

"It's—"

"M-A-N-E-E. It's a Thai name, it means 'jewel.'"

God, Stephanie, let me get a word in edgewise. I shoot her an irritable look, but at the same time, my heart speeds up at the thought of Stephanie looking up what my name means. Well, she does know some Thai.

"Thai! I thought you looked kinda like you're from Taiwan!" Emma said, as if she'd solved a great mystery.

I groan internally. Every freaking time, seriously.

But again, before I can say anything, Stephanie rises from her seat, slamming her hands on the desk. "It's *Thailand*, not Taiwan, they're completely different. If I meant Taiwan, I'd say Taiwanese! Also, she's not from there, her grandparents were! *She* was born right here in this town!"

Emma shrinks back. "I'm sorry."

Jackson looks up from his paper at last with the expression of someone watching a mildly interesting debate program.

"Is there a problem?" Mr. Barnes asks from across the room.

I tug at the corner of Stephanie's sleeve. "Steph, do you want to leave?"

"No," Stephanie huffs, sitting down. "I'm good. Art club is good for you. Us." Her face is flushed and her eyes unfocused.

I'm not sure what to do. It's not like I feel bad for Emma or anything, but it's unusual for Stephanie to be flustered like this.

Wanting to break the awkward silence, I cast around for something the comment on. My eyes fall on Emma's art and I'm surprised at the quality. There's about eight half-finished drawings all stacked up, but her style is really fluid and nice looking. It's all high-fantasy stuff. The dragons and lady knights were so well constructed I'm envious.

"Hey, that's really nice," I say, nodding at her.

"Thank you," Emma cries, positively beaming. Wow, she bounces back quickly.

"What are you drawing?"

I'm bent over my art, shielding it from view. "Nothing, it's terrible, you don't want to see," I tell her hastily, hunching over even more.

"It's not terrible, it's good," Stephanie says irritably. I see out of the corner of my eye she's drawing stick figures getting anvils dropped on them.

"That's right! I'll bet it's great!" Emma chirps.

"You can't be ashamed of your art," Jackson mutters without looking up from his own.

I stare pointedly at his eraser-marked sketch.

"Yeah, I know," he says flatly, sensing my look.

"I wanna see!" Emma reaches over to pull my hand out of the way. I jerk back to avoid contact, nearly toppling my chair over. In the same instant, Stephanie reaches over and slaps Emma's hand away.

"She said she didn't want you to!"

A heavy blanket of silence covers the room. Emma rubs her bright-red hand, her lips trembling. Jackson is hunched over in his seat, his face strained. Mr. Barnes rises and comes toward us.

I jump to my feet. "It's okay, we're leaving," I tell Mr. Barnes. Grabbing the purse strap dangling from Stephanie's shoulder with one hand and my bag with another, I jerk her upright and march us both out of the room. Mr. Barnes calls after us, but I ignore him.

When we're finally safely outside the school, I turn, hands on my hips. "What was *that?*"

"What? She was way out of line!"

"Yeah, she was, but people have tried to touch me before and I've never seen you lose it so much!" I decide not to bring up the fact *she'd* even been one of those people once. "You know that if we draw attention during arguments like that, we're the ones who get in trouble while people like her get all the pity points."

"Well, maybe I'm sick of it!" Stephanie kicks the brick wall of the school. "Maybe I'm sick of everything! Why can't people just leave us *alone*?!"

"Us?" I raise my eyebrows.

Stephanie freezes. "You. I meant you."

"Stephanie, what are you really mad about?

Stephanie's shoulders slump. "I don't know," she says in an exhausted voice, staring at the ground. "Everything, I guess.

Everything's spinning out of control." She looks at me with drooping eyes. "Manee, are we okay?"

"Us? Of course." I lick my dry lips. It's unnerving to see Stephanie acting like this. She's supposed to be the strong one. "Steph, why don't we forget about all this and go on a trip downtown tomorrow? I know you've been wanting to."

"Downtown?" Stephanie draws her eyebrows together. "But you hate it downtown."

"I hate it a lot less when I'm with you," I tell her. "In fact, I kind of like it." That's a lie, but maybe if I tell it loudly enough, it will come true.

Stephanie's face breaks into a beatific smile. "Okay. Let's do it."

I bathe in the warmth of that smile. I don't get what's going on with her right now at all, but if I can still make Stephanie look like that, maybe things will be okay again someday. Maybe.

Chapter Twelve

I TAKE A deep breath, reminding myself this is for Stephanie. She was so happy I suggested this trip. I have to tough this out for her.

It's easy to see why she loves it here so much. Our downtown area is famous for being artsy and quaint, with all different types of people populating the streets, tourist buses, and folks with traveling backpacks snapping photos. Both homeless people and teenagers attempting to be "urban" camp out on the sidewalks. On one corner, there's a gaggle of young women with dyed hair and ripped clothing screaming with laughter. On the other corner, an eighty-year-old couple is holding hands as they take small, toddling steps on the sidewalk.

It's colorful enough even I want to get out my sketchbook every few feet. But I also can't help but be antsy. The sidewalks are glutted with people and sometimes they all blur together dizzyingly. Every time someone shouts as they walk by, I flinch away from them. I can't stop thinking that someone's going to grab me out of nowhere.

Stephanie looks over, apparently sensing the tension pouring off me. "We can leave if you want to," she tells me softly.

I shake my head. "Nah, I'm fine. Gotta get used to crowds someday."

Stephanie grins. "What heroic resolve! Worry not, fair maiden, I will make sure it's not in vain. Tonight, we take on this town together!"

I giggle as Steph bows with her arm outstretched toward the sidewalk, like a knight gallantly clearing the way for the lady in her charge. Steph is true to her word and takes me to see all the sights. We gaze at a street performer pretending to be a statue for a while, in awe of her perfect stillness and elaborate silver makeup. Near a real statue of a girl leaning over a water fountain, we happen across a magic show and chuckle together as the performer desperately tries to convince a skeptical seven-year-old his tricks are real. After this, we go to the town square and watch old people and young people alike facing off in heated chess matches. Nearby stands a man attempting to juggle for tips.

"I'll give you a dollar if you drop it on your head!" A bulky man heckles him.

Stephanie turns and looks directly into the man's eyes, hitting him with the full force of her icy glare. The man glares back at first, but then he quails and breaks eye contact. I don't know how she does that. I wish I could just intimidate any sort of person with a look like hers.

In the center of the town square, a drum circle gets going. We watch it from afar, standing near a soft pretzel stand across the street. Steph sniggers slightly. She's watching at a couple at the edge of the circle who are clearly feeling very passionate. "Making out" is really too tame a description—it's like they're trying to merge with each other. My ears go hot and my heart beats faster. I try to hide my lame embarrassment and laugh like Stephanie.

"Ah, romance," Steph trills. "You ever think about it?"

"What? No!" I goggle at her. "Why do you suddenly wanna talk about something like that?"

"C'mon, we've talked about it before. Remember when we did the 'who would you date' game last summer?"

"Remember how I chose the X-Men and then you chose Cthulhu because you wanted to one up me in the 'power couple' department?"

"Ah, yes. I guess we were too young to have a serious discussion. But we're mature now."

I snort. "Yeah, six months makes so much difference."

"But like really, is there a reason you don't want to talk about it?"

I throw up my arms in exasperation. "Do I have to spell it out? I don't want to do it because of the touching thing. There, I told you what you already knew."

"Then *I'll* state the obvious: limiting yourself like that will only lead to badness."

"What, because I can't do *that*?" I snap, gesturing to the two currently climbing all over each other. "Yeah, I'm perfectly fine with friends." *Or friend, singular.*

"Friends you can't touch?"

"Nobody wants to touch me anyway."

"I wouldn't mind," Stephanie mutters with a sidelong glance.

I suck in some air through my teeth. "Yeah, but you're a complete weirdo. Is there any reason you're talking about this? Do you have a crush on somebody or something?" My throat closes up at the thought. Is it Mr. Barnes, maybe?

"Mm, I think I still haven't moved on from Cthulhu. You never forget your first," Stephanie says with an exaggerated dreamy sigh.

I chuckle. "So much for maturing."

We stand in awkward silence for a couple seconds. Stephanie fidgets. Then she gestures toward the drum circle.

"I just want to go up and put something in a donation box and tell them they're doing a good job. Is that okay?"

"Sure." I force a smile. I don't want to be alone on a street so full of people, but clearly Stephanie needs a moment. Maybe I do too. "I'll just stay here and have a pretzel or something. Take all the time you need."

"You sure?"

"Positive. Get going." I watch Steph cross the street and only let my smile drop when she fully disappears in the crowd. My eyes dart through all the people milling around the sidewalk, people I don't know at all. My head fills with a strange buzzing. I take a big breath and try to pull myself together. Focus on getting a pretzel. Just do that. Nothing else matters.

I walk up to the stand, hands shaking as I take out cash for my purchase. Once I successfully get the snack, I direct all of my might toward finding a place to sit and eat it. Overdramatic excitement bursts through me when I spot an empty bench a little ways down the street. I settle down, placing my purse beside me in hopes of deterring anyone from sitting next to me. I take off one glove and place it in my lap before slathering the pretzel with mustard. When I take my first bite, my mind is wonderfully blank of everything but the savory saltiness and the warm baked bread topped with a spicy tang.

That doesn't last long. A pale girl with dyed red hair that sticks out every which way drops her shopping bags and collapses next to me, shoving my purse out of the way. Her hand comes an inch away from brushing mine.

I shrink away instinctively and scramble for my glove. Cold sweat breaks out on my forehead. Talk about a close call.

The girl notices my discomfort. "What's your problem?" she asks sharply.

I quail under her scarily annoyed look. I get up unsteadily from my seat, clutching my food and glove. "Um, nothing. I have to go."

"What, do you have an issue with me or something? It's a public bench!"

I start backing away quickly. People are staring at us now and their gazes weigh me down. It reminds me too much of that time with Callie. This girl is going to grab me and everyone will just watch and it will start all over again.

"Whatever," the girl sneers. "Don't forget your purse." She picks it up and throws it at me. The purse hits me in the arm and I squeak and drop my pretzel on the ground. The girl snorts.

I bolt, gripping my purse tightly to my chest. I weave in between a pair of buildings and come out on the street at the other side, breathing heavily. I look frantically around for someplace, any place, where I can just be alone. But there are people everywhere, everywhere I look, I can't escape them.

I stumble down the sidewalk and put a hand against the buildings to keep myself upright. A sudden harsh noise makes me gasp. I fall to a crouch on the ground, hands over my ears. I don't even know where I am right now. Stephanie won't be able to find me. I'm all alone. I shake with suppressed sobs.

"Manee!"

My eyes snap open and my heart leaps—Stephanie is crouched beside me, eyes round and worried. A gust of relief sweeps over me and tears leak out. "H-how did you find me?"

"I was already coming to find you when I saw you running away. I just followed you. I'm so sorry. I shouldn't have left you alone."

"No, I'm okay," I wipe my face. I want to sink into Stephanie's arms so badly, just lose myself there, but I settle for hugging myself instead. "I was doing okay, it just got overwhelming."

"Yeah, I want to go find that girl and kick her ass. I saw her throw your purse at you." Steph clenches her fist.

I smile weakly. Here I wanted to take care of Stephanie for once, but it ended up the other way around, just like always. I blink my tears away and finally look around me. We're in the middle of the sidewalk, near a bike rack with a black-and-white dog tied to it. It barks.

"Oh, that was the sound that startled me," I groan, moving closer to the building entrance off the sidewalk so people don't have to walk around me anymore.

"Aw, he just wants attention," Stephanie coos, scratching him behind the ears. The dog responds by happily licking her face. "C'mon, you should pet him, it'll make you feel better."

"I can't."

"Why not? You can't see animal's deaths, can you?" Stephanie stares intently into the dog's eyes.

"No, but I get a kind of headache for a few seconds and sort of this weird feeling." I put my hand to my forehead. "I think it's like, well, when I see a vision, it's sort of like my mind travels through that person, through their brain and body. It's like I'm scanning their soul almost. I guess I just can't read an animal. We're incompatible because we're different species."

"Yeah," Stephanie tilts her head thoughtfully. "Have you ever wondered what that means?"

"Huh?"

Stephanie taps her finger against her lips. "Well, if you have to 'scan their soul' or whatever, doesn't that mean your powers are sort of 'x-raying' to figure out the most likely death for that person based on how they are? So, what you're seeing is just the most likely option, not their set-in-stone fate. And you can't see an animal's because they don't really make decisions like we do. Or something."

That's a hell of a theory for Stephanie to come up with off the top of her head. "I'm not sure that makes a lot of sense."

"Makes as much sense as scanning someone's soul does."

"I just don't really want to think about that stuff."

"I know you don't. That's why I've tried not to bring it up." Stephane sucks her cheeks in and I know she means, not since Callie. "But there's some stuff I want to—" She pauses for a long moment. "I—I mean, don't you think it would make you feel better to understand it? Talk it out once in a while? It's a part of you."

"I don't want it to be a part of me." I twist at my gloves irritably. "I don't want to understand. Look, I get you're trying to help, but can we just not talk about this right now?" *Or ever.*

"Okay, okay." Stephanie lowers her eyes, shoulders slumping. A few seconds of silence pass and then she looks back up again, suddenly sporting a bright-eyed smile. "But I know a few seconds of headache wouldn't be reason enough for me not enjoy animals. I'd go through the fires of hell for a fluffy doggy. I really think it'll make you feel better!"

I can't hold strong, that smile always makes me melt. "Well, I guess it does only last a few seconds. It's more the idea I almost see them die that creeps me out."

"Girl, just think of it as allergies! Or like petting their soul!"

I giggle. "You're such a weirdo. Okay, fine."

I place my hand on the dog's head. My brain twinges, but it doesn't hurt as much as I remember. The soft warmth of the dog flows into me, and I want to bury my face in its fur, glory in being able to freely cuddle another being for once, but I restrain myself. I return the dog's silly, sloppy grin. I let it lick my bare knuckles.

After a few minutes of cuddling, I'm finally well enough to get up off the curb and put my glove back on. Stephanie hits me with a smug smirk. "See, wasn't so bad, was it?"

"No, it wasn't. Actually, I'm wondering if I should get a dog. It'd be nice to cuddle something once in a while."

"Sure would! Glad I'm expanding your horizons. Now let's get you home!"

"Oh, are you sure? I mean, I'm fine now! If you want to stay and have fun a while longer, don't worry."

"I think we've had our fill of fun for the day," Stephanie says. She gives me a tender look. "But thanks." She gestures to the bus stop up the street. I follow her resignedly. When we reach it, Stephanie flops down on the bench, her eyes twinkling. She pats the spot beside her. I sit down, keeping a decent-sized space between us. The twinkle in her eyes flickers. It's a small flicker, but I still catch it.

"I'm sorry," I mutter.

"For what?"

"For a lot of things. For making you leave early." I stare through the glass of the booth. There's another couple out there, two guys casually holding hands. "I'm sorry I couldn't just be normal for you for once."

"Hey!" Stephanie says empathically. "I'm not normal. Just ask my parents."

I look away from the couple and directly at her. "I would if you ever let me see them."

Stephanie goes stock-still. I shift uncomfortably in my seat. I didn't mean to say it, but I'm not surprised it burst out. I've never been able to shake that nagging suspicion why Steph won't take me home or introduce me to her parents. That it's because she's ashamed.

"They're just not very accepting." Stephanie rubs her eyes. "The way you dress and things. I know they'd give you a hard time about it."

"See?" I lean back. "You may think you're not normal, but you are compared to me. It always comes back to that."

"If," Stephanie's voice wavers, "if you found someone like you, would it make you feel better? Would you rather have a friend like that? Someone who understands?"

There's a weird squeezing in my chest. Stephanie's shoulders are bowed, her mouth pinched, her hair falling limply over her face. It's one of those rare moments where she looks vulnerable. It reminds me strongly of that night back on the porch when Callie died. Steph always tries to act tough, but, in some ways, she's the same as me. Both of us worry that we're not enough.

"Stephanie, I like you just the way you are. I would never want to be friends with someone like me," I say vehemently. "If I was friends with someone like that, I'd just be constantly reminded of, you know. I love that I'm friends with someone who's just like everyone else but accepts me anyway. It makes me feel like part of the regular world. You have no idea how much that means to me."

Stephanie presses her lips together. She looks almost like she's holding back tears. "Oh. I see." She rubs her eyes again, more vigorously this time. "This is not worth talking about. Sorry."

It's all I can do not to slide down this bench and take Stephanie in my arms. I bite the inside of my cheek. Hold back. Hold back. Instead, I lean as close to Stephanie as I possibly can without risking touch. "You're not going to lose me," I murmur. "You're stuck with me. Nothing could ever change that."

"Okay." Stephanie's voice is small. "But you don't have to push yourself and go on these trips or whatever. Having you with me is enough. You're the one person who makes me feel less alone. That's everything."

My skin's going to cook off my face. "I, yeah, me too."

Stephanie snickers. "I get the picture, ya awkward turtle."

The bus pulls up, but my face keeps on burning as I follow Steph on. There's so much more I want to say, but I just can't get the words out.

Chapter Thirteen

THINGS ARE CALMER the next few days. Stephanie doesn't get into any more fights—in fact, she even waves at Emma and Jackson when she sees them in the hallway. They seem startled by this but wave back nonetheless. She continues acting distracted, but I'm hoping this will pass soon too.

Then one rainy night, my sister comes home late with a drenched and worn-down-looking Stephanie in tow.

I'm sprawled out on the couch when they come in. As soon as I see Stephanie, draped in Mai's jacket and shivering like a wet cat, I jump up and run to the bathroom for towels.

"What happened?" I ask, handing the towels over to Stephanie, who thanks me in an uncharacteristically subdued voice before drying off.

"Beats me," Mai says. Steph remains silent, her head bowed, her face hidden by a towel. "I just found her outside Ms. Carnahan's house when I came to visit, sitting in the rain. She said she didn't want to go home. And then Ms. Carnahan wouldn't let me in." Mai lets out a long sigh.

"Sorry. That was my fault," Stephanie mumbles, her face still buried. "I was just trying to help, but I upset her earlier."

Mai shakes her head. "Don't apologize. I know how easy it is to set her off right now. I'm glad someone's still trying to help her." She gives me a very pointed look. My cheeks burn.

There's a few seconds of awkward silence, then Mai lets out another, even louder, sigh. "I've gotta go take a shower." As she passes me, she hisses, "I know being comforting's not your thing, but it would be great if you try for once, considering she's your best friend and all."

I grind my teeth. I dearly wish to snap back at her, but Stephanie's more important right now. I lead her up to my room and make her change out of her wet clothes into some of my nice dry pajamas. They end up being pretty tight around Steph's chest, which is pretty tough to look at, but at least she's not shivering anymore.

"So." I sit down on the bed beside Stephanie. "What happened with Ms. Carnahan?"

Stephanie tucks a still-sodden lock of hair behind her ear. She looks so much smaller with her curls reduced to wet, limp strands that stick to the sides of her face.

"Like I said, I upset her earlier. She's been so frustrating and we got into an argument. Tony walked in on it and got really pissed at me for making her cry. So I didn't want to go home."

"Oh." My stomach churns. "Why didn't you call me?"

Steph shrugs listlessly. "I dunno. You don't seem like you wanna talk about Ava ever."

I gulp. Guilt crawls up my spine. "If you need help, I want to be there."

Stephanie grips her knees hard. "Then, I didn't want to ask this, but could you come with me next time? Maybe?"

I hook a finger in my glove. I want to say yes, but I still hate the thought of going back into that house so much. Sitting at the little coffee table without Callie studying by my side felt so wrong. Her presence hung in the air, filling the room so much it was hard to breathe. I tried to open my mouth to say something to Ms. Carnahan, but I just started crying instead. And that, in turn, made Ms. Carnahan cry, though simply "crying" is an inadequate way to describe it. Each sob came out as a harsh, hacking retch that rattled her entire body so much I feared it was going to fall apart. I ran straight out of the house, terrified.

My second visit was even worse. The place smelled like death. And there was Ms. Carnahan, waxy and skeletal-looking. The coffee table was like a casket we were both standing over. I tried to say something, anything this time, but it took everything I had to hold back another sob session.

Ms. Carnahan just looked at me with those hollow eyes and said, "You don't have to come back here. We can't help but remember when we see each other. And neither of us want that."

That was the last time I saw her.

"I'd go, I really would, but I don't think she wants to see me. I think I just make her feel worse."

"Look," Stephanie says, twisting her fingers together. "It's not about how you make her feel. I know you won't want to do this. But I'm desperate right now. I just need to know if she's going to *do* anything. I just need you to check."

It takes a second for what Stephanie's saying to truly sink in. I reel back.

"You think it's that bad for her?"

Stephanie pinches the space between her eyes. "I'm not sure. But I need to know if it's coming. If there's anything I can do at all to keep it from happening"

"No!" The word bursts out with such an intensity that even

I'm surprised by it. "No, Stephanie. We're not doing this again. That shit is what got Ms. Carnahan into this mess in the first place. If we try to screw around with her life again she'll get hurt. You'll get hurt even more. I refuse to repeat wh-what happened with Callie."

Stephanie turns away. "I knew you'd be this way." The disappointment in her voice is palpable.

As we sit in strained silence, I try to sort through everything that's so mixed up inside me. I want to finally tell Stephanie about my biggest fear, the one that still haunts me, that when I'm anxious or disturbed about the people I touch I make them have horrific deaths. The theory's just gained more and more supporting evidence as time wears on.

I thought of Grandma as so fragile when I touched her that time. Did those thoughts cause her to die during that operation? Deep deep down, did I fear Jocelyn was going to have the worst death possible for her and so I made that happen? And I was so scared and angry when Callie grabbed me. I probably wanted something bad to happen to her.

There's really no point in sharing this with Stephanie, though. She'll just dismiss it. Say it's paranoid. Just more of my self-loathing nonsense. But I can't think of it like that. These tragic, premature deaths are too much like a disease I'm spreading. I can't let it spread to Ms. Carnahan. I've done enough to her already.

I break the silence at last. "Maybe it's best to just back off from Ms. Carnahan for a bit. It seems like the best move if things have gotten this heated."

"Why don't you just admit you don't want to deal with it?" Stephanie snaps. "You're scared of going back to that house, you're scared to talk to Ava, you're so scared of yourself and your powers that you never *do* anything!"

"Of course I'm scared! I have no reason not to be!" I blink furiously. "I'm scared that you're getting all fixated on 'helping' a person no matter how much it upsets them again and I'm scared of being dragged into another horrible thing! Even though you promised you wouldn't do that to me ever again! What are you trying to prove? Who are you trying to prove it to?"

Stephanie doesn't answer. She simply crosses her arms, her cheeks puffed out in anger.

I don't want to say it, but it looks like I have to. "If this is about T—, about someone's approval or something, you don't need it."

A long hiss of air, like a balloon deflating, escapes Stephanie. Her face sags. Once again, I'm reminded sharply of that night more than a year ago. The night of Callie's death. The night when she told me everything.

"I don't care about anyone's approval," Stephanie says. "I just want to be able to fix what I break." She rubs the back of her neck. "But I get it. I shouldn't have tried to drag you into it again. I'd just feel better having you by my side for things like this. I wish I could explain to you. I wish you could see." She trails off, her eyes slightly glazed.

"Um, well, I definitely can't see whatever you're staring at right now." I finally cut in. I scoot just a tiny bit closer to Stephanie. "I am by your side, though. Right now and forever. And if you're afraid to go home, well why don't you bring me along? I can finally meet everyone. Your parents and Tony might go easier on you if I'm there. Maybe I can even put in a good word for you."

Stephanie's whole body tenses. My heart sinks to my stomach. "Unless you really are ashamed of me or something."

Stephanie shakes her head vigorously, her hair slapping the sides of her face. "Like I told you, I'm not ashamed. I'm not. It's just scary. There's a lot of stuff. I feel like if you see this side of my life, everything will change between us. I don't want that to happen."

"I just told you, it won't."

"Well," Stephanie's voice quavers, "I guess you're right, it's not fair.

There's a short silence as Stephanie's eyes flick back and forth, back and forth. Then, finally, she closes them and breathes in deeply.

"Okay. How about you come home with me tomorrow then? Tony shouldn't be home till dinnertime, so we can deal with him and my parents all at once."

I just barely restrain myself from squealing. Without even checking to see that my glove's secure, I grab Steph's hand and squeeze it hard. "Thank you!"

"Well, if I knew I'd get that reaction, I'd have caved sooner!" Stephanie laughs.

Realizing what I'm doing, I quickly let go. Steph pouts but still looks pleased. I readjust my glove, stunned by my own daring. I can only imagine how furious Mai would be if she knew I'm able to touch Stephanie without spiraling into anxiety but not her. But it's different with Stephanie. I can't quite explain how, but it is.

There's a thump and then a male voice sounds downstairs. "Ah, Dad's home. Better tell him you're staying the night and all that." I get up.

"Are you sure you want me to?" Stephanie's still uncharacteristically shy.

"Of course. You're Dad's favorite daughter, after all, remember?"

"Oh yeah, that's right!" Steph's demeanor lightens and she jumps up from the bed to follow me out.

"Don't be too happy about that. It means you'll have to put up with his fussing and nagging."

"So that's where you get that from. You're like a mini version of him."

I wince. "Ugh. How dare you?"

"You're much cuter, of course."

"Well, I would hope so!"

We bicker and tease each other all the way down the stairs, and, for a while, every wound and worry fades away.

Chapter Fourteen

AS THE BUS rolls into Stephanie's neighborhood, I'm sort of comforted that the cookie-cutter suburban houses haven't changed in the year or so since I was last here. Stephanie's house hasn't changed either; it still rests on the hill overlooking it all, stately and imperious. The bus pulls to the foot of the hill, and Stephanie and I are let out.

"My parents get in at six, and Tony's got a thing with his girlfriend till seven. We'll have the place to ourselves till then!"

I nod. I'm getting serious butterflies at the thought of meeting Stephanie's parents at last, so I'm glad to have some time to prepare mentally.

I see Ms. Carnahan's house out of the corner of my eye and my stomach lurches. I wonder what's inside, how bad Ms. Carnahan looks. Guilt gnaws at my insides.

Just when we scale the hill and are almost at Stephanie's house, she stops dead in her tracks. I nearly crash into her and swear under my breath.

"What's wrong?" I ask.

Stephanie points at the sports car parked in her garage. "Tony's here. He's not supposed to be here!" She's shaking slightly.

"Hey, it's okay. We can just hole up in your room and play video games. No need to bother with him."

"Yeah," Stephanie mutters, her shoulders slumping. "Just be on your guard, okay?"

I follow Steph to the door, nerves jangling. What is going on between those two?

As soon as we open the door, a deep voice bellows from the depths of the house. "Get out!"

"No!" Stephanie shouts back, closing the door behind us. "And Manee's here, so you'd better behave yourself!"

Tony thunders into the hallway, a listless looking white girl with stringy black hair and mascara-caked eyes trailing behind him.

"If Manee had any sense, she wouldn't be hanging around you." Tony trains fierce eyes on me and I immediately shrink back. He's gotten bigger since I last saw him. The hallway shakes with each angry stomp.

Stephanie glances despairingly at me, then turns her attention back to her brother. "Are you seriously gonna come in here, throw a fit, and insult my friend? Isn't it embarrassing at all for you?"

"Isn't it embarrassing for *you*, being a remorseless little psycho?" Tony snaps. "Does your little friend really know anything about you? Does she know you assaulted Ava a few nights ago?"

Stephanie puts a hand to her head and groans. I stare at Tony. There's no hint of a lie in his expression. He radiates hatred and wild grief. His girlfriend only looks bored by the outburst.

"I don't know what you're talking about," I say in a small voice. "But I know Stephanie wouldn't ever hurt Ms. Carnahan."

"Yeah?" Tony sneers. "Why don't you ask Ava, then?"

"Manee and I are going up to my room now," Stephanie cuts in loudly. "You can keep ranting and raving if you want, but do it away from us."

She starts down the hallway, beckoning me after her. As she approaches Tony, he stands protectively in front of his girlfriend.

Stephanie stops, burning red patches appearing on her face. "What, do you think she'll melt from contact with me?"

"I'm not letting you hurt anyone else I care about!" Tony snarls.

Stephanie's face burns even brighter. She reaches around Tony and taps the girl lightly on the arm. "Whoops!" She backs away, her hands held up in mock surprise. "Looks like I touched her! The dangerous criminal strikes again!"

Tony shoves Stephanie away with all the force he can muster. She's sent stumbling into the wall on the opposite side of the hall. Her head cracks against it.

"Hey!" I cry, my voice coming out way squeakier than I'd like. "Leave her alone! She didn't do anything!"

Stephanie rights herself, rubbing her head, her eyes glittering with rage. Her mouth twists into a dangerous smile. "Hey, Sage," she says to Tony's girlfriend. "Does it bother you that Tony has a huge crush on Ava Carnahan?"

For the first time, Sage's expression of detached disdain flickers. Her heavy-lidded eyes narrow at Tony. He goes beet red and grabs Stephanie by the wrist, jerking her forward so hard it's a miracle her shoulder doesn't pop out of her socket.

"I'd watch my goddamn mouth if I were you." The air around him seems to crackle. "I've got things I could say too, you know. I bet your little friend would leave you if she knew how insane you really are. I bet she doesn't—"

Stephanie interrupts him by slapping him in the face. She seems to realize immediately this is a mistake and her eyes go round with terror. "Uh, um, I'm sorry!"

Tony howls like a wounded animal and slams her against the wall. She squeals in pain.

"Stop it!" I scream desperately.

Tony's girlfriend just stands there, her lips pressed together in anger as she watches Stephanie try to squirm free from her brother's grip.

I stumble forward, my hand outstretched. My instinct is to try to pull Tony off from Stephanie. But then I see the thin, transparent glove on my reaching hand. My heart seizes as I consider how easily it could be ripped in a fight. I drop my arm. I can't risk it. There has to be something else.

I fumble in my purse for something to help. Maybe I can threaten to call the police on my cell? My hand bumps against a bulky bottle. The mace!

As Tony raises his hand to punch Stephanie, I jerk the bottle out and scream, "Let her go right now or I'll use this!"

Tony tenses up when he sees the pepper spray pointed at him. His grip on Stephanie slackens.

"Come over here, Steph, we're leaving," I command. Stephanie wrenches away from her brother and runs to my side.

Tony sneers, "That's all I wanted in the first place."

I jerk open the door behind us with my free hand, still keeping the mace trained steadily on him. Then, we turn and run as fast as we can. We don't stop until we're at the bottom of the hill.

I check behind me to make sure Tony hasn't followed, and when I see he hasn't, I fall to my knees.

"Well, you wanted to come over," Stephanie sighs. She's already composed herself. She stares up at the sky with a sort of practiced detachment, rocking back and forth on her feet. "Hope you enjoyed your stay."

"What—what was he talking about?" I pant. "Saying you attacked Ms. Carnahan?"

Stephanie runs her fingers through her hair. "I did sort of argue with Ava a couple nights ago. She wasn't listening to me and I lost my temper. Her glasses had gotten all dirty and smudged because she's not cleaning them. I sort of snatched them off her face and I yelled that she needed to take care of herself. It really upset her."

"Oh." That *is* something I can see Stephanie doing. "He's not always like this, is he?"

"Not until recently. He's gotten way more annoying since Ava's gone down a bad road."

What can I even say to any of this? It's so much worse than anything I expected.

"You can stay with me tonight and whenever else you want," I promise. "You don't have to be alone with him."

I force myself to my feet. I'm still unsteady. I can't stop looking back at the house, afraid Tony will come bursting out any minute. I put the mace back in my purse and root around for my phone, finally extracting it. "I'll get my sister, she'll come pick us up."

Steph grins and nudges me with her elbow. "Heyyyyy, you were pretty cool back there, y'know."

"Ah, thanks," I blush and dip my head while speed dialing.

After a lot of groaning and grumbling, Mai agrees to come get us.

"You're so lucky you have a nice sister," Stephanie sighs.

I don't really think of Mai as "nice," but after what I've just seen, I may have to reevaluate my standards. "You might not have such a good opinion of her after the ride back," I say, attempting a light tone. "She's gotten a new boyfriend. I'm sure she'll want to talk your ear off about him."

"Looks like everyone's finding their match, huh?" Stephanie laughs. "Except us, of course."

I duck my head again. The motion causes her my hair to brush my lips and I automatically start to chew on it, then make myself stop and spit it out.

As I predicted, Mai regales Stephanie with tales of her beloved all the way home.

"He's so passionate and dedicated! And he has these eyes, like they know your very soul."

"I think Steph has eyes like that myself," I say without thinking.

"How flattering," Stephanie bats her eyelashes coyly at me. "Do they penetrate you?"

"Ahhh," I sputter, my brain bluescreening. I respond the only way I know how. Flip hair forward, activating face shield mode. "Ah! Don't be like that in front of my sister, she'll get the wrong—"

"Wrong idea?" Through my hair, I see Stephanie's eyes lose their playful sparkle and become flat and hard like wood. She straightens up and turns her face away from me. "I see."

I don't know what to do. My mental processors are still flatlining. I knot my fingers. Gauzy fabric rubs against sweaty flesh. Fortunately, my sister distracts Stephanie with further love talk.

"We're actually thinking of applying to the same college."

"Sounds serious!"

The car ride continues like that, with Stephanie speaking like I'm not there. When we get to my place, Stephanie follows me up to my room so we can do homework up there like usual.

The awkward silence between us is oppressive. There's so much I want to say, to ask her. Like "Why didn't you tell me it was this bad?" and "Can't your parents do anything about him?" But her expression is so cold that icicles are practically forming on her eyelashes. I can't come up with the words to melt that. So instead, I draw a happier version of Stephanie, trying to catch the playful sparkle her eyes had before everything froze over, the lively tilt of her lips, as if by drawing it, I can bring it back.

Stephanie notices the drawing, and soon she reflects the picture. I want to leap in joy. It actually worked!

"Well, well, well. There's a beauty. Should I model for you?"

"Go right ahead."

Stephanie strikes a provocative pose, long legs crossed, chest thrust out, hips delicately curved, hair a silky curtain over one eye. "Draw me like one of your French girls."

"You'll get sore if you stay like that!" I laugh.

"Beauty knows no pain, darling!"

It soon turns into a sexy pose-off between us, and that keeps us entertained until dinnertime. During the meal, Steph is a whirlwind, firing off a joke a minute. But it feels so canned and forced now. I can see the emptiness behind it. It makes me wonder how often she's faked being happy and I just haven't noticed.

When it's time for bed, I grab Stephanie's usual air mattress out of my closet, only to find it's been punctured somehow.

"I'll just have to wear my stuff to bed then," I say, slipping on my gauze gloves. "That way we can sleep next to each other in peace."

"Look, I can just sleep on the couch."

"No way, that couch is a lumpy nightmare. I have a full-size bed, so we might as well use it."

It was going to be a sweaty night. I groan inwardly. Usually, sleep's the one time I don't have to wear this stuff.

"I'll wear it," Stephanie declares. "It's the least I can do."

"You'd do that?" A heady sort of heat flows through me and I'm all floaty. I shake myself back to my senses. "I mean, no, you can't."

"No, I insist. I won't let you wear it."

"Sleep on the couch if you're gonna be like that."

"Nope, I'm determined now. I wanna know what it's like to be you. I want us to share this." Steph gives a sly smile. "Besides, I'm looking forward to sleeping with you."

I put a hand over my face to hide my blushing, and Steph laughs, pulling the veil off me and slipping it over her own head.

She's really serious about this.

"You know," Stephanie says as we slip into bed. "You ever wonder why you never thought of this?"

"Huh?"

"I mean, you went around for years in those heavy sleeves and gloves, and you never thought of just wearing a sheer cloth instead?"

"Jeez, sorry I'm not as smart as you!"

"You're plenty smart, it's more than that. You were punishing yourself."

"What?"

"Just think on it. You never thought of a way out because you didn't want one. And someday, that's not just gonna hurt you, it'll hurt people around you."

"Look," I interrupt. "We need to talk about you right now, not me. About what happened at your place today."

Stephanie sighs loudly and rolls over, showing me nothing but her back. "Don't worry about it. I'm usually not alone with him like that. Ava will get better and he'll get over it all soon enough."

"Yeah, but—"

"I'm gonna go to sleep now. I'm pretty tired."

"Okay then. We'll talk tomorrow," I murmur. Maybe by then, I'll actually know what to say.

Chapter Fifteen

STEPHANIE DROPS OFF immediately, but beads of sweat glisten on her forehead. The sheer veil looks so uncomfortable. I can't stand it. I lift it up carefully, uncovering her face. Then I just gaze at her, enjoying her peaceful expression, watching her full lips ripple as she takes soft breaths.

I've suspected, no, I've known, that Stephanie's home life was pretty bad for a while now. But I did nothing about it. Now I've seen a little piece of the horror Stephanie deals with.

I'm not sure what my next move should be. Maybe I should tell Dad about Tony. But his solution will probably be to call Stephanie's parents. And from the way Stephanie talks about them, I'm not sure they can be trusted. A cold hand clenches over my heart as I remember Callie. *Whatever happens, whatever you guys say, my parents are going to blame me. It's over.* I squeeze my hands into fists, wishing I could just choke that memory into submission. I can't deal with the thought of losing Stephanie like I lost Callie.

If I can't figure out how to fix it, I wish I could at least comfort Stephanie by holding her. I lie here awake, every inch of me aching to reach out and touch the girl sleeping beside me. But I can't give in. If I do, I'll experience the worst thing imaginable.

I've had this conversation in my head so many times. Over the year and a half I've been friends with Stephanie, I haven't touched her once. Not even one lone fingertip briefly brushing skin. Just a short while ago, I told Stephanie this didn't bother me, that I didn't even want to touch her, that I would be happy to go the rest of my life without doing it. But of course that was a lie. The desire is always inside me, thumping like a heartbeat. And now we lie together on this soft bed, only inches apart.

I watch Stephanie's chest rise and fall. She's almost intimidatingly beautiful when she is awake, but sleep softens her sharp edges. Her jaw, usually strong and jutting, is slack. Her chin isn't raised in sharp defiance, but small and delicate. There's still some tension in the way her mouth twitches, though. It's clear just from her slight frown that she's gone through a lot today, too much to escape even in sleep. And she's carrying it all alone.

I stretch my hand out slowly.

I want there to be nothing between me and Stephanie. I want to press against her until I don't know where she begins and I end. I want to know every curve and crevice. I want to feel the smooth dips with my fingers. I want it so badly it burns in my gut like a match struck against the lining of my stomach.

My fingers are so close now. They tremble.

I stop, my hand suspended in the air. The skin on my fingertips tingles. I'm aware of every cell, every nerve, every breath. I've never felt this alive. Yet I can't push forward. It's as if Stephanie's surrounded by a thin field of radiation. If I touch it, it will burn me to the bone.

I can't throw it all away like this. I can't.

I grit my teeth. Slowly and painfully, I inch my hand back.

Then Stephanie whimpers in her sleep, her face scrunching up. The small, tremulous cry pierces me. Every other thought flees. I lean forward and gently stroke Stephanie's cheek. I open my mouth to speak some generic worlds of comfort, maybe the classic, "It's okay, I'm here." But before speech can even form, it begins.

A dark tunnel sucks in my mind. I grope around desperately for a thought, any thought, that can keep me anchored to the present, but nothing is that powerful. In an instant, Stephanie's essence envelopes me completely.

Slipping through Stephanie's shadow is hell. I no longer have lids and lashes to shield my eyeballs. They boil in my sockets but I can't even cry to release the pain. I'm tugged in a million different directions, stretching and stretching until I snap. A fireball roars, threatening to consume everything. And then it happens.

It's some sick, dark empty lot. It should be too dark for me to see, yet of course I can anyway. A body crashes to the ground in front of me, as if dropped directly from the sky. It's Stephanie. She lies there like a smear in the wet grass. She doesn't look a day older than the Stephanie sleeping back in my room. Blood pools around her, and her breath comes in short, ragged bursts, her chest bucking and heaving. A figure emerges from the darkness and crawls on top of her, pinning down her broken body.

Stephanie looks up at the person straddling her, half-smiling. The assailant is small. Short dark hair shrouds her face, shielding it from view. She puts her hands around Stephanie's neck. Her stubby fingers dig into Stephanie's flesh. She chokes her.

Stephanie clumsily puts her own hands over the assailant's, trying to pry them off her. But it's no use. Her grip slackens. Her smile is soft as she gazes at her strangler. The serenity doesn't leave her face even as her eyes flutter closed.

The murderer lets go of Stephanie. She tilts her head back and looks up at the sky, her mouth half open. Her arms are limp at her sides, and her shoulders are loose like a great weight has been lifted. She closes her eyes and lets out a soft moan of contentment.

I look so peaceful, sitting there on top of Stephanie's corpse.

Chapter Sixteen

I'M BACK IN my bed, completely drenched in cold sweat and staring at Stephanie. I think for a wild second I'm looking at her corpse, that I've already killed her, but the easy rise and fall of her chest assures me I haven't. I looked down at my hands. No blood.

For a full minute, I can't move at all. Then, a switch inside me suddenly flips on. I frantically scramble backward, putting as much space as I can between me and Stephanie. I don't stop until I'm threatening to fall off the bed.

I am going to kill my best friend.

There is nothing else in the world right now but that thought, pressing down on the top of my skull. It's going to split my head in two, bruise my brain, make everything spill onto the floor, my frontal lobe floundering gray and pulpy like a jellyfish.

I slide out of the bed. As soon as I hit the floor, my ankles turn under my weight, and I fall, my knees slamming down on the carpet with a deafening thud.

Stephanie doesn't wake, though she stirs. I start dragging myself forward with my elbows. My legs are just useless lumps of flesh right now, but acid's rising in my throat; I can't let the sound of hacking wake Stephanie up. I can't face her right now.

I manage to crawl to the bathroom. Once I vomit everything up, I just sit there staring at the disgusting toilet bowl.

I saw our future. It's going to come true. I can't deny this. I've seen the evidence my visions are real too many times. But I've never had a vision as *impossible* as this one.

I'm suddenly horizontal, my cheek pressed against cool tile. My head won't stop spinning. How can this be? How can it be that I'd ever kill Stephanie, the person I love most in the world?

Calm down. Calm down. I have to think. I can figure this out. Just think. There has to be an explanation, right? This can't possibly be how it all ends. Not after everything we've been through together.

I cover my face with my hands, trying to keep my breathing steady. It's hard to focus while addled by vomit fumes. Flushing the toilet will at least get rid of some of the rancid smell, but I can't move. Maybe that's for the best. The stink sets the atmosphere so well. A perfect fragrance for the total shit-show that is my life.

But it's not just vomit I'm smelling. A crisp, copper scent hangs in the air as well. The smell of Stephanie's blood burns my nostrils. I can feel the wetness of it on my hands, as if I've already killed her. I wonder if I should scrub myself raw, Lady Macbeth style. No, that's stupid.

So, instead, I stuff my hands under my armpits and curl up on the cold floor. Maybe if I try hard enough, I can curl into myself until I disappear completely. Maybe I can just stay here forever, invisible.

I know that's just a fantasy. There's no escape. I have to figure this out. Figure out what circumstances could possibly lead to me killing Stephanie.

There's a sudden noise outside the bathroom door. I snap into a sitting position, cracking my head on the sink. I moan and rub it, then jump again when the doorknob starts jiggling. Someone's trying to get in.

I shrink back against the wall, heart banging in my chest. Is it Stephanie? I can't be in the same room with her right now! What if I suddenly transform into that remorseless monster I was in the vision the second I get near her? Or maybe I'll just burst into tears. The latter's obviously preferable, but still pretty awkward.

The doorknob stops jiggling. I hear a deep sigh and know immediately it's Mai on the other side of the door. I've made her sigh in exasperation so many times over the years it's impossible not to recognize the sound. The sound of footsteps follows the sigh. They soon fade away and everything's silent once more.

I slump, my chest still heaving. I have to get out of here. It's no use sitting around and trying to figure out why I'd ever kill Stephanie, I'm not going to find an answer to that. The important thing is to prevent it from happening. How can I make it *impossible* for me to kill Stephanie?

The only way to *really* ensure that would be to kill myself. The thought is a vein of icy water running through my head. I shiver. It's not like I've never considered doing it. My future has always loomed like this shapeless, threatening thing. Whenever I think about what I'll have to do to survive in the adult world, I get exhausted and utterly hopeless. Even something as simple as getting a job seems impossible. Who would ever hire this nervous, charmless woman who can't even stand to touch anyone? I'm a burden to my family now, but I'll be even more of a burden when I inevitably fail as an adult. I sometimes think the only future that awaits me is that of a phantom haunting this house, a shut-in who accomplishes nothing but draining life from my family. A crushing disappointment.

The weight of that bleak future made me swallow a handful of pills once, shortly after my return from the mental hospital. But then I remembered the raw terror in Jocelyn's eyes just before her heart finally stopped, the way her body jerked around. I vomited every pill up. Death is just as shapeless and threatening as life, and I'm scared to face that alone.

Thoughts of suicide stopped almost completely after meeting Stephanie. Life was so much less scary with her at my side. There was even that spark of hope, one I only dared entertain in my weakest moments, that we could have a future together, that we could live in a little apartment and make it work.

That faint hope is gone now. Not only do I not have a future, I might steal Stephanie's future. Doesn't that leave me with nothing to live for?

I look over at the medicine cabinet and swallow hard. Now I don't just see Jocelyn's eyes, but Callie's. The swollen agony, the accusatory glare. I can hear her snarling, "You think you can just go to sleep after what you did to me? If you're going to say goodbye, at least do it out there, where no one will have to see you again."

There's a thought. I can just run away. I can put as much distance between me and Stephanie as possible. Make it so we can never meet again. It seems like the best option. I can wait until I'm far away from here to make the decision about whether I should die. Heck, maybe I'll get killed by someone or something out there before I even have the chance to do it myself. That's a weirdly comforting idea. There's a sort of poetic justice in it.

A strange energy flows through me. I'm almost excited. The longer I think about it, the better the plan sounds. I mean, if I kill myself here, my family and Stephanie will find the body, or worse, walk in on me before I finish dying. I don't want to see the looks on their faces. I know all too well how awful it feels to see such a thing.

Yeah, it's time to move. Take action. If I want to run away, I need to do it now.

I grab the edge of the sink and slowly, painfully pull myself up from the floor. Now I'm standing! And my legs are only shaking a bit! I have to work fast. I've only got a little time here. Money, clothes, whatever food and supplies I can scrounge up. I'll figure out the rest later.

The hardest part of preparing to run is sneaking back into my room. I'm only in there for a minute, but, the whole time, I'm terrified Stephanie will wake up. I grab the savings I bundled up in my sock drawer, my backpack, two pairs of shirts and pants and underwear, along with my phone and wallet, sweating bullets all the way. But Stephanie's a heavy sleeper, so I'm able to get out unscathed.

I can't even bring myself to look over at Stephanie before leaving. I close the door behind me gently and take a deep breath. After changing in the bathroom, I tiptoe carefully downstairs, more worried about alerting Mai than anything. Dad sleeps like the dead. I take a messenger bag from the living room closet and rifle through all the coats there for extra cash. I can't find much. I go into the kitchen and stuff all the snacks I can find into the bag, along with a few bottles of water.

I heave my backpack up and sling my bag over my shoulder. I'll figure out how to get more food later. I can't afford to dawdle here any longer. I march out the door and into the night.

Chapter Seventeen

AS THE COOL breeze hits my face, the fear inside me lessens. It's nice to be outside. I've always been a "night owl" as Dad puts it. That's partly down to insomnia. My mind has a hard time calming down enough to let me sleep. But I'm also just more at home with the night. Everything's so still in a way that's both beautiful and unsettling. It's really like the darkness is a blanket over me. It has a peaceful, heavy softness that envelopes me.

The streets are mostly empty too, so I don't have to navigate around people and their noise. It's a nice change. I find myself humming as I walked along, using my phone's flashlight to see around. I imagine I'm tromping along with a handkerchief on a stick, like one of those hobos in those 1930s-style movies. Stephanie showed me one once, and we spun out a whole scenario where the two of us were running from the law on the back of a moving steam train.

My fingers tighten on the strap of my bag. It's no use imagining adventures with Stephanie anymore. I'm on my own from now on.

I walk on, all impulse to hum like a happy hobo extinguished. The muscles in my legs are beginning to burn. Where's the bus stop? I should be there by now. Did I take a wrong turn somewhere? I start to check my phone's GPS and then notice how low the battery is. Shit. And here I even forgot my charger. I'm not that far from home and already running into trouble as a runaway. How pathetic is that?

This is what I get for trying to be a confident girl of action like Stephanie. But I can't stop now. If I really want to be like her, I've got to adapt. Don't worry about any complications that arise. Just keep the end goal in mind and steamroller over everything else.

When I finally find the bus stop, I practically collapse onto the bench in relief. I pant, my chest rising and falling, as I sit there. Now there's nothing to do but wait.

All night.

Because the buses don't run this late.

I put my head in my hands and moan. How stupid could I get? Buses generally stop running at midnight. It's like two o'clock in the morning right now. I'm better off calling Uber or something. I look despairingly at the flashing red light blinking on the side of my phone. Is it going to hold out long enough for me to download the app? I start punching in the search terms with fumbling fingers. Ugh, it's so slow. Why is this phone such a piece of garbage?

"Hi."

I nearly jump out of my skin. A man's standing next to the bench. Where did he come from? I can't make him out very well in the dark, his face is just a blank, black shadow.

"What are you doing out so late?" His voice is soft; it sends chills down my spine. The inside of my mouth and throat are like sandpaper. I try to answer but only a scratchy sound comes out.

He moves to sit down beside me, and I bolt. I can't even see what's ahead, but I run as hard and fast as I can. I can't feel anything but the air rushing past me and I can't hear anything but my own shallow breathing. My feet seem disconnected from my body, thumping along under me in a dangerous whirlwind. I'm just doing my best to keep up as they drag me along.

But I can't do it forever. My feet get away from me, hit a crack in the sidewalk, and I launch into the air. I hit the concrete like a baseball player sliding for home, but not all of my skin slides with me. My elbows and knees rip open and bleed.

I flip over and look frantically toward where I came from. I left the bench far behind and the man doesn't seem to have followed me. I exhale loudly, weak from relief. Then I wince. Blood runs thick and fast down my legs.

I've got to admit it at this point, I'm not cut out for life on the streets. It's been maybe an hour and I've already hurt myself. That's got to be some kind of record. Maybe I can win a "most pathetic runaway" award.

The street beneath me starts to vibrate. I stumble to my feet as quickly as I can but it's not fast enough. A car careens toward me at unbelievable speed.

I stare at the advancing metal monster, completely frozen. I see Callie reflected in the car's window, her eyes glinting with the headlights. An awful scream fills the air and the earsplitting noise reverberates through me, snapping me back to life. I fling myself off the road.

I crash-land on the sidewalk. The car zooms by so fast the wind it leaves in its wake whips my hair around. I lie there, shaking. It takes a second to fully comprehend what just happened.

When I do, the heaving and gagging starts. Nothing comes

out, of course. I used up all my vomit reserves earlier tonight. I just cough up spit. Callie's all I can see. Was she really there?

I wipe my mouth, trying to reassure myself Callie had just been some fear-fueled hallucination. But it feels like a sign. A warning that like Callie, I can't escape fate.

I fumble around in my backpack, hoping against hope I remembered to bring a first-aid kit. Turns out I did. Well, at least that was one thing I got right.

I apply the stinging medicine, bandage myself up and stumble to my feet. I am utterly defeated. It's time to do what the world is telling me to do and go home. I begin the walk of shame. Each step is slow and painful. The rhythm of my footsteps turns into a singsong little chant. *Why go back? You know you can't stay.*

I really can't. I'm an infection that needs to be removed from Stephanie's life. Even if that sick little voice in my head is right and I can't stop what I see for Stephanie's future, I can at least do her the favor of staying away from her.

But I need to regroup. I need to plan and prepare. I need to get things to help me survive on the road and I need to figure out exactly where I'm going to go. Or maybe all that's an excuse. Maybe no matter how I try to rationalize it, all I'm really trying to do is escape the specter of Callie for a while. I'm just scared. I'm sad and stupid and scared and that's all.

The walk home feels like an eternity compared to the walk earlier. The frantic running really sped things along for that one. By the time I reach my house, weak rays of sunlight break up the darkness.

I stand there for a minute, taking slow breaths in and out. I'll see Stephanie in there. How will I possibly look her in the eye? How will I keep everything from boiling over? I'll have to drive her away somehow.

At least I know I can't kill her right this minute. The Manee in the vision had weird short jagged hair. As long as I don't look like that, nothing can happen. I touch my hair. Still safely shoulder length. Good.

After another minute of psyching myself up, I grab the handle to the front door and turn. It doesn't move. The door's locked now. How the hell did that happen? I check under the Buddha statue beside the doormat where the spare key is usually kept. It's gone.

I groan. Of course. A perfect end to a perfect night. I only have one choice now. I go around the side of the house and find the tree that stretches up to the bathroom window. It's still slightly ajar. Good. I throw my bag to the ground and begin to climb, hand over hand. It's a lot harder than when I was eight, especially since I'm weak with exhaustion and aching all over. But I manage it by going branch by branch and double-checking each foothold.

By the time I reach the top, I'm trembling all over. Maybe I don't have to even worry about seeing Stephanie. I'm just going to pass out for a week on the bedroom floor.

I stretch out my right leg until it rests against the windowsill. Then, keeping one arm firmly wrapped around a branch, I stretch my hand until I'm hanging halfway out of the tree. I shove the window up, bit by bit, sweat dribbling down my brow.

"Manee?! What are you *doing*?

I gasp and my foot slips from the sill. I swing wildly in the air and my arm strains painfully. I just barely manage to grab onto the branch with my other hand, and I'm left panting and dangling from the tree.

I crane my neck and see the source of the startling yell: there's my sister's car stopped in the middle of the street with her hanging out of it, gaping at me. Her boyfriend is in the passenger seat, also staring.

What am I doing? I want to yell. *You're the one who clearly snuck out with your boyfriend tonight!* I struggle to pull myself back up onto the tree.

"Shit!" Mai flings her car door open and leaps out. "Wait!"

But it's too late. My hands slide off the bark and I plummet to earth. There's a split-second of air rushing by me, I hear my sister scream and then there's nothing.

Chapter Eighteen

AM I DEAD? Everything's so dark and heavy. There are distant noises and after a few minutes, the faint sound of voices. Stephanie? Mai? What are they doing?

A thick fog covers everything. All these blurry shapes flit around me, but I'm too dizzy to follow them. I want to tell them to stop, but I can't move my mouth. I'm so tired.

I hear voices and feel someone pick me up. It hurts. I hurt all over. I want it to stop. I feel rumbling beneath me and vaguely know it's the car. There are a bunch more noises happening, but they're pleasantly far in the distance. I open my mouth to say something, but the words get all tangled together. I can recognize now that one of the blurs is Dad, but I can't really understand what he's saying to me. So I give up talking and close my eyes again.

After a while, I feel fingers poking and prodding. I don't like it, they feel all plastic. But at least I'm not seeing anything bad. I still hear voices, but they aren't familiar. Where is everyone? Can they please come back? I close my eyes tighter and tighter, my whole body tensing up.

The prodding stops. I wait a long time before I open my eyes again. When I finally do, everything is white and wispy. I can't be sure, but I think I'm in a bed. There's a Stephanie-like shape beside me. Is she another dream? A memory? I try to reach out but Stephanie is a shadow I can't quite touch. Maybe I really am dying.

Steph's voice is soft and echoey. I try to focus on what she's saying. Something about being together, but it's all a murmuring mumble. Even so, the words cradle me like I'm a baby. I drift away. I wish I could stay with Stephanie. I really do.

WHEN I FINALLY return home from the hospital, I immediately retreat to my bedroom. I kinda wish I could stay concussed forever. A broken head really beats having a broken mind; all it takes is a knock on the skull and the world gets less vivid and much more manageable. I should hit my head more often.

I still felt out of it when they released me. All the doctor's talking and Dad's worrying just washed over me. Stephanie was gone by that point. Apparently, after the doctors confirmed the concussion wasn't serious, she was sent off to school. Mai probably personally dragged her there.

Mai also somehow managed to cook up a decent story that covered everything up. She told Dad I was startled when she suddenly entered the bathroom and slipped, and I fell right out the open window. It would be unbelievable coming from me, but since it came from the *perfect* daughter, Dad bought it. I assume I'm expected to keep quiet about Mai sneaking out in exchange.

Dad's nervous coddling is finally working in my favor. All I have to do is groan about the pain and he won't hear of me going to school. I tell him I need quiet and rest to cut down on his hovering. I also turn off my phone so I can't get texts or calls. Now I have nothing getting in the way of executing *Manee Runs Away 2: Second Time's the Charm.*

I work feverishly, mapping out my exact route, calculating the amount of supplies I'll need to survive a certain number of days and coming up with plans for every emergency I can think of. I even look for employment, scouring the Internet for shady places that might give a kid a job with no questions asked.

This sort of planning wasn't really my thing to be honest. It's hard, boring to think about, and worst of all, involves math. But distracting myself with planning beats actually thinking about why I'm doing all this. If my mind isn't occupied, I remember how I'm never going to see Stephanie again and get all torn up inside.

And I still can't shake the suffocating feeling it will all be pointless in the end. But I've got to try anyway. What else can I do?

On the fifth night of my self-imposed isolation, it's finally time. I've discovered all the places spare cash was hidden in the house. I've carefully stockpiled enough food and water to survive at least a week and gathered every weapon I can find for self-defense. I have a first-aid kit and several changes of clothes, including stuff I can use to disguise myself. My phone is fully charged and I have several backup chargers. I've also got a physical map marked with my exact route, emergency stops, and places I can stay at. I've even got my depression and anxiety meds this time. Sure, they'll run out eventually, but I looked up how to lower the dosage slowly so I won't be as screwed up as I would if I suddenly went cold turkey. I've managed to pack it all so it isn't horribly heavy too.

I'm ready.

Ready for anything except for the guilt that smacks me in the face when Dad comes in to check on me before going to bed. He has a cold cloth and a glass of water for me.

"Do you need anything?" he asks, his eyes shining with anxiety.

I respond with a close-lipped smile and a shake of my head. "No, I'm good. Thanks. Thank you for everything you do for me. I really do appreciate it."

He blinks, blindsided. Then he positively beams. "Of course, sweetie."

His smile is almost too much for me. I want to give him a hug for once, but doing something out of the blue like that will definitely make him suspicious.

I can't stand to watch him anymore, so I close my eyes as he leaves the room. I wait until his footsteps have completely retreated before I open them again.

"I love you," I mumble at the closed door. "And I'm sorry."

Of course I couldn't look at him. I'm going to steal from him. I'm going to leave here and never see him again. He's going to be so hurt. And here I can't even hug him goodbye. I know that a hug is what he wants more than anything. It seems so petty now that I've denied it so long. But it's too late to change any of it.

I wait, my heart beating fast and guilt eating me alive. I hear Dad and Mai exchange good nights. After an hour, I change out of my pajamas. I pull my backpack and overnight bag out from under the bed and take a deep breath. Time to go.

I creep into the hall, stepping as softly and silently as I can. I cringe as I slip past Dad's door. He's going to freak when he finds me gone. But he'll realize he's better off without me. Eventually.

Mai's door is shut tight. I don't spare any guilt for her. She'll probably be relieved.

I put a sneakered foot down on the first stair step and it creaks loudly. I wince and look back, but neither Dad nor Mai come looking for the source of the noise. I peek out over the stairs, making sure the living room is empty before creeping down. When I reach the front door, I just stand there for a few minutes. Finally, I square my shoulders and thrust it open.

"Hey."

I gasp, jumping back. Mai is standing in front of me, stone-faced, arms crossed.

"What are you doing out there? Are you sneaking out again?" I sputter.

"Of course not. I've been waiting for you."

A book's lying on the stoop by her feet. She was just sitting here reading until she heard me open the door. Then she jumped up to be all intimidating. How theatrical.

"Did you think I wouldn't notice you scurrying around stealing all you could for your big adventure? I knew you were going to try to run away again. And here we are."

I snort. "You know, I've been in the house this whole time. You didn't have to wait until now to talk to me about it."

"I wanted to catch you in the act. I didn't want to hear any stupid excuses."

"Why?" I throw down my bag in frustration. "Why do you care so much?"

"*Why*?" Mai hisses. "Do you know how much trouble you cause pulling stunts like this?"

Of *course* it's that. "Yeah, I'm the troublemaker. Meanwhile, I'm sure you've totally got permission from Dad to go out all night and bang your boyfriend, right?"

Mai's face turns beet red. "That was the only time. I just didn't get to see him in school that day."

"Aw, is it too hard on you not to see his beautiful face every waking hour of the day? I feel so bad for you!" I snarl at her. I don't know why I'm so angry all of the sudden.

"Shut up." Mai's lips twist up like she's eaten something sour. "You're just jealous."

"Oh, gosh, yes, of course I am," I say, rolling my eyes. "He's just sooooo dreamy."

"No, you're jealous of me because I have a life. Because I have people I want to go see, because I have more than one friend," Mai advances as she says this, her eyes narrowed. I'm forced to take a few steps back into the house to avoid touching her. "But you could have all that too! Instead, you push everyone away. Then you feel all lonely and pull little stunts like this for attention."

"I'm not doing anything for attention." I can barely keep my voice steady. I knew all along my problems were never real to Mai, that she thought of me as some anti-social nuisance acting out, but it still hurts to hear. "And I don't push people away, I get pushed away."

"Then what about Ms. Carnahan? You just left her to drown in her grief."

"Maybe I just have my own goddamn grief to deal with, Mai, ever consider that?" I growl.

Mai scoffs. "What happened to 'I didn't even like Callie and I don't care at all?'"

I don't say anything. I'm sick with anger now. I can feel it like poison in my veins. It's taking everything I have to resist screaming at her.

Mai stands in the doorway, gripping both sides of it tightly. "You just throw people to the side when you can't get what you want from them. First, you abandoned Ms. Carnahan. Now you're abandoning us. You're just like Mom."

It's as if Mai just kicked me in the stomach. The edges of my vision go gray.

Mai has everything I've ever wanted. It comes to her so easily, so effortlessly. She can kiss and hug her boyfriend anytime she wants. She never has to think about watching him die, she never has to smell his blood on her hands, she doesn't see his mangled corpse when she closes her eyes. She has *everything* and she thinks she has the right to self-righteously judge *me*? She thinks she has the right to compare me to *Mom*?

For the first time in my life, I really want to hurt my sister. I want to make Mai understand just a little slice of the agony inside me right now. It'd be so goddamn satisfying to sink a fist into that smug face.

"Get the fuck out of the way, Mai," I hiss. My fingers flex, aching to make a fist. "Or else."

"No," Mai says firmly, blocking the doorway. "I don't care if you tell Dad I snuck out. I'm not letting you do this selfish, horrible thing. You've caused everyone enough misery."

The thin thread restraining me snaps. Mai senses it too. A shudder runs through her. Her mouth twitches nervously and her eyes dart around. I savor her fear, savor finally having power over her. My hand forms a fist.

I take a step forward and she flinches. I realize vaguely I've never seen my sister scared like this. It's strange, just like it was strange seeing Stephanie flinch and tremble when Tony terrorized her. I feel sick at that sudden memory. *What the hell am I doing?*

I bite down hard on the inside of my cheek. I taste blood. With a great effort, I turn away from Mai. "Fine," I mumble. "You win. I won't do it."

"Oh, um, good." Mai's voice shakes slightly.

I walk away with heavy, dragging steps. But halfway up the stairs, I look back at her. "But don't pretend you did this for my own good or some shit. You don't care about me. You don't care about Dad. You only care about being the golden child."

"That's not true!" Mai cries, a flush rising on her swan-like neck.

"Yeah?" I reply dully. "If you really care, why didn't you bother to ask me why I want to run away?"

I've rendered my sister speechless for the first time in my life. At least I can take satisfaction in that.

When I get to my room, I throw my bags down on the floor with a snarl, then collapse on my bed, massaging my shaking, clenched fist.

I was really going to tear Mai apart back there. My sister, who I once slept with in a huddle of pillows under a blanket fort we built together. My sister, who tied my shoes for me, taught me how to braid hair, and even helped me with my math homework when we were little. My sister, who was, in many ways, my first friend.

What am I turning into? Tonight, I took another step closer to becoming that monster I saw in my vision. I'm standing on a razor's edge here.

I stare blankly at the ceiling. Too bad Mai would never take the time to understand that. She can't see how dangerous I am to her. She's caging herself in with the monster.

I know when Mai sets her mind to something, she's impossible to get around. I peek into the hallway and confirm she's now sleeping with the door wide open. There's no chance of sneaking past her anymore. Bet she'll make me go to school tomorrow too.

I rub my eyes as exhaustion settles over me. I'll have to figure this all out later.

Chapter Nineteen

THE NEXT MORNING, Mai is just as intense as I expected her to be. She not only makes me go to school, she even inspects my backpack to make sure I'm not smuggling supplies to run away with. There are none, so I'm marched to my sister's car. We ride along in stony silence only broken by Mai's bubblegum pop music.

Things really look bad for my great escape now. Mai informs me she's going to pick me up from school as well, so I'm not allowed a second without supervision. I could always just try to run after Mai drops me off at school, but I've already learned the hard way I won't get far without supplies or preparation. I've got to rethink this whole thing now. I reassure myself that as long as my hair isn't short, I'm safe to take some time to come up with a new plan. I instinctively reach up to feel it again. Still good.

Mai pulls up in the school parking lot. The building looms intimidatingly, a gray monstrosity. I get out of the car with a groan.

"You better be here when school lets out."

I hit my sister with the hardest glare I can muster.

Mai snorts. "Honestly, Manee, I know you think your angst is so special and nobody can understand it, but I can promise you whatever you're dealing with, someone's been through it before."

I don't know whether to laugh or cry at this. Maybe going to school isn't such a bad prospect if it means getting away from Mai. I walk away as fast as I can.

I stop at the threshold of the school, my hand tightening around my backpack strap. Stephanie will be in there, but I can't talk to her. I can't. I have to cut her off completely. A lump rises in my throat at the thought. I swallow it down as best I can and moved forward.

I lurk in the dark corner of the hall, delaying homeroom until the last possible minute. After the bell rings, I walk toward the classroom, each step feeling like I'm wrenching my feet up from sticky mud. When I finally stumble in, Stephanie's right there, sitting in our usual spot. She shoots up from her seat like a lightning bolt as soon as she sees me.

"Oh my God, finally! Where have you been? Why haven't

you called?"

"Aw, her wife has come home from war," a girl with a ponytail snickers.

I do my best to keep myself from showing any emotion as laughter echoes around homeroom. Steadfastly ignoring everyone, I walk away from Stephanie to the other side of the room and park myself in front of the girl with the ponytail.

Stephanie strides after me, paying no heed to the morning news starting up on the classroom TV.

"What's with you?" Stephanie looms over my desk, eyes snapping and hair bristling. "You're *avoiding* me? Your dad said you were too sick to talk!"

"Was it the clap?" Ponytail girl whispers in my ear.

"That's *enough!*" The commotion has caused our teacher to do the unthinkable and put down his paperwork. "Go back to your seat!" he snaps at Stephanie.

"Not until she talks to me!"

The teacher sighs the sigh of someone who had endured enough high school drama for a lifetime. "I'm *very* close to sending you to the principal's office."

"*Fine,*" Stephanie huffs. "I'll catch you in the hall." She tosses a glare over her shoulder at me as she stomps back to her seat.

As soon as the bell rings, I sprint out of the room. I nearly see the deaths of three people as I weave around them like marathon obstacles, but it's an acceptable risk. I don't think anything could top the vision that ruined everything, anyway. My next class isn't with Stephanie, but I'm still worried she might follow me. My phone vibrates almost angrily when I enter the classroom. I know who it's from before even looking.

```
WHAT IS UP WITH YOU!!
```

I check to see if the teacher has come in yet. He hasn't. I hunch over my desk, carefully punching in my reply.

```
I don't want to talk to you anymore so leave me
alone. Don't ask why or try to convince me
otherwise. This is what's best for both of us.
```

I suck air in through my teeth. My entire being is protesting what I just typed, but finally, I force myself to hit send.

It takes two seconds to get the totally expected reply:

```
WHAT? AFD WHERE THE FK DOES THIS CME FROM?
```

I write:

```
I'm sorry, but please accept it and don't
contact me again, I'm turning my phone off.
```

Before I can turn off my phone I get another text.

```
WAIT IS SOME1 BLACKMIALING U TO KEEP US APART IS
THIS LIKE A NBLE SACRIFICE BC THAT IS THEONLY
LOGICAL EXPLANATION BUT UKNOW THATNEVERWRKS
```

I laugh so weakly it sounds more like a whimper. Stephanie really does act like she's in a Hollywood drama sometimes. Like anyone cares enough to blackmail me. My eyes sting as I turn off my phone. I'm going to miss being a part of Steph's ridiculous world. Not that this will be enough to make her give up. I know her better than that. I'm just putting off the inevitable here.

Mr. Barnes ambles in. Looks like Stephanie's heartthrob is still subbing. I shove my phone hurriedly into my backpack. He probably sees me do it but he says nothing. He goes to his desk and begins speaking to the class. I can't really focus on what he's saying. Honestly, why does Stephanie think he's so hot? Well, objectively, I guess his face is nice. He's got that crooked, full-lipped smile, though Steph's lips are fuller. His eyes are kind of big and reflective like Stephanie's too, and his skin is really smooth and warm looking, like Stephanie's. He has all those good features, but in *my* opinion, they don't come together for him as well as they do for Stepha—

Jesus Christ. I've got to stop this.

When class ends, I slowly pack up my things as the other students stream out. Mr. Barnes takes his time clearing the dry-erase board. When I pass him, he says, "You seemed a little distracted during class, Manee. Something bothering you?"

"Oh! No, not really." I start to hurry out the door but stop short when I spot Stephanie out in the hallway, waiting with eyes like burning coals. Either Steph has developed super-speed or she cut out of class early just to confront me. I slide back toward Mr. Barnes.

"Uh. Actually! I was, uh, thinking of going back to the art club?" I shift from side to side. "I enjoyed it a lot."

He looks at me very skeptically. Can't say I blame him.

"So you enjoyed art club in the *very* short time you were there," Mr. Barnes says slowly. "Well. I'm happy to hear that."

"I—I kind of want to hear more about it, though. How it started and stuff."

I manage to get Barnes to walk me to my next class that way. I also get him to agree to meet me during lunch period so we can talk more about it. This is how I end up stuck with him in an empty classroom, desperately trying to keep him talking long enough to avoid Stephanie without committing to *actually* rejoining the art club. I go on about how I want to so badly but my sister would never let me, but I'm completely steamrollered when Barnes decides we should call Mai to ask her permission.

"Well, we're good to go!" he says after he gets off the line with her. I stare at him with my mouth open, but he just keeps smiling at me like the expression is permanently carved on his face. This level of positivity and tenacity is almost creepy. But at least he's useful. His constant presence seems to have dissuaded Stephanie from following me around. It's probably the calm before the storm, though. Maybe Stephanie will crash art club and we'll have an incident even worse than our *first* club meeting.

When I come in, though, only Emma and Jackson are there. Emma waves energetically. I smile nervously in return.

"Hi, Manee! I'm really sorry about last time," Emma says.

Correctly pronounced and everything. "Thanks," I say shortly, sitting down.

"I won't ever touch you without your permission again either," Emma assures me. "Mr. Barnes really read me the riot act."

"Okay, cool."

"Where's Stephanie?" Emma looks around as if expecting her to suddenly pop out of a dark corner and yell "Surprise!"

"Not coming," I mumble.

Emma's eyes widen. "Did you guys have a fight?"

"Sort of." I pull a paper over and start drawing hard and fast. I decide my piece will be my sister being pelted with tomatoes. "It's not worth talking about."

"Oh no! What happened?" Emma cries.

"Not worth talking about means she doesn't want to talk about it," Jackson whispers in her ear.

"Oh, yeah. I get it."

Good ol' Jackson. Everyone should have a friend like him. Except for me, obviously. I murder friends who look out for me. I press my pencil down even harder, my strokes getting more jagged.

"You know I can actually see your art, right?" Emma says,

tilting her head.

"Oh." I pause. I've been so consumed by angry drawing I neglected my usual hunching. Oddly, now that I've realized it, I don't even care. I don't care about anything anymore. I return to basically stabbing the paper with my pencil.

"I like it!" Emma declares. "You've got kind of a manga style, huh? But you don't shirk on the detail, that's good! I like the sharp angles you use. It's kinda, hmm, it's full of emotion, you know?"

"Oh." Heat rises in my face. That actually sounds like a sincere compliment. "Thanks. I really do like your art too, you know. It's so intricate."

"You're a sweetheart," Emma beams.

She's clueless if she really thinks that.

We continue drawing for about an hour. It's not as bad as I expected. Emma chatters the whole time as she goes through five different drawings, but it kind of becomes soothing background noise after a while. Emma also squirms in her seat and jiggles the table a lot, but she stops whenever she notices she's doing it and peeks nervously over at me. I give her a reassuring smile and she looks relieved. Well, at least we can relate about one thing. I know all about struggling with a body you can't control.

Eventually, the session ends. Emma gives a loquacious goodbye, Jackson a stiff nod, and they exit the room. I take my time getting my stuff together, not looking forward to the ride home with my sister. I wonder if Mr. Barnes thinks anything about my slowness, but he just says that he hopes to see me at the next meeting when I finally do leave.

I scurry out of the classroom, walk for a while, then, upon spotting the out-of-order bathroom, figured I can take a moment to myself without being interrupted. I lean against the patch of wall next to the door with the sad marker-scribbled paper sign, closing my eyes and massaging my forehead. Well, it was a pretty stressful day, but I got through it without anything too dramatic happening with Stephanie. Maybe I *can* pull this off.

"Manee."

My eyes fly open. Stephanie has materialized from the shadow itself, dark eyes ablaze. I squeak, but before I can even find my feet to run, Stephanie cuts off my escape, cornering me against the wall, planting her arms firmly on both sides of me. I'm boxed in with just a few inches of space between my body and Stephanie's.

"Have you been waiting here this whole time?" I choke.

Stephanie ignores the question. "Tell me what's going on."

"I told you. I just don't want to talk to you anymore." God, her body heat is suffocating.

"Unless this is some B-movie where hitting your head caused your personality to change, that doesn't make sense." Stephanie's gaze is hard and unrelenting.

"Stephanie, you need to let this go. You're acting really creepy." I try to keep my breathing even.

"I want the *truth*."

"That is the truth."

"It's not!" Stephanie slams her hand against the wall right next to my head, making me flinch. "I *know* when you're lying!"

"How? I'm always honest with you. I've told you more about me than anyone else in the world!" I snap. She's the one who never tells *me* anything.

"That's how I can tell when you're keeping something from me. It's not natural."

I try to duck under Steph's right arm, but she moves it down. "I'm not letting you go until you tell me!"

I let out a slow gust of air. She's going to make me say it. Those eyes, so intense and focused, almost dare me to. *Can you do it?*

I can. If there's even a chance it will save Stephanie, I can.

"Do I have to spell it out for you?" I force the words out.

"Spell what out?"

I ball my hands up into fists. Now or never. "I know how you feel about me. I've tried to ignore it, but I can't anymore. I don't feel the same way. And you feeling like that, it grosses me out, honestly. We're never gonna be together the way you want, okay? I can't take being around you anymore."

I immediately feel nauseous, like I puked those words up. It takes a second for Stephanie to process them. Then her eyes lose their hardness and her mouth drops open. She blinks and shakes her head.

"You think — ?" Her brows contract. She looks utterly lost.

"Don't try to deny it. You're pretty obvious," I snap. But my stomach is coiled in knots. Is she honestly shocked? Oh no, she really was joking all those times. Oh God, I'm wrong, I knew it, I'm wrong. I'm such a loser. Okay, stop it, I tell myself. It doesn't matter anymore. It doesn't.

Stephanie laughs softly. She bows her head, shoulders shaking with mirth, a curtain of curly hair covering her face. "You really think that?"

I brace myself for the blow.

Stephanie lifts her head and reveals a sneer so twisted she looks ugly to me for the first time ever. "You *really think* you can pull that crap with *me*? You think I'm blind? I *know* you want me as badly as I want you."

I'm caught in a swirling storm of fear and relief. Stephanie really looks like she wants to incinerate me or something, but on the other hand, *she feels the same way!* As much as I might tell myself that doesn't matter to me anymore, it does. It really does. I have to bunch up my lips to keep from smiling.

"You're wrong. You're wrong a-and *gross*, and I don't want anything to do with you," I finally manage to say. It sounds fake even to my own ears.

Stephanie snorts. "You damn liar."

"I'm not at all attracted to you. You repulse me." God, now I sound like a robot or some character in a bad old movie.

"Yeah?" Stephanie slowly leans her face closer to mine, her smile hard and mean. "Do I *really*?"

"What are you doing?"

"Does this give you the creepy-crawlies?" She's an inch away now, and her breath's hot on my face. "If I kiss you, would you just *throw up*? You can tell me stop anytime. Go ahead."

I can't respond. I'm too entranced by the freckles on her nose. They form a tiny, perfect constellation. The two of us are so close now our combined body heat makes little beads of sweat to form on our foreheads.

I can touch Stephanie now. There's nothing stopping me. I've already had the vision; the worst has already happened. Stephanie's leaning in, tilting her head, her chin jutting out hard, her lips open partway. It won't be a gentle kiss, it's going to be angry, Stephanie's tongue shoving into my mouth, our lips scraping roughly. Stephanie will probably pin me against the wall, and I'll grab handfuls of curls, lose myself in that mass of hair, slide my hands down to her waist, burrow under her shirt, squeeze warm handfuls of flesh, maybe squeeze so hard her bones break, claw into her flesh and rip it open; I'll bring Stephanie weeping to the floor and then I'll stand there alone with the knowledge I've killed her, killed the only person who ever wanted me.

"Stop it, Stephanie," I say hoarsely.

Stephanie freezes. I feel our lips brush, just the slightest bit, and it sends a shiver through me. I wonder if Stephanie notices. Probably not. She looks like something's pulsing under her skin, ready to rip its way out from under her, the flesh stretched tightly across her face.

"You've always been a coward," she hisses. "I don't know why I even tried. I always knew you'd run. I *knew* if I ever told you *anything*. I knew it would be like this. After all, your true love has always been your own beautiful, lonely suffering, hasn't it? How could *I* ever compete? How could *anyone*? You goddamn *weakling*."

Her words steal the air from my lungs. She's like a stranger. Her eyes are so dark and cold it's as if they've retreated to the back of her skull and all I'm looking into are the black tunnels of her empty eye sockets. Her mouth's a thin jagged line, and all the flush has drained from her face.

"Seems weird to me you're so hung up on such a weakling," I croak.

Stephanie just stares at me. Her arms go limp and she drops them to her sides.

"I hate you." Her voice cracks.

I look down at me shoes. I feel completely hollow. "Then why even bother with me in the first place?"

Stephanie shakes her head, eyes downcast. "Hell if I know." She turns and walks away, her strides stiff and deliberate. Her footsteps echo through the hall.

I slide down the wall, hitting the cold, flat floor with my tailbone. My sobs come out as little croaks and peeps rather than the shuddering gasps I expect. All I can do is hiccup mournfully and let the silent tears fall. Stephanie is right. I'm just too weak.

Chapter Twenty

"MANEE! MANEE, ARE you here?"

My sister's clomping shakes the wall behind me. I wipe desperately at my face but can't stop new tears from streaming out.

"*There* you are! I waited forever out front, I was starting to think you'd run off! Then I saw Stephanie stomping out and knew you had to be in here somewhere." Mai strides forward, her lips pushed out in consternation.

She stops dead, close enough to see me properly now. For the first time in my recent memory, Mai's expression softens as she looks at me. "Hey, what's wrong?"

"N-nothing." I try to hide my face with my hands.

"Did something happen with Stephanie? She wouldn't even stop to talk to me."

I'm too exhausted and sad to hide it. "We're not friends anymore, that's all."

Mai squats down in front of me, brow furrowed. "C'mon. You two have fought before, haven't you? You'll work it out."

I shake my head "No. We can't work it out this time."

Mai bites her lip. "It might seem that way *now*, but if you step back from whatever the problem is, you might be able to find a compromise or something. *I've* had arguments with friends before and—"

"It's not that kind of problem," I mutter. I don't even have the energy to get angry at her presumption.

"Then what *is* it?" Mai sighs.

I hug my folded legs tightly. "It's that I'm no good for her, okay? We're not good for each other. We could have *never* been together the way we wanted. Now we can't be together at *all*, no matter how much I wish." I bury my face, finally smothering my outburst. Everything is just spilling out of me now, I'm falling to pieces.

"Oh." Mai's eyes widen slightly. "*Oh.* I see." She clasps her hands in front of her and bounces on her toes. A flush crawls up her neck and cheeks. "Oh, God, was this why you were trying to run away?"

"Yeah, sort of," I mumble into my knees. "I was just pushing her and everyone away, like you said. It's all I ever do."

"Shit. Manee, *no*, I didn't mean it like that. If I'd known this was what was going on! You were right, I didn't understand, I thought you were just trying to jerk me and Dad around. I should have asked you why." Mai's face is fire-engine red now. She covers her eyes with her hands and takes a deep breath. "Look, were you, like, scared Dad and I would react badly to this or something? Because I would never! I—I have no problem with it." She takes another big breath. "And I'm sure Dad too! He'll always accept and love you, okay. He'd never ever reject you over something like that!"

I can't help a phlegm-filled chuckle at Mai freaking out like this. It's been a long time since I've seen her act this awkward. "Thanks, that's good to know, but it's not about you guys. There's a lot of complicated stuff. It's us as people. We're just not right for each other. I thought I'd just end up hurting her."

I can't believe I'm actually having this conversation with my sister, and what's more, that she's actually listening.

The red fades from Mai's face and her breathing returns to normal as she stares at me thoughtfully. She purses her lips. "I don't get what you're saying. You always seem to make each other happy whenever I see you together."

"Yeah, but, it's not that simple. It's not really something I can talk about."

Mai hisses through her teeth. "*There* it is. Well, fine. Thanks for actually telling me *something* for once. I understand better now." She winces. "Ooh, I guess it must have been pretty annoying to have me getting all into my boyfriend while you were going through this."

I open my mouth to try to deny it, but I can't. I've been jealous and I've got to own that. "That's not your fault. I shouldn't have blamed you for it."

"Still, I'm sorry. And look, I might not know much about this whole thing, but I don't think you should give up if you really want to be with her."

I shake my head. "Like I said, you don't understand."

Mai rolls her eyes. "Of course I don't." She straightens up. "I'm *not* sorry enough to cancel Zack coming over for our family dinner next week, by the way. I want you on your best behavior for that. He needs to get a good impression of my family."

I groan, but Mai ignores that, holding out her hand. I take it gingerly and get jerked to my feet. Sisterly sympathy time is over. At least something's still normal.

I CAN'T SLEEP at all that night. I keep thinking about what happened in the hall. Stephanie was like a different person. Her words keep echoing in my head: *Liar. Coward. Weakling. I hate you.* It's not like I haven't been told those things before. I say them to myself all the time. And a part of me always wondered if Stephanie shared that opinion, deep down. Now I know.

I force myself up from my bed and walk across the room, floorboards creaking with each step. I open the window slightly and stare out into the darkness. There's the tree I fell from in the distance. The jagged, broken branch looks pitiful.

I wonder what Stephanie is thinking right now. Is she sleeping soundly, glad to be free of me at last? Is she regretting ever meeting me? Is she wishing she could erase every memory of me? Wishing she'd never given me anything?

A breeze wafts through the window, making the transparent, silky coverings hanging in my closet flutter. I reach out, rubbing the silk between my finger and thumb. This was the first gift I ever got from Stephanie.

I want to cry just remembering it. *You deserve to be happy.* I'm sure Stephanie doesn't believe that anymore. And she's right. *She's* the one who deserves to be happy. She deserves to be happy and alive and whole. And she won't get any of that if I stay in her life.

I let go of the silk and turn away. In the end, it doesn't matter what Stephanie's thinking right now. All that matters is whether she's still here to think it.

THE NEXT FEW days are a struggle. Before I met Stephanie I was comfortable alone, but now it's unbearable. I want to voice every stupid observation that occurs to me, and I feel like I've been punched in the gut when I remember I have no one to voice it to. My classes with Stephanie are the worst. I can feel her staring at me. It's a constant burning sensation on the back of my neck, and it's a Herculean task not to look back.

I'm not sure if I can handle Stephanie approaching me one-on-one again. I came so close to ignoring the danger and just giving in to my desire to be with Stephanie, so close to kissing her. The memory still makes my heart race. I need to distract myself from it by any means I can. So when Emma waves at me in the cafeteria, I barely hesitate to go sit with her and Jackson.

Emma's certainly very distracting. When I'm with her, all I can think about is how overwhelming she is. Even how she addresses me is weird. She's taken to calling me "Neenee."

"What's the point if the nickname's more letters than her actual name?" Jackson asks.

"The point is that it's cute!"

"Got me there," he mutters.

I'm not really sure how to feel about Jackson. He rarely talks, so that at least makes him tolerable. He's always absorbed in some private world of his own.

I don't mind the fact I don't really fit in with them or completely understand them, though. It's safer that way. Every time I get close to someone, it ends in tragedy. It's best to keep my relationships distant.

"So, are you coming to the art club meeting tonight?" Emma asks during lunch a few days later.

"Yeah, my sister's decided I'm a permanent member," I grumble. I had an argument about it with Mai this morning. "It'll be good for you to branch out and make new friends!" Mai said, and that was that. Why is it I can never win against her?

"Do you not like it?" Emma inquires with a frown.

"I like it okay, it's just, y'know." I trail off. I'm watching Stephanie eat lunch alone out of the corner of my eye. Why isn't she sitting with anyone? She shouldn't have any problem making new friends. She's pretty, she's vibrant, and a hell of a lot more social than me. But here she is, hunched over in a corner, scribbling in a notebook. It looks so sad.

It's taking everything I have to restrain myself from running over there and cheering her up. Stephanie's face is one of the few I can always reliably put a smile on. I indulge for a second in a fantasy of rushing to Stephanie's side and offering to take her downtown. Our last trip was pretty nice, after all. Well, *mostly* nice.

"Neenee? Helloooo? Are you listening?" Emma's waving her hand in front of my face. I jerk out of my reverie.

"O-oh yeah, I'm fine! I was just thinking about something. Um, continue with your story."

For once, I try to listen to Emma as she rambles on. I've got to stop obsessing about Stephanie. It's all over now. We're done. There's nothing I can do.

Despite telling myself this, I can't stop thinking about it. Even when art club rolls around, I'm still trying to come up with ways to cheer up Steph covertly. I look over at Mr. Barnes, wondering if I can get him to take his shirt off in front of Stephanie somehow. God, that's a disgusting thought. But anything to make Stephanie smile.

"If you're feeling unhappy, you shouldn't bottle it up. Let it loose in your art," Jackson says quietly, interrupting my inner turmoil. I blink at him in surprise.

"You're unhappy, Manee?" Emma asks with a comically overdone frown.

"No, uh, how come you think that, Jackson?" I boomerang it back at him.

Jackson shrugs. "You keep looking over at Barnes and making a face like he just stabbed you in the heart."

Emma's eyebrows shoot sky-high. "Do you have a crush on Mr. Barnes?" she asks me in a whisper that somehow manages to be louder than her normal speaking voice.

I sigh. Emma and I will clearly never understand each other. "No. Do you?"

Emma scoffs and flips her hair. "Any girl who says she doesn't have a crush on that piece of man-meat is delusional or lying."

"Emma, your voice is way too loud," Jackson says, his eyes darting toward Mr. Barnes, who's very intently focused on his paperwork. I can tell from the redness on the tips of his ears he's hearing everything being said.

Emma ignores Jackson. "If you ever need advice on how to deal with men, you can come to me," she tells me. "I'm very experienced."

"I see." I turn my attention back to my painting, trying to disengage gracefully from the conversation.

"You've never dated." Jackson shakes his head at Emma. "How are you experienced?"

"I have dated, and you know it."

"I keep telling you first grade doesn't count."

"Wow, you guys have known each other forever," I half-mumble.

"Yep. Really can't imagine what it would be like *not* being with her," Jackson says with the slightest smile.

"Life without me would be an empty desert for you." Emma throws her arms out grandly.

My heart is strangely heavy. Do I even know *how* to have a life without Stephanie anymore? We're "broken up," but I still spent most of my time thinking about her. Who even am I anymore without Stephanie by my side?

I look down at my painting. It's a boring, bare landscape. *An empty desert.*

I crumple it up and reach for another piece of paper. I'll do a portrait of my dad or something.

When it's time to leave the art room, Emma sticks annoyingly close to my side. It's like I have a brand-new elbow attachment. Jackson drifts slightly behind us.

"So did you enjoy art club a little more this time around?"

"I guess," I say, shifting away. Putting space between me and Emma without banging into the lockers as we walk is a difficult task. "It's helping me do some, uh, self-reflection."

Emma's eyes practically sparkle. "Cool!" she chirps. We pass through the front entrance to the school steps. "Because I was wondering if you wanted to — is that your sister?"

Mai has pulled up in her Camry directly in front of the steps. She waves at us.

"Yeah, that's her. Guess I'll see you guys later." I hurry down the steps, but Emma rushes after me.

"Wait! I was wondering, do you want to come over to my house and hang out with me and Jackson sometime?"

I stop in front of the car and turn to face Emma. Her face is red.

"Oh." I'm not sure how to respond. The thought of going to visit someone I barely know makes my throat dry up. What if Emma's parents try to hug me? What if she has an army of identical siblings who can easily overwhelm me and hold me hostage forever?

"Our family is actually having a big dinner next Friday!" a loud interjection comes from behind me. "My boyfriend is coming over. You two could be Manee's guests if you like!"

I spin around. My sister is hanging out of her car with a big smile plastered on her face. "C'mon, Manee, it'll be fun."

Well, it's better than going to Emma's house at least. I force my own smile and let Mai make the arrangements.

"That was pretty damn nosy of you," I grumble as we pull out the parking lot.

"Aw, come on, I did it for you," Mai says with a self-satisfied expression. "Besides, you could stand to socialize a little."

I want to snap at Mai that she's supposed to be my sister, not my mother, but I restrain myself. Mai really is trying to think about my feelings for once. In her own smug way.

"Well, at least I'll have some people I can make fun of your boyfriend with."

"Hardy-har-har."

I lean back in the car and close my eyes.

Chapter Twenty-one

THE DAY OF the dinner party, Mai is a nervous wreck. Her face is pinched and her hands are sweaty against the steering wheel as she drives me, Emma, and Jackson to the house. I know she's probably overthinking everything and convincing herself that Zack's going to dump her over her weird family. I don't really know what to say to comfort her. This dinner party hasn't even started yet, and I'm already exhausted.

As soon as we get to the house, Mai runs up to her room to get ready. Dad comes out to greet Emma and Jackson and leaves refreshments on the coffee table before going back to the kitchen to prepare dinner. I'm left alone with my guests. Jackson's looking around the living room with interest, but Emma is watching me closely. She's been doing that a lot this week for some reason. It's starting to bother me.

I clear my throat and paste a smile on my face. "Please, sit down and enjoy the drinks." The words sound robotic to my ears. Playing hostess is bizarre.

Emma looks over at the drinks and is instantly transfixed. I inwardly sigh in relief. One good thing about Emma, she is always easy to distract. "What *are* they?" Emma asks, pointing at the orange beverages.

"*Cha-yen*," I stammer. "Dad's really good at making it, so you should give it a try."

"What's 'cha-yen?'" Emma knits her brows in confusion.

I'd automatically used my dad's terminology for the food. "Oh, uh, Thai iced tea. Milk tea."

"That doesn't seem anything like iced tea, though," Emma says, crouching down by the table and examining the glass closely, eyes narrowed suspiciously.

"It's really tea with ice and milk in it, I promise," I say through gritted teeth. "It's not going to poison you."

"Emma, chill out and drink it." Jackson says as he sits down gingerly. He shrugs at me. "She's just a really picky eater. It's tough to take her to restaurants."

"Yeah, sorry," Emma says. She picks up her tea cautiously. I blow out a shaky breath. Did I fail Hostess one-oh-one just now? Ah well, screw it, it's a stupid course, anyway.

I sit down on the chair opposite the couch, clasping my hands in my lap. Very quickly, I realize I have nothing to talk with them about. The only thing I know for sure we have in common is art club. And I don't want to bring up Mr. Barnes because Emma might start harping on about crushes and all that. I wring my hands. What am I gonna do?

"Holy crap!" Emma interrupts my thoughts, tea dribbling out of her mouth. "This is so good! It's like a milkshake or something! I love it! Wow! Your dad made this?"

I blink at Emma's smiling face, taken aback. "Yeah, he did."

"Will he be making dinner, then? Will it be more Thai food?" Emma seems pretty excited.

"Yeah, probably," I say. "He likes keeping in touch with our heritage and stuff and he worked at a Thai restaurant when he was younger, so he makes it a lot. He makes other stuff too, of course."

"So we're gonna be getting food cooked by a professional?" Jackson says, raising his eyebrows. "Dang, you didn't tell us that."

"I can't wait! Man, I would've gone to a Thai restaurant sooner if I knew!" Emma sloshes some tea out of her glass and onto the table in her excitement. "This is great, I'll tell him it's great!"

"I'm glad you liked it," I say, and for a second, my fake smile becomes real. It's hard not to be swept up by her enthusiasm. "I like it a lot too."

"Can you cook too?" Emma says, eyes shining.

"I'm no good at it." I realize I can just lob these questions back at them. "Do you like to cook?"

Emma laughs. "I burn everything I cook!"

"My parents taught me a lot about cooking," Jackson says. "So I'm okay."

"He's *amazing*," Emma says, clapping him on the back. "He makes the best friggin' lasagna in the *world*."

Jackson goes beet red at this and scrunches his head into his shoulders. I can't help but giggle. It's like a turtle retreating into his shell.

Before I can say anything else, the doorbell rings. There's racket on the stairs like an approaching landslide as Mai comes down. Dad comes out of the kitchen, his stance defensive, his mouth pressed into a thin line. It's time to meet the boyfriend.

Zack is cherubic-looking with his blond curls and sparkling brown eyes. He's also aggressively clean cut, all decked out in a suit and tie. He even holds a bouquet of roses.

"Damn," Emma whispers way too loudly behind me. "I'm glad I'm not in your shoes. Having a guy like that in my house would drive me bonkers with lust. I wouldn't be able to stand it."

"I'll manage somehow," I respond dryly.

"Hello," Dad says shortly, sticking out his hand. "I'm Sakda, Mai's father."

Zack is carefully polite with his greeting. He goes on to shake everyone's hand, except mine. He simply smiles at me. Mai must've given him the rundown. When he takes Emma's hand, she giggles nervously and runs to hide behind Jackson after he lets go. He raises his eyebrows at this but says nothing.

"Well, your house is very nice looking and whatever's cooking smells great! Who's the chef? Is it you, Mai?" He looks over at her.

"It's me," Dad says, crossing his arms. "Is that a problem?"

"O-of course not."

"Dinner's ready, right? Let's all go have dinner!" Mai interjects hurriedly, clapping her hands. She herds us all to the dining room. Mai put a side table against our regular dining table to make it bigger. Mai, Dad, and I serve the food, and we all sit down on the mismatched chairs. We barely get through the first bite of the meal when Dad starts in on his interrogation.

"So Zack, what is your home life like?"

"My parents aren't around much. We definitely don't have home-cooked family meals like this!"

My father's face softens. Aw, Zack's gotten all sweet and pitiful and knocked down those protective father walls in an instant. That's disappointingly anticlimactic.

"And you're like, a master chef!" Emma interrupts while digging into her dish with great enthusiasm. "This is so yummy! What is it?"

"Oh!" Dad straightens up. He clearly forgot there were other guests. "That's a seafood curry in coconut. It's called *hor mok ma prow awn*. See, you've got a lot of seafood in there, but also things like coconut cream and red curry paste."

"So this is really a coconut shell?" Emma asks, banging her fork against the small white thing that served as a bowl. "That's so cool! This is like, the best dinner I've ever had."

"Well!" Dad beams. "You have excellent taste in friends, Manee."

I shake my head. Dad is way too easily won over. Mai's smiling to herself. Clearly, everything's going according to plan.

As I watch my father recite the entire history of Thai cuisine at Emma, a hollow pang shoots through me. Usually, it's Stephanie who's sitting at our dinner table, asking Dad all kinds of questions. Sometimes I got tired of our dinner talk constantly turning into a dissertation on Thai culture. But I realize now how special it was for Stephanie, to have someone to talk to her and teach her about that part of herself. Her mother never bothered to do it. And Stephanie was just so desperate to know more, to have something large to connect with, to *belong*. I remember how transcendently happy Stephanie was when Dad offered to take her along on our next trip to Thailand. Now she'll never get to go. She'll never get to be part of our family again. She's stuck with the family she was born with now.

I ball up my fists in my lap. Stephanie might be alone with Tony right now with no one to come to her rescue for all I know. I remind myself that I'm far more dangerous to her than Tony is.

But still the guilt weighs on me, especially when I take Emma and Jackson upstairs to my room after dinner. Stephanie was the only person outside my family who was ever allowed in here before. I feel like I'm betraying her somehow by letting other people inside. But I make myself open the door, and the two of them follow me in. Jackson whistles when he sees the long box of comics at the foot of my bed, and Emma squeals over my fairy-themed calendar. Heat crawls up my neck, but it isn't a bad heat.

"Go through whatever you want," I tell them, sitting on my bed. "Make yourself at home. If you want to watch something, I've got a little TV up here and some DVDs."

"I didn't even know you were into comics," Jackson says, still fixated on the long box. "Can I take a look?"

"Yeah, sure," I say distractedly. I've noticed that Emma is peering in my garbage can. That's bizarre, even for her. "Emma, what are you doing?"

"Oh!" Emma looks abashed. "Sorry. I was being bad. I saw something that I thought was a, uh, love letter."

Is she *still* on about Mr. Barnes? I sigh. I really do want to get along more with Emma, but this is getting annoying. Coming clean will be the only way to move forward with her. "Okay. Emma, I want to make this clear to you. There are no love letters in here. I don't have a crush on Mr. Barnes and I never will have a crush on him. Or any guy, probably."

Emma's mouth forms a little "Oh."

"Yeah, I'm a lesbian. Take me or leave me."

Emma just stands there for a second, her lips pursed. I'm determined not to feel self-conscious, but it's difficult.

Emma finally speaks, "So, Stephanie's a lesbian too, right? You guys were a couple and then you broke up? That's the deal?"

"What?" I say, thrown by this unusual perceptiveness. I almost respond with "Actually, I'm pretty sure she's bisexual," but then think better of it. Emma doesn't need to know Stephanie's private business. "Uh, no, we weren't really together. I kind of wanted to be, but it didn't work out."

"Oh, I see," Emma looks satisfied, like she's solved some great mystery. But then her triumph fades and she squints at me suspiciously "Wait, are you saying *she* didn't want to be with *you*? Because I don't think *that's* possible."

"Uh, that's sweet, but I don't really see how you know that."

"Maybe it was a misunderstanding. Have you tried talking to her?" Emma persists. She walks to the bed and sits down. She remembers to put space between us, but it's still too close to me for comfort. "Because she misses you. I mean, she must. And I know you miss her."

I scoot away, readjusting my gauze. I'm glad Emma's taken my confession well, but she's getting a little *too* supportive for my taste. "Look, Emma, I really don't want to talk about it, okay?"

"I have something more important to talk about anyway," Jackson cuts in, holding up a comic. "Who's your favorite X-man? My guess is Rogue."

I grin. "Right on target! You're good."

"Well, it doesn't take a genius to figure out you might connect to someone who doesn't like to touch people if she can help it."

"Ah cahn't kiss you, Remy!" I warble in imitation, clutching my heart. Then I flush. But Jackson is doubled over laughing.

"It's great to have someone to dunk on comics with!" he says. I've never seen him so animated.

"Yeah, for me too! Steph mostly just liked indie comics and horror manga and stuff, not much with superheroes."

Emma pouts. "Great, now you two can shut me out while you geek out together."

"You can always read some comics, then you'll know what we're talking about," Jackson says.

"No thanks. The way some of those artists draw women physically pains me," she snorts.

"Can't argue with you there," I say with a shrug.

"That's why you should become a fan!" Jackson laughs. "The more girls at comic conventions, the more artists will be forced to see what they actually look like! I try to go as often as possible to remind them black folks exist."

"At least they remember that *once* in a while. I don't think I've ever seen a Thai superhero," I sigh.

"You should create one," Jackson says. When I open my mouth, he puts up his hands. "I don't it mean in a nasty 'if you don't like it, you make one' way. I just notice you draw heroes a lot and I think you could do it. I'd read it."

"Yeah, I'd read a superhero comic if it was by you!" Emma cries. "We should do an art-club anthology!"

"Yeah?" I tug on my hair thoughtfully. "You really think so?"

"I know so!" Emma declares, already so pumped up she's practically dancing at the thought. "You just wait! We're gonna put all the other clubs to shame!"

Funnily enough, I almost believe her.

We talk for a solid hour after that. Then the time comes for Zack to leave and Mai to drive Emma and Jackson home. As I wave them off, I realize I'm actually sad to see them go. Weird.

I go to see if there's any further cleanup needed in the kitchen, but it's spotless. Dad's surveying the clean sink with utter contentment. "He was very helpful. I was worried, but Mai seems to have found herself a good boy."

"Yeah, he seems all right."

"Your friends are good people too." Dad gives me a slightly sad smile. "Mai told me you were having some problems with Stephanie. And that we needed to look after you."

Ugh, of course she did. "I'm fine, Dad, honestly."

"Well, I do miss having Stephanie around here. But whatever happens between you two, you have my support. If you need help, I'm here."

"Thanks," I mutter, looking at my feet.

I return to my bedroom. As I put back the comics Jackson pulled out, I find I'm humming. I get up and start straightening up my closet. Emma went through my clothes and left several half-off their hangers. But I honestly don't mind. Everything seemed so dark and empty these past few days, but right now it looks brighter. Maybe I can do this. Maybe I can live without Stephanie.

My hand brushes against something silky.

I pull out a slinky red dress and instantly know it's Stephanie's. It must be a leftover from one the millions of times she came over with outfits scavenged from thrift stores and who-knows-where and tried them on for me. It's so vivid. Steph parading around my room grandly while I sit and watch, struggling with the desires the sight awakens in me. It feels like another life now. One I'd give anything to have back.

A faint trace of lavender tickles my nostrils. The dress still smells like Stephanie. The gnawing ache I've been trying so hard to suppress tears through me. I'm forced to sit down. I hold the dress tightly against my body. The fabric is soft. I stroke it, skimming my fingers along the red expanse, trying to feel some vestige of Steph there. No, I've got to stop this now. I'll be making out with it next if I'm not careful.

My chest hurts. How could I think, even for a second, that I can ever get over Stephanie? All it takes is one measly piece of cloth and I'm fantasizing about running over to Stephanie's house, liberating her, and carrying her back here. I want Stephanie to be lying on the bed across from me, I want to feel her heat, stare into her eyes.

It's not only a stupid fantasy but a dangerous one. After all, I've seen how that will end.

I inhale deeply. It doesn't matter if I'm making new friends and starting to feel comfortable again. It doesn't matter if things are finally getting better between Mai and me. It doesn't matter if I actually want to stay. I've still got to leave. I've got to do everything I can to protect Stephanie. It's time to come up with a new plan for running away.

My cell phone buzzes out of the blue and startles me. I drop the dress and pick it up, thinking for a wild moment it might be Stephanie, but I'm nonplussed when it's Jackson instead.

I need your help

With what? I reply.

Its important. about Emma. I need to talk 2 u about something going on with her but I'd rather do it face 2 face

OK

We need to talk in private somewhere when Emma's not with me

She's always with you, Jackson

I know. could u maybe meet me after school tomorrow in the art room

```
I guess. Around 4?

K see u then
```

I stare at my phone for a while before sliding it shut. My nerves are jangling. What on earth could Jackson want to talk about? It's weird he can't tell me over text. But he said it was important, and Jackson strikes me as the kind of person who really means it when he says that. Is Emma in some kind of trouble?

I groan and fall back on my pillows, exhausted. Well, whatever it is, I can't allow myself to get too wrapped up in it. I'll be saying goodbye to both of them soon. But I've got to admit I'm curious. Might as well see what he has to say before I leave for good.

Jackson acts as he normally does the next day, quiet and barely attentive. I can't stop trying to guess what is going on. Is he planning on rekindling his first grade romance with Emma and wants some advice? What advice does he think I can possibly give? Honestly, Jackson doesn't seem like the type of person who asks for help with stuff like that. Maybe her birthday is coming up and he's planning a surprise party. He doesn't seem like a party person either. But still, better something like that than Emma secretly being a criminal or whatever.

When four o'clock rolls around, I approach the art room cautiously. I can't help but feel I'm making a mistake, that whatever Jackson has to say will be more than I can handle right now. Shaking off my doubts, I thrust the door open.

The room is empty.

Jackson's late to his own appointment. Rude. I step inside.

A strong arm wraps around me from behind, pinning my arms to my sides. Someone presses against my back, I feel their hot breath. I hear a snipping sound, cold metal bumps against my neck and my head becomes lighter. Before I can process any of this, I'm released. I whip around just in time to see the back of Jackson's gray hoodie as its wearer dashes out of the room. My hand jumps to my hair and I feel the jagged edges. It's been cropped to chin level. I glance down. Black locks litter the floor.

What the hell?

Only this thought burns in my mind as I launch myself after Jackson, screaming his name. Shock, outrage, and disgust are all mixed together, but mostly it's the burning question of *why* that propels me forward. I'm not going to let him get away before I get an explanation.

I follow the hooded figure as he races up several flights of stairs, running so fast that I bang off the wall each time I turn a corner. I let each ricochet carry me up the next flight. My chest constricts painfully and I wheeze but force myself to keep going. Something's nagging me about the way Jackson's running. The graceful loping movement is oddly familiar.

When we reach the third floor, I think that Jackson will finally be forced to stop, but instead he makes another sharp turn and thrusts open the door leading to the roof, kicking aside a wooden doorstop that prevented the door from locking automatically. Did he set that up earlier somehow? I don't let myself wonder too long, I grab it before it slams shut behind him and propel myself up the small staircase, bursting out of the little metal door at the top onto the roof.

Jackson finally comes to a halt and stands, back to me, near the edge of the building. He's looking at the grassy expanse spread out below. The track and football field is visible from this vantage point, stretched out in the distance. As I stare at the figure's back, gasping and heaving, it finally dawns on me.

Jackson was running just like Stephanie.

Chapter Twenty-two

THE PERSON TURNS. Yes, it's Stephanie in Jackson's sweatshirt, looking perfectly calm, if out of breath. She pulls down the hood and shakes out her wavy hair. I stumble back against the door, numb with shock.

"What the — ?"

"Whew, I can't believe I pulled that off!" Stephanie gasps, wiping her forehead.

I can't process this, there are only questions. "You have Jackson's hoodie?"

"Yeah, I took it along with his phone."

"You took it?"

"I'll give them back, don't worry."

"You stole Jackson's phone and hoodie, ambushed me, cut my hair, and made me run after you to the roof? I don't get it!"

"Yeah, I know, kinda weird." Stephanie shrugs off the hoodie and drops it on the paving. Her expression is so placid it's unnerving. "But desperate times, desperate measures. I'm going to finally end this. I don't care what I have to do."

My senses are returning to me. I'm still dazed from the bizarre string of events, but it's windy up here and with the breeze against my neck I remember that my hair was short like this in the vision. And now I'm alone with Stephanie. This is bad. Solving whatever's going on will have to wait.

"This is just screwed up, Stephanie. I don't know why you'd do something like this, but you know what, I don't care." I force the words out shakily. "I'm out of here."

I turn and grab the handle of the little metal door.

"You know that door at the bottom of the stairs locks automatically when it closes, right? You're stuck up here with me."

I whip around. Stephanie's teeth are bared in a grin that looks almost like a snarl. I swear and dash to the edge of the roof where Stephanie is standing. The ground is three stories down. The windows don't offer any significant footholds. The building's fairly squat, so it's *possible* I could survive the fall, but I'd definitely break some bones hitting the ground.

I look around. We stand on a flat roof, nothing but solid gray concrete beneath our feet. The door I came through is on a much higher section of the building than the one we stand on, and there's no way to climb up there. But on the side directly opposite there's a building with a lower roof. I can jump down onto that one and get closer to the ground. I stride toward the edge, fumbling in my purse for my cell phone. I need to call Mai for help.

"I finally figured it out, you know," Stephanie calls after me as I walk away.

Ignore her. Keep walking. My fingers close around the cell phone.

"You must have touched me. You must have seen how I die."

My fingers slip and my phone drops back in my purse. I slow my walk. She knows? I shake myself and pick up speed again. She's always been smart. She just guessed right. It doesn't matter. Keep ignoring. Keep walking.

"And you should know," Stephanie pauses here and takes a deep breath. It rattles in her mouth.

Keep walking.

"I saw it myself a long time ago. You killing me."

I stop so abruptly I almost trip over my own feet. I spin around and gape at Stephanie. She's standing just a few feet from the edge of the roof, her arms crossed over her chest. She's smiling, but it's a tight, empty smile.

"I finally said it!" Stephanie lets out a hoarse little laugh. "That wasn't so hard."

I feel like I've been clubbed in the back of the head. Stephanie *knows*. But how?

Stephanie slowly sinks to the ground, arms still clasped tightly around herself as she settles into an awkward sitting position. "Might wanna sit down. This conversation will probably take a while."

I couldn't sit down even if I wanted to. I'm completely paralyzed. "I don't understand!"

"You never *tried* to understand," Stephanie snaps sharply. Her fingers dig into the soft flesh of her arms. "I thought you might guess it on your own someday, but that was a pipe dream. You're too self-absorbed for that. Just *think* about it, okay?"

"Stephanie," I trail off. I can't make sense of these words. They race around inside my head, bouncing off the walls of my skull with dull thuds. "What are you saying?"

"Guess I have to spell it out," Stephanie says hollowly, lowering her eyes. "I'm like you. Well, not exactly like you. When I look into a person's eyes, I see all the deaths that person will ever witness. That includes murders, naturally. So when I met you, I saw you murdering me."

I shake my head with a nervous squeak of a laugh. "No! How could that be?"

"I didn't see any of your other visions, though. Don't really know why. Guess the deal is that you've got to be there in person. See it with *your* eyes, you know?" Stephanie's voice has taken on that mechanical affect it always does when she's trying to solve a particularly difficult math problem.

"But no, this doesn't make sense. If you saw a vision of me killing you, why would you want to be friends? Why would you even want to get *near* me?" I'm honestly surprised I can still speak, the question escapes from within without my permission.

"Because I don't believe it *has* to happen!" Stephanie cries. She takes several heaving breaths, squeezing the sides of her shoulders so hard that they start to turn inward, threatening to cave in on themselves. "That's always been the difference between us. I *knew* I could save you from whatever made you become a killer. I'd become your friend and show you that you didn't have to kill me. I could finally change fate. And even if I couldn't, well, that'd just be like my comeuppance, I guess. For not helping Matt when I saw what was going to happen to him. That's fine with me."

I just gawk at her, my mind full of static.

"And then I found out you had powers like I did. Someone else like me! It was such an amazing discovery. I can't describe it. I don't believe in destiny, but wow, we just fit perfectly together, don't we? You can see how someone will die, I can see any other deaths that person would be a part of. It's like we're meant to be! Maybe we were drawn to each other because of our powers, maybe that's like a side effect. Whatever. I just, I wanted to find out more about you. Me. *Us.* I was hungry for it, and somewhere along the way, I realized how I felt about you was more than just a fascination with your powers. It was much more than that."

She finally loosens her vice-like grip on herself, letting her arms fall to her sides. Now that her hands aren't clenched tight, they begin to shake. Stephanie blinks rapidly and takes another deep breath, still looking down at the roof beneath her.

"B-but," My whole body quakes, like the earth is rumbling beneath me. "Why wouldn't you tell me?"

"I tried!" Stephanie says, her voice cracking. She's rubbing her wrists now. They both have angry red marks on them. "I started to so many times. But I was so afraid! You always said you just wanted a normal friend. You hated your powers so much! If you knew I was the same, I thought you'd push me away! You'd be like him! And if I started, I'd have to tell you everything, I'd have to tell you that I saw you kill me. And I knew you wouldn't believe we could change it, I knew you'd *leave* me!"

I try to speak but it comes out like a whimper. I raise my hands in the air, trying to push away what Stephanie was saying.

"See?" Stephanie says dully. "Even now, you're trying to run away, aren't you?"

I am. I can't handle all of this. I need to be somewhere to be alone and think. I need to go. My eyes dart around, looking for escape, but there was nothing. I'm trapped.

Stephanie snorts, the snort turns into a laugh and the laugh to a convulsion. A horrible, rasping cackle rings out and her entire body rattles with it. Finally, she settles, breathless. "Nothing for it then," she mutters, wiping tears off her face. "I have to do it." She wrenches her head up, finally meeting my eyes.

I instinctively take a step back, panic rushing through my numb body.

Stephanie's gaze bores through me. Her eyes look sunken again, and they're trembling in their sockets. She looks like some kind of wraith.

She stumbles to her feet, lurching and swaying as she does so. I jump at the sudden movement, tripping over myself. I fall as Stephanie rises, landing hard on my rear.

My breath comes quickly now, too quickly, I can't control it. I'm choking on air. "Wait," I try to say but can't spare breath for the words.

Stephanie takes a step forward and when her foot hits the concrete, it splits my world in half, snuffs it out. For a second there's just blackness.

Then, slowly, the world comes back into focus, fuzzy around the edges. Cool fingers brush against my cheek. Stephanie's gazing down at me, cradling my head. The sunken look is still in her eyes but it isn't quite so frightening. She's crying as she traces my jaw with her fingers.

"Did you seriously black out over this?" she says with a shaky little smile.

"It was a panic attack, okay?" I croak. "Don't make a thing of it."

I want to tell Stephanie to stop, to let go of me. But even in the middle of everything, the feeling of Stephanie touching me gently isn't something I can bring myself to stop. I haven't allowed anyone to touch me like this in years. I want to feel it even more deeply, this softness, this slightest trace of warmth.

I pull off one glove, then the other, and take Stephanie's hand in my own. Stephanie lets me, even squeezing back. It's clammy and sweaty, but it feels right, somehow. It feels *so* right. Regret and longing fills all my hollow places. Why can't it just be this simple, as simple as the fact that our hands fit together? Why can't we forget the tangled mess of everything and just exist for this one thing?

"You lied to me, Steph," I whisper. "All this time."

Stephanie doesn't answer right away. Her eyes are glazed, distant. "All relationships are built on lies."

"I don't need a Goth kid's t-shirt slogan, I need you to explain yourself," I hiss. Stephanie raises her eyebrows. I'm also surprised at the venom in my own voice, but I hold my glare.

"I just did, didn't I?" Stephanie mutters, twirling a lock of hair around her finger. "I mean, at first not telling you was just me being careful. I wanted to keep my distance and observe you first, build up to it, you know. But then we really became close and I didn't want you to run away. And the longer I didn't tell you, the harder it was."

"I meant explain cutting my hair and luring me up here," I say, pushing myself up out of Stephanie's lap into a sitting position. I don't trust myself to remain there without giving into temptation.

"Oh, that," Stephanie sighs. She crosses her legs and leans back, looking as if she's contemplating the heavens. "Well, I'm just giving you every opportunity I can to kill me."

"*What?*" I cry, recoiling.

"Yep, I've given you everything you need for a good, clean murder. We're alone up here and I'm totally vulnerable." She extracts a bag from the front pocket of Jackson's hoodie. "I've got a knife in here you can use."

"Give me that!" I snatch the bag from her and throw it as hard as I can. It sails over the edge of the roof. "What is *wrong* with you? Seriously!"

"My grief journal was in there." Stephanie looks wistfully in the direction I threw it. "I hope you didn't mess it up."

I jump to my feet, my hands balled into fists. "Stop playing games! I can't deal with you, with any of this! It's like you're a complete stranger!"

"Yeah, it must all be pretty frustrating," Stephanie says,

getting up and dusting herself off. "Like you said, I lied to you. You don't even know me anymore. Maybe I didn't even love you, right? How can you believe anything I'm saying? Doesn't it make you mad?" Stephanie tilts her head inquiringly. "Admit it, deep down, you really want to hurt me."

"What?" My hands go slack. My heart beats fast, and goose bumps rise on my flesh.

Stephanie's expression settles into that placid, blank mask-face again. "Take your best shot." She holds her arms open and juts out her chin as if readying herself for a punch.

"I'm not gonna hurt you."

"Why not? It's fate, right? Can't change destiny." Her face twists into a grimace. "You know it has to happen. So admit it. You were lying when you said you loved me. You're lying to yourself right now when you say you don't want to hurt me."

"I don't!"

"Of course you do. Why wouldn't you?" In the time it takes me to blink, Stephanie grabs my wrists. She slowly, almost lovingly, places my hands around her own throat.

"Don't you realize?" Stephanie says. "If you don't kill me, it means the visions weren't inevitable fate after all. It means all those people, you, no, *we*, let them die." Stephanie gives a high-pitched titter, almost like a scream, her throat vibrating under my thumbs. "Can you live with that?"

"Stop it."

"Do it!" Stephanie yells, her voice harsh and terrible. I jump back, panicked, and jerk Stephanie forward by her throat in the same motion. An airless grunt escapes Stephanie's lips. I gasp and let go, my hands trembling.

"Knew you had it in you," Stephanie says, rubbing her neck.

"No." I stumble back. My legs feel like they're made of squishy rubber. It's all I can do not to fall down again "No, no I *don't*. You're wrong. I'm not angry and no part of me wants to hurt you." And it's true. I'm too exhausted, too empty to feel any outrage. "You can say whatever you want, you can even attack me. I *won't* do it."

I wobble away from Stephanie. I look over again at the smaller building next to the one I stand on. I can probably make it if I jump down. Maybe break my ankle, but I'm willing to risk that. I take a shaky step in that direction.

"You won't kill me even after all this," Stephanie mutters.

I wish there was a way to shut her out. Maybe I should put my fingers in my ears and start humming really loudly.

"Well, see then?" Suddenly, Stephanie's tone is cheerful. "Point proven. There's no reason we can't be together from now on."

I spin back toward Stephanie. "*What?*"

Stephanie's image shimmers before me. Her face is flushed and she smiles hesitantly. She's fidgeting, standing with her knees turned slightly in as she rubs her elbow. She looks awkward.

"You asked why I did all this," she says softly. "I did it to show you what you just said yourself. Your hair's cut, we're in the perfect place, might even start to drizzle soon." She looks up at the sky, which is getting gray and cloudy. "I dropped this big bombshell on you, I did everything I could to provoke you, and you didn't break. You didn't even come close. So the vision isn't going to happen, Manee! We can change fate!"

"*That's* what this was? You tried to provoke me into *killing* you over something like *that*?!"

"I got it all out in the open. Now we know where we stand. I showed you that you don't have to be afraid. We don't have to avoid each other now!" Her eyes are luminous.

I stare at her. A full minute passes. I've been on an endless roller coaster this whole time and all the twists and turns have me sick to my stomach. Is this it? Is this the end of the ride, or are we headed for another steep drop?

"Hello?" Stephanie's smile fades.

But really, does it even matter? The answer is clear.

"No," I say. My voice comes out raw and scratchy. "No. We can't." The words hang there, a noose around my neck.

"Why not?" Stephanie asks.

The noose tightens. I gulp and force my answer out. "Because we could never be sure. It'll always hang over us, what could happen. I'd just be worried and scared the whole time. If there's even the slightest possibility, I can't do it."

"So you really have no faith in yourself. In us." The flush on Stephanie's cheeks burns brighter with anger.

I groan in exasperation. "Look, this should cinch it! All this that just happened, this whole thing, the way you're acting, even me, it's *not normal*. We're both so messed up we bring out the worst in each other. I feel like, at this rate, the vision is going to happen. I just can't risk it!" I plead, tears pricking her eyes. I can't stand the wounded, furious look Stephanie wears now. I want to break away, but Stephanie's gaze holds me.

"You're seriously still going to cling to this?" Stephanie's chin quivers and tears glitter in the narrowed slits of her eyes. "I've always felt like you were a part of me. But you're the weak part. You'd rather live in fear than be happy. It's just too easy and self-satisfying to be miserable."

"Think whatever you want about me." I press my thumbs against my eyelids. Little lights pop in the dark. I inhale deeply. "Goodbye, Stephanie."

There's a long silence, then, "Heh. So that's it. I'm trapped after all. It's just decided. That someday you really will do it. Just because they told you." Stephanie doesn't sound angry anymore, or hysterical. Her voice is dead, emotionless. "I guess it's actually true, what I said. You never really loved me, huh."

Tears force themselves through the cracks between my eyelids. "This is *because* I love you! Just forget it." I leave Stephanie where she's standing, finally managing to walk to my original destination, the edge of the roof overlooking the smaller building. I don't care if I break my ankle jumping down there now.

"There's nothing else left now." Stephanie doesn't seem like she's talking to me anymore. Her voice is distant. "They took everything. Like always. God, I just wanted this *one thing*! I wanted to show you, show him, show *them*! But I can never win."

I can hear her walking around. I resist the urge to turn and see what she's doing. I instead focus on readying myself for the jump, backing up slowly. How much of a running start will I need?

"I'm tired. So, so tired. I'm sick of losing. I want to have a choice for once. They don't get to choose the way I die."

Something about the way Stephanie's talking chills me. I slowly look over my shoulder. What I see nearly makes my heart stop.

Stephanie stands with her toes over the edge of the roof, her face a sick gray color, her eyes fastened on the grassy ground three stories below.

"This is the only way left. I'm going to choose, no matter what." Stephanie's voice wobbles. Her body wobbles too, trembling on the ledge. "I'll show you all."

"Stephanie, no!" I gesture wildly at her. "No, don't do it! C-come this way." I'm afraid to move. It's like the faintest gust of wind will knock Stephanie over.

Stephanie turns her head toward me, smiling faintly. Her eyes are like a doll's, nothing but empty glass. "It's fine. Don't be sad. I'll set us both free, okay? I'll show you the future is yours to make. Watch me, Manee."

She jumps.

I erupt into a high-pitched whine, like some weak imitation of a siren's wail. I rush forward. Stephanie is splayed out on the grass below. She isn't moving.

I run full tilt to the other side of the roof and make the jump to the smaller building, my ankle folds under me as I land, my knees crash into the concrete, but it barely registers. I get up and look down at the side of the building. I'm only two stories up now, and the window ledges are large enough to be good footholds. I waste no time climbing down. I fall from the first story window, but I hit the ground rolling and scramble immediately to Stephanie's prone body.

A pool of blood is forming around Stephanie's head. Her leg sticks out at an odd angle. I drop down to my knees. Check for a pulse. I have to check for a pulse. I can't remember how, though. Something with the neck. I put my hands on Stephanie's neck, trying to feel her heartbeat. Stephanie's eyes flutter half-open at my touch. With a great effort, she put her hands over mine. Her eyes close, and she's gone again.

I recoil with a gasp. For a second, I can't move. I just sit there like a lump on a log, mouth half open. Then I jerk into action. I try to staunch the wounds on the side of Stephanie's head, but blood streams through my fingers. I rip my jacket off and wrap it around Stephanie's skull. I finally remember my cell phone. Fingers slippery with blood, I drop it three times, but finally manage to dial nine-one-one.

I'm not sure exactly what I say or even what the person I talked to on the phone sounds like. I feel like I'm having a vision, trapped outside myself, just watching everything happen, a helpless invisible bystander.

I grab Stephanie's hand with scrabbling, numb fingers, holding on as tightly as I can. She's warm. Still warm. "Don't let go, please, don't let go," I whisper over and over.

I don't know how much time passes before the ambulance arrives. The medics have to pry my hands off Stephanie. They wear gloves, and I'm briefly tempted to touch their faces, so I can escape into visions of their deaths. No matter how horrific, watching the death of a stranger is preferable to what I'm watching now.

I follow, zombie-like, as they lift Stephanie into the ambulance, but they hold me back.

"I have to go with her. I have to make sure she's all right," I tell them, over and over again.

"We are going to do our best to help her, there's nothing more you can do."

Eventually, I stop struggling and sink to the ground, cold drops of water pelting me again and again. It could have been raining for a while but I've only just started to feel it. Distantly, I can hear them asking me questions, but their words echo into nothingness. I notice one of the medics staying behind has picked up a little red tote bag. Stephanie's bag, the one I threw away.

"That's mine," I find myself saying. The medic hands it over. Inside it are scissors, a knife, and a little journal. It's that one Stephanie's been writing in lately, the grief journal. I quickly take it out and put it in my purse. I won't let them have it, not her journal.

My eyes drift to the knife. Then I look at my hands. There's blood all over them — under my fingernails, in the grooves of my knuckles.

I should have been the one to do it, I think through a dizzy haze. The second I had that vision. I should have been the one to kill myself. It shouldn't have been Stephanie.

"Manee!" Two clammy hands clamp around mine. I'm pulled into a smothering embrace.

Mai's here now, I guess.

"Dad's coming, he's right behind me. Can you hear me? They say you're in shock, please, I know it's hard, but please, please just answer me."

Chapter Twenty-three

WHEN I WAKE, for a second it's like I've simply had an unsettling dream. Then I notice the white regulation bedsheets and how my arms feel like they have fishhooks in them. I'm connected to a bunch of tubes and a beeping machine. And above me is that blank expanse I hate so much. I put manga drawings up on my own bedroom ceiling so it could be as different as possible from the white void of a hospital ceiling. But here it is again, like I never left.

Something feels weird about how my neck rests on my pillow. I move my head side to side without lifting it, trying to figure out what's wrong. Then I reach up and feel it. My hair is short.

It all comes back to me.

"Stephanie!" I shout hoarsely, sitting up. A stabbing pain shoots up my arm.

"Whoa!" Dad's here and a doctor is forcing me down. Have they been in the room this whole time? I can't keep track of time or space anymore, everything's spinning around me.

"Thank God you're awake!" Dad sobs.

The doctor gently presses down on my shoulders, trying to get me to lie flat.

"Manee, I need you to calm down," he says.

"*I* need to see Stephanie!" I struggle, clawing at him and pounding at his chest like a three-year-old. There's no strength left in my limbs. "Dad! Dad, how is she? Is she dead?"

I can hear Stephanie's voice in my head. "You killed me."

Dad looks startled by the bluntness of the question. "I'm sure she's not dead, honey."

"You don't even *know*?" I cry, struggling harder. Stephanie's dying alone somewhere and I've just been sleeping through it!

"They wouldn't let us see her."

"Manee, if you keep this up, I'm going to have to call for another sedative," the doctor speaks in an infuriatingly calm voice, like he was just *so* used to dealing with hysterical people like me. I'm ready to punch him in the face; I wouldn't mind seeing his death at this point.

"Her family wouldn't talk to me, but I can see if Mai can track them down for you." Dad takes out his cell phone, trying to calm me.

"Her *family*! She hates her family! They don't even care about her!" I spit. "I'm the only one who cares." I shove the doctor hard in the chest, but he still doesn't budge. When I try to go for his face, his gloved hand catches my wrist and he forces my arm down. Why do I have to be so weak?

"I'm going to call for a sedative," the doctor sighs.

Dad holds up his hand. "Please! Manee, I'm getting Mai to find out about Stephanie. You need to settle down if you want to hear anything."

I close my eyes and take a deep breath. My body feels so heavy I don't know if I'll even be able to get up, much less find Stephanie. I need to wait either until I find out or until I'm strong enough to shove the doctor aside. Whichever comes first.

I let go of the doctor's coat.

The doctor releases me but stays at my bedside as a looming threat.

I realize hollowly that I'll probably never be strong enough to get past him, no matter how long I wait.

"Paralyzed by weakness, same as always."

It's Stephanie's voice. It bites into me, but at the same time, I treasure how the words sound in my head, I treasure hearing the dancing lilt of her words, even if it's only a hallucination.

Mai comes in. She explains that Zack, who's out in the waiting room, called Tony for her, as he's on better terms with him than she is. Tony gave him the rundown: Stephanie is comatose. She broke her leg in the fall as well as a couple ribs, but the real problem is her head injury. She's stable for now, but the doctors can't say for sure when or if she's going to wake up.

I know I should be grateful Stephanie hasn't died yet, but I just feel dread, like the inevitable has only been prolonged. My vision already became reality. Things played out just like I saw them. True, there wasn't anything about going to a hospital, but that probably just means my visions focus on the cause of death, rather than the exact moment. Now that I think of it, I didn't actually see Jocelyn die during her vision either, she was still twitching at the end. So Stephanie hanging on a little longer doesn't mean anything.

"Don't you dare come up with an excuse to give up like you always do."

Stephanie's voice in my head. Again. It's disturbing that I'm hearing it like this, but I don't want it to stop. It's like a fragment of Stephanie is still with me. Does hearing her mean there's hope?

Some part of Stephanie is hanging on? It probably just means I'm losing it.

They take my IV out after a while, but want to keep me overnight for observation.

"She's been through a lot. With her history of mental illness, we want to make sure she's stable. She really needs some rest," I hear the doctor saying. "Especially since I'm sure the police will want to question her about what happened. She needs to be strong enough for that."

I cover my ears with my pillow, tuning out the rest. Normally, being treated like a mental case would bring out the old bitterness in me, but I'm glad for it right now. I want to be in the same place Stephanie is. Tonight will be my only chance to sneak out and visit her.

The problem will be getting my father to leave my side so I can get it done. He's clearly afraid I'll hurt myself if he leaves me alone, so he takes off work to stay with me all day and night. This typically would annoy me and make me snipe at him, but he doesn't try to talk to me after I make it clear I'm not interested. Instead, he asks me if it would be all right for him to read aloud to me, like he did when I was a kid. I agree, since I know being occupied will help him be less anxious. Mai brings some books from my room and he reads *Harry Potter* to me in a soft, soothing voice. I wish I really could just be a little kid again and lose myself in the story, but I can only pretend to listen. I just can't stop reliving Stephanie's fall over and over in my head.

When night falls, I feign sleep. After an hour of this, Dad finally leaves the room. As soon as I hear his footsteps receding, I sit up. I'm going to have to work fast, Dad's likely just taking a break to eat.

I slip out of bed and quietly pad down the hall.

The hospital is dark and unfamiliar, and I'm constantly checking behind and around me so I can remember the way back. I note room numbers carefully. I come across a map of the hospital near the front desk on my floor and read silently, cold in my flimsy gown, standing stock still so as not to catch the attention of the woman at the front desk. The ICU is on the third floor. It's likely that's the ward someone with a head injury-induced coma would be in, so I double back and find an elevator at the other end of the hall. It makes me shudder to be in this small, silent space at night, rising slowly upward. But all that's left now is finding Stephanie's room.

I scan room after room and the pit in my stomach grows

deeper and darker with each motionless person I lay eyes on. Some are a mass of bandages. Some of the rooms smell like rotting flesh and the patients look like living skeletons. I fear, irrationally, that Stephanie will look like this too. Just being here might have shriveled her up already.

Finally, I find the right room.

Stephanie's not a shrunken skeleton or a mass of bandages and rot. But I inhale sharply when I see her. Half of her head is shaved and tightly wrapped in gauze. The right side of her face is swollen purple. Her leg is in a cast.

I used to enjoy looking at Stephanie. Now it's painful. I can't stand seeing her face so shattered. I wonder if Stephanie herself would be horrified looking in the mirror. I manage not to close my eyes. I focus on the left side of Stephanie's face, the familiar dip of her nose, her swooping eyelashes, and the brown shine of her unbroken skin. Her hair will grow back. Her face will heal. If she lives that long.

After a while, I find the strength to speak. "So, I guess we both got haircuts." My voice quavers as I sit down in the vacant chair near her bed.

A part of me expects Stephanie to miraculously respond with a snarky comeback. It doesn't happen. Even the voice in my head won't respond. I put my hands together, suck in a breath, and blow it out.

"I need to talk to you, I guess. Even if you won't hear me. Though I think it was you who shared this fact of science with me: Don't they say comatose people can sort of hear? That talking to people in comas is good for them, that they'll reach for your voice?" I laugh sadly. "I doubt you want to hear my voice, though. I'll probably just motivate you to sleep longer."

I pause for a second, trying to decide what to say next. I watch Stephanie's chest rise and fall rhythmically. I'm seized with a sudden fear that her breathing will stop. I squeeze my clasped hands together so tightly they shake.

"I'm not sure what I know anymore. I'm not sure what to believe. But I still know one thing: I don't want you to die." The second I say it, the desire fills me up completely, threatening to overflow. It gives me this strange, manic energy. "No, I *need* you not to die. You can't just leave me after turning everything upside down. I still have so many questions for you. I feel like there's so much of you that's a stranger to me now, so much of you that scares me. But I still want to get to know you again." I reach over and my hand hovers above Stephanie's. "Because you're still the only person who knows me. You knew what a terrible person I am, what a coward, but for some reason, you stuck around. That has to mean something."

My hand trembles. "You're right about me: I *am* self-absorbed. I knew you were struggling with something, I knew you were suffering, but I didn't see how bad it was for you. I didn't try hard enough to help you."

I swallow a sob.

"Some part of me probably *did* enjoy the idea of being the most miserable person in the world. I didn't want to deal with the idea there might be other people like me. I'm not like you, I never wanted to think about my powers and how I could use them. But I do now. For the first time, I want to know *why*. I want to know what I can do."

I bow my head.

"I'm still not sure I believe we can really fight back against our visions. But if there's any hope, any hope at all that I can stop your death from coming true, that I can make you happy again, well, I have to try. I would die trying."

I'm embarrassed about how dramatic this sounds. I'm pretty sure under normal circumstances that Stephanie would just burst into laughter, hearing that. But she doesn't stir. I can't touch her. I fear that if I do, the hand will be cold. Or maybe I'll see another vision, depicting the moment Stephanie will die in this hospital bed, just to taunt me. I pull my hand back.

"You said you'd prove to me we could change fate, but you didn't, really. You just ended up playing out what I saw in the vision. I want you to show me for real this time. I want you to show me your way works. You're not off the hook yet. Prove me wrong by surviving this. Do that and I'll let you rub it in all you want."

I stand up, my throat constricting as I look down at this person I love and can barely recognize now. Because the Stephanie I know isn't prone and silent and perfectly behaved. She's only really Stephanie when she's talking a mile a minute, steamrollering over everything else in her path.

"I'll do my best, Stephanie," I murmur. "So please. Don't let me kill you."

I slip out of the room softly, noiselessly, like a phantom passing through.

Chapter Twenty-four

THE OFFICERS COME to talk to me before I'm discharged from the hospital the next day. I tell them the closest to the truth I can. I tell them that Stephanie got me up on a rooftop and tried to convince me that we could be in a relationship but I rejected the idea out of fear. Stephanie responded to that by jumping off the roof.

Surprisingly, the whole thing's pretty painless. I have to repeat the story a few times and clarify a few things but the police don't act as if they doubt me. They speak in soft voices and looked at me with sympathetic eyes. One officer takes me aside afterward and treats me to a long, rambling speech about how her daughter is a lesbian so she understands how difficult it must be. She gives me the phone number of a support group.

When I tell Mai and my dad about the police's strange cooperation in the waiting room afterward, Mai gets shifty.

"What's up?" I ask sharply.

"Well, for some reason I can't figure out, Zack's always been pretty friendly with Tony, so they talked and he told him," she hesitates. "Stephanie apparently, uh, left a note at home saying she was considering something like this. So, you see, it really was nothing to do with whatever happened between you two, and the police know that!" Mai's talking so fast now that her words run together. She's giving me this watery desperate look I can't stand. I block her out, my mind whirring.

Stephanie *planned* this? How long was she thinking about this? Was this always her backup plan if I refused to fight fate with her?

"Or maybe I was giving you an alibi for if you *did* end up murdering me," Stephanie's voice volleys back.

Ridiculous. There's no way anyone would go out of their way to give their murderer an alibi. Stephanie definitely wouldn't.

"Yeah, I bet you never thought I'd jump off a building either," the voice inside my head scoffs. "You clearly don't know me as well as you think you do."

I squeeze my eyes shut. No. The head-voice is just messing with me. Stephanie was sincere about not believing in the vision. She must have been. But try as I might to shove the doubt away, I feel like I'm losing my grip on Stephanie more and more. I can't be sure about anything. The Stephanie I cling to is becoming smoky and indistinct, and soon there will be nothing left.

The car ride back home is bursting with tension. Mai and Dad regard me like something that might shatter with the slightest nudge. Every question is posed in hushed voices. It's even worse than when I came home from the institution.

I shake my head when they ask me if I need anything and if I want to talk.

"I just want to rest in my own room," I tell them in the most stable sounding voice I can muster. "I need a little alone time to get my head together."

They exchange nervous looks.

"I'll keep the door open, okay?"

So when I get home, I'm allowed to convalesce in my room with a plate of my favorite foods: *gai pad med ma muana*, fried rice, and potato chips. I don't touch any of it. Instead, I sit at the edge of my bed, staring around my room, an electric sort of energy thrumming through me. My skin quivers and strains around my body, like I'm about to burst out of it. I flex my fingers, clenching and releasing, clenching and releasing. I need to get my hands on something. I need *answers*. I need to figure out how to help Stephanie, or I'm going to tear myself apart.

Then I spot it, propped in the corner of my room. My purse. Stephanie's notebook is inside it. I lunge across the room and open the purse so violently the metal zipper comes off in my hand. I throw it aside and tear open the notebook. Then a noise makes me jump.

Mai's peering through the open door, but when I glare at her she mouths, "Sorry," and nervously backs out of view.

I return my attention to the notebook in my hands. For a few minutes, I just trace the words written in Stephanie's careful, precise hand with my fingers. I want to cry just at seeing it. But finally, I force myself to actually read what's on the page.

It looks like Steph attempted to do actual "grief journaling" at first; there are a lot of sentence beginnings like "I feel" and "I wish." However, she quickly gave up on all that and just decided to devote the thing to strategies for fixing the situation with Ms. Carnahan.

If Ava was going to kill herself, would I see it? She'd be her own murderer and all… Maybe I would and her glasses are just blocking me. I didn't see Callie's death when I looked at her, after all.

She's written and crossed out various schemes to get Ms. Carnahan to take her glasses off. Ask her if I can clean her glasses and so on. Apparently, they were all unsuccessful. The final one is, throw a drink in her face, then she'll have to take them off to clean them. It's crossed out and under it is She just sat there, didn't even care! Lost it and just grabbed them—she got mad and then Tony came in. What am I going to do?

Then on the next page: I messed up. He won't even let me see her now! What if she dies? I need to fix this somehow. I need to show him I'm not what he thinks I am. I need to do something right for ONCE!

I grip the notebook hard, my fingernails making little crescent indentations on the paper. She really did tear herself apart trying to redeem herself, in her own eyes, in her brother's eyes. She worked herself to the bone, all because she was so desperate to be treated as family. She *needed* it so much.

Why couldn't I have seen that? Why couldn't I have seen how much it meant to her? I could have helped. I should have helped!

Tears spill out of my eyes. It feels like I've spent more time crying than not these past few days. I rub my eyes roughly. It doesn't do any good to wallow in self-pity. I've done enough of that already. I grind my teeth, glaring down at the notebook. The best thing to do is get to the source of it all. Tony's the one who drove her to this. He's at fault just as much as I am.

I remember the last time I saw Tony. "I bet your little friend would believe me if she knew how you really are," he said.

Did he know about Stephanie's powers? That would explain why he was so afraid of her. He probably knows other things too. He has the answers and I'm going to get them all, even if I have to bash his slimy head in to do it!

The edges of the notebook tear under my grip. I quickly let go and smooth it out clumsily.

"Manee?" My sister stands at the door, a picture of concern.

"What?" I say, more sharply than I intend to.

"Can I talk to you for a minute?"

Her sister's eyes have this needy, naked look to them, like *she* was the one who saw someone jump off a roof. I sigh, kneading the space between my eyes with my knuckles. "Fine. Come on in."

Mai shuffles into my room and sits down on the edge of my bed. She leans forward, fixing me with an achingly sincere gaze.

"I want to help you."

"I've got all the food and water I need and I don't want to talk," I groan.

Mai shakes her head. "I mean *really* help you. I feel horrible for what I said when you were trying to run away, how I said that you were just looking for attention. Nobody should have to deal with what you're dealing with right now. Maybe if I'd let you run, you wouldn't have had to go through what you did." Mai looks down at her feet.

Unexpected. I make a clumsy sort of "calm down" gesture. "Mai, I don't think you should feel bad. I mean you were just trying to help."

But Mai interrupts me. "So when I say I'll do anything to help you, I mean it. I'll help you run this time, but like, safely. If you want to get away for a while, Zack's uncle owns a hotel."

"I'm not running anymore," I interject shortly.

"But don't you think you should take a break? After what you went through."

I just shake my head. "What's going to help me is taking action." I look back down at Stephanie's notebook. "Taking action to help Stephanie."

"Take action?" Mai looks like a lost kitten.

I brace myself for the inevitable "but there's nothing you can do, please calm down."

"Okay," Mai straightens up, her expression focused. "What action are you taking then? Tell me what I can do."

I stare at her. "Are you serious?"

"I said I'd do anything to help you and I meant it." Mai has that familiar glint in her eyes. "You should know by now that I stick to my convictions."

I glance down at the notebook again. "If you really mean it, I want to go talk to Tony. Can you arrange a meet-up with him?"

"Talk to Tony? Why?"

"I think he's part of the reason Stephanie jumped," I mutter. The words burn my throat on the way out. "He has some answers I need."

Mai observes me for a long moment. Then she exhales and claps her hands together. "Fine. I'll talk to Zack about it and he'll help me get you over there. But in the meantime, you focus on resting and recovering, okay? You need to be ready for this. Dad will let you take off as much school as you need."

"Yeah," I say eagerly. "Thanks a lot, Mai."

"Sure thing." Mai gets off the bed. "Let me know if you need anything else, okay?"

"I will."

Mai leaves the room and I shake my head in awe. A few

months ago, I wouldn't have been able to imagine my sister coming to my aid like this. Now I don't have to worry about sneaking out to find Tony.

I'm going to find out everything, Stephanie. So just hang on.

I turn my attention back to the notebook. There's still some writing left.

What I see hits me like a quick jab to the jaw. This part of the journal is about me. Or rather, about Stephanie dealing with being without me. There's a list of theories for why I'd suddenly ended our friendship. She really is a self-hating homophobe is one, but it's been crossed out. There are ones that make me hate myself all over again, like I'm asking too much of her lately and she's tired of me and The thing with Tony made her not want to be around me—she knows he's right and angry ones like I'm eating way into her moping schedule. But near the end, in different colored ink is she's afraid she won't be able to restrain herself from touching me and then she already touched me. She knows.

This one is circled, and under it is Stephanie piecing together when it happened, noting that I started avoiding her after we slept together.

The last few pages of the journal are devoted to "the plan" to corner me. Stephanie even went so far as to try to write out her confession. It's all ridiculously poetic and nothing like what she actually ended up saying. Yes, when I looked at you I saw my death with you, but now when I look, I see a life with you—the only life I want.

Jesus. Total schmaltz and melodrama. That's just classic Stephanie! It would make me laugh if it didn't hurt so much. Instead, I struggle not to turn into a creature made entirely of tears.

Sleep eludes me that night. I can't stop looking up facts about comas and head injuries on my phone. Apparently, the longer someone stays in a coma, the less likely they are to wake up. The thought makes my stomach shrivel. It's already been three days.

"You're just going to worry yourself to death," Stephanie's voice rings in my ears.

If that could happen, I'd be long dead.

I decide to do research about my powers again. But even searching as hard as I can, I can't find anything worthwhile. Nothing about Stephanie's powers either. I grind my teeth in frustration.

My phone buzzes suddenly, scaring me so much I nearly

drop it. It's just an alert telling me that my text storage is full. "I. don't. care!" I growl, throwing it as hard as I can. It hits the floor with a satisfying crack.

I sit on my bed, panting for a minute. Then I get up and go over to my closet, pulling out the dress Stephanie left. I hold it in my hands and just stare at it. I can't stop for some reason. By the time morning comes, I have a stuffed nose and aching body and what feels like heavy bruises under my eyes.

I trudge over to look in the mirror. A horror movie nightmare greets me. I really haven't gotten a chance to look closely at my new hair until now. It's like my head is covered with uneven porcupine needles. That combined with my hollow, shadowed eyes gives me the look of a zombie girl.

I run my fingers through my hair. On other girls, this patchy look might come off as kind of punk rock. But on me, it's ragged and pathetic. I can't bring myself to feel upset about that, though. It's the truth after all. I'm a torn-up little ragdoll.

"I'm not going to cut it until Stephanie wakes up," I tell my reflection defiantly.

"Wow, now I'll really have to speed up my recovery. You might get arrested by the fashion police, taking such a bold risk!"

I ignore my inner Stephanie's snark and undress. Stephanie's crumpled gown is still in my hands. I pull it on and stare at my reflection in the mirror. It looks completely mismatched, like I'm wearing somebody else's skin. But I'm oddly okay with that now. Everything about me is mismatched at the moment. I might as well own it.

I dig through my closet, looking for more of Stephanie's clothes. Soon I have a small pile of clingy tops and elegant skirts. It's as if Stephanie had decided this was her closet too.

"Hey, maybe I just left you this stuff to improve your sense of style. Do you have any idea what a sad existence it is, being attracted to someone who only wears baggy shirts and sweatpants?"

I smile to myself, letting the voice wash over me. I pull on a little black jacket from the pile—it's one of those useless, super-short ones that stop just below the ribcage. I step into my only pair of shoes, some ratty sneakers. It clashes horribly with the rest of the ensemble.

Satisfied, I make my way downstairs for breakfast, where a glass of milk and cereal is already waiting for me at the table, as are my father and sister, who both stare at me.

I smile blandly back at them.

"Are you planning on going somewhere formal today?" Mai asks dubiously.

"Not really," I respond. I notice Dad has a perplexed look on his face. "What? Is the dress really that big an issue?"

"No, it's just you aren't wearing the gauze you normally wear," Dad says hesitantly.

"Oh." I look down at my bare arms. "Yeah."

It hadn't even registered with me I'd left my gauze behind. I know without it I'll see all sorts of deaths but the thought brings no kick of fear. I saw my best friend jump off a roof. I wasn't there as an invisible, voiceless spirit but as a solid presence, someone whose words and actions caused the event. In comparison, hazy visions of the deaths of strangers seem so small and far removed from me. I feel like I've entered a different world where there's only one thing I can focus on. Everything else is not important.

I rub my palms and feel a certain roughness there. Yes, my skin is hard as iron now. Visions will just bounce off.

"Ah, well," I say with a shrug. "I guess I don't really need it anymore."

My father and sister exchange worried glances.

"Jeez, I thought you guys would be over the moon," I grumble, swirling my spoon around in my cornflakes.

"No, it's great, sweetie. It really is. I'm glad you're taking that step," Dad says unconvincingly. "It's just a bit of a sudden change, so I hope you aren't pushing yourself."

I can't be annoyed at my father's dithering. That kind of thing is also trapped in my old world, the world where Stephanie isn't in a coma.

"Are you planning on missing work today?" I ask quickly. "You don't have to, you know. I'm fine on my own. I just don't want to go back to school quite yet. It must be annoying for the other people at the museum."

My father shakes his head. "No, they're all perfectly fine with it. They know I need to be with my family right now."

"In other words, nice try, but you're not getting rid of him," Stephanie sniggers.

Mai gets up from the table, her eyes still fastened on me and clouded with concern. "Well, I've got to get going to school. See you two when I get back. Manee, remember our promise, okay?"

"What promise was she talking about?" Dad asks after Mai leaves.

"Oh, just to be good and get well. That kind of stuff," I say as we put away the dishes.

"Ah." I can tell Dad doesn't believe me, but he doesn't press the subject. "Would you mind having a little talk with me, Manee?"

There's no fighting the inevitable. I nod silently and follow my father to the living room.

Dad sits down on the couch, hands clasped on his knees. I just stand there, facing him. He looks at me searchingly.

"I'm worried, honey."

"You don't have to be," I respond automatically. "I'm not going to hurt myself or anything."

"I know," he sighs.

I'm thrown by this response. "You do?"

"You're trying to act tough right now. Hurting yourself would go against that." His eyes soften as he gazes at me.

I bristle. "I'm not 'acting' like anything. Don't patronize me."

"I'm not. I just know it from experience. When someone you love leaves you, you want to change yourself." There's a touch of bitterness in his voice. "You try to become the person you think would have been able to keep them from going."

I stiffen. "You're talking about you and Mom." It's rare to hear him mention her.

Dad nods wearily. "I didn't know what to do when she left. She was always the one who would take charge and handle you girls. I was so lost and I'm still lost. I don't know what I'm doing. I want to help you so badly. I can't imagine what it must have been like to see what you saw. I wish I could erase what happened for you, I wish I could make the hurt go away." His voice cracks slightly. He takes off his glasses and rubs his forehead, eyes closed. "But I can't. I can only try the best I can to reach you any way I know how."

I swallow. My mouth is dry and I'm nauseous. I don't like talking about this, I don't like hearing this from him, but I also long to know so many things about Mom.

"Then explain it to me. What's wrong with trying to be the person who would have kept them from going? What was wrong with becoming that person for Mom?"

The lines under Dad's eyes deepen. "Like I said, your mother was always the one who handled disciplining you girls. She always said I was too soft. So, when it came to handling your breakdown, I tried to be harsh and decisive like she would want me to be. But that wasn't the right thing to do for you at that moment. It just made you feel even more disoriented and displaced. I hurt you trying to become the person I thought your mother wanted. And I'm sorry for that."

It was the first time he's directly discussed my hospital stay with me in a long time. It's all I've ever wanted for years and years, an apology. But for some reason, I find no joy in it, no closure. Instead, something begins to burn inside me.

"So, what are you saying? You think we're the same? You think I'm going to hurt someone like you did?" It sounds meaner than I intend, but I don't take it back.

He just gives me this tight sad smile. "Not exactly. But I am worried that you're blaming yourself for what happened to Stephanie. Like I blamed myself for your mother leaving."

I blink at him. "You blamed yourself? But it was my fault, not yours."

Dad makes a noise that's somewhere between a laugh and a scoff. "Of course it wasn't your fault. Why would you think that?"

"Because of how I am." I gesture at myself. "I figured she didn't want to deal with it anymore."

"No, honey, no." He groans. "You see, we both fell into that trap of blaming ourselves for something we couldn't control. That's just how people are. It's self-centered, honestly."

"Self-centered?" I repeat in confusion.

"Yes. It's us wanting to believe we had some sort of control over another person. But *we* didn't make your mother leave. She's her own person and she made her own choices. Acting like we could have stopped it is giving ourselves too much credit."

I'm silent at this. I really wish I could believe him.

"That's why I hope you're not blaming yourself for what happened with Stephanie. You weren't responsible for it."

"You don't know anything about that," I cut in harshly.

"We may not talk as much as we used to, but I know my daughter and I know you're a good person. You would never do something abusive to Stephanie or egg her on in doing what she did. What happened wasn't your fault."

"You're wrong!" I snap. My eyes burn, but once again I refuse to let the tears out. I don't deserve the release of crying. "Do you want to know what happened? Steph wanted me to stop avoiding her, she wanted to be together. She made it clear she needed me so badly. She gave up everything, she gave me all her secrets and fears to convince me. And I said no, I said I could never see her again. Not because I wanted to. But because I was afraid. She needed me and I turned away and she had no other choice." My voice hitches slightly and I can't continue.

"She had a choice, Manee," Dad says softly, leaning forward. "This wasn't *your* choice. It was *hers*. You were confused and afraid and that's not a sin. Stephanie wouldn't have done this if she wasn't struggling already. You couldn't have known how bad it was."

"Yes, I could have!" I cry. "I should have! I knew something was going on, but I was too wrapped up in myself. As someone who loved her, I should have known and I should have *helped* instead of making it worse!"

My father stands up too. "You did your best, honey. I'm sure of it. You're just a kid and you have your own problems. It's the adults in Stephanie's life who were in the best position to help her. She's their responsibility, not yours."

"Oh yeah, and clearly I was in good hands with my parents," Stephanie laughs in my head.

"You just don't understand." I can't stand to look at my father and his eyes full of pity I don't deserve. I turn away from him and glare at the wall.

"Then help me understand, Manee. Tell me what you need. I can't stand seeing you hate yourself for this. Tell me what I can do to help."

There it is, the offer for help. The one Mai gave me. He says it with such raw sincerity.

But I know I can't tell him what I've planned. I can't say that I'm going to confront Stephanie's brother and possibly her parents. I can't tell him I'm going to get answers about what was going on with that family even if I have to beat it out of them. He'll never allow it.

I certainly can't tell him that I'm determined to find out if there's any way I really can prevent the deaths I see. He'll just see that as "delusion" and I can't afford to be institutionalized again. Not now. No, I can't take my father's support. I can't trust him with the truth.

"I just need some space and time," I finally mutter, still turned away from him. "I need some time alone to figure things out."

I can almost hear my father deflating behind me. "If that's what you need. I'll just watch over you. But when you do decide you want to talk, I'll be right here."

"Thanks." I turn around and force a tight-lipped smile. "I didn't sleep last night. I'm going to go take a little nap."

"Sure," he says, his face sagging.

A pang of sorrow shoots through me, but I ignore it. I march up the stairs at a clipped pace, my jaw set.

It's for the best. I'm not lying, after all. I really do need to get some sleep. I have a lot of work ahead of me.

Chapter Twenty-five

THE SOUND OF the doorbell ringing jolts me awake. I'm sprawled so awkwardly across my bed that I nearly fall off it when I try to sit up. I spit out locks of hair that got stuck in my mouth. My brain's wobbling inside my head, weighed down with whatever dreams I was having. I can only remember faint snatches like running after Stephanie, screaming her name but never catching up, blood, a lurching corpse.

I glance at the clock. It's around four. I only got to sleep a couple hours ago. I hear Dad open the door, then I hear a familiar chirpy voice. What is *she* doing here?

Dad calls for me. I've got no choice but to deal with this. I force myself up off the bed and make my way down. Emma and Jackson are standing nervously by the foyer, next to my frazzled-looking father. Their eyes widen in alarm when as they see me descending the stairs.

"Hi, Manee!" Emma says, a little too loudly. Jackson raises his hand in a vague sort of greeting.

"Hi," I respond flatly. I stop at the foot of the stairs, and for a minute, we all simply stare at each other.

Dad clears his throat. "I'll go make some tea. You just sit down, make yourselves at home, have a nice chat." He hurries off to the kitchen.

"Why are you here?" I ask as soon as he's gone.

"Well, we heard about what happened, and you weren't answering any of my texts, so I was worried." Emma scuffs her foot against the floor awkwardly.

"Texts?" I think for a minute, then I remember the alert. "Oh yeah. I didn't get those. I threw my phone at a wall."

"Oh." Emma gives a shaky facsimile of a smile. "No biggie."

"Maybe we should sit in the living room like your dad said," Jackson finally chimes in.

I shrug and lead the way. I sit in the armchair while Emma and Jackson sit on the couch across from me. It's just like we were before the dinner party, which seems like years ago to me now.

We just sit there in silence for a few seconds, staring at each other. Emma fidgets while Jackson looks wary.

Finally, Emma breaks the silence. "You look ah, it's not your usual look, but it's nice!"

Jackson nods vaguely.

I look down at my dress, which is hopelessly wrinkled now that I've slept in it.

"God, if they think you'll buy such a pathetic lie, they really don't think much of you, do they?" Stephanie's voice echoes sadly in my head. I clench my jaw.

"So how've you been holding up?" Jackson asks softly.

"Fine," I reply. I'm not up for another conversation about my feelings. I search around for something else and land on it. "Stephanie stole your phone, Jackson. And your hoodie. The phone's in my room if you want it."

"Oh, that's where it went. Thanks." Jackson gives me a small smile.

I narrow my eyes at him. His face didn't show even the faintest flicker of surprise at the news. There's no confusion either. He isn't asking why Stephanie stole it or when or where. A sick dread fills me.

"You knew she had your stuff."

Jackson's smile drops. He glances over at Emma, who's pale and sweaty. She takes a deep breath.

"I-it wasn't Jackson's fault. I was the one who convinced him to let me borrow his phone. I-if I'd known what would happen!" Emma squeezes her eyes shut. "I just wanted to help. I just wanted you two to be happy."

"You were in on it. You were talking to Stephanie behind my back. You gave her everything she needed to trick me." I can taste something sour in the back of my throat. It burns.

"It wasn't supposed to be like that. I wasn't trying to! We have a class together and she just seemed so sad and desperate. She said you wouldn't talk to her, but she had something really important to tell you, something that would fix everything. I just thought I could help."

"It's my fault just as much as hers," Jackson cuts in, his voice small and barely audible. "I'm the one who ended up letting them borrow my stuff." A slight flush colors his cheeks. "They made it sound like it was going to be some really romantic surprise. And after I heard you say you wanted to be together with her, I thought you'd like it."

"Oh, I was surprised all right," I speak in a rasp as thin as a razor's edge. I can barely breathe. My eyes sting. The bile is rising, thick and quick, scorching my throat. "Was it fun, manipulating me? Have you just been laughing at me this whole time? Laughing at me as you used me and kept things from me?"

"Of course not!" Emma says frantically. "We were just—"

"Just putting one over on me." I get to my feet, shaking. "I gave you my secrets. I gave you my trust. And I got nothing in return. I wasn't even worth the truth to you!"

"Manee, we're sorry, okay?" Emma says, her mouth quivering. Jackson is silent again, hunched over and looking at his feet. "We shouldn't have done it, we should have told you, we know that now."

"Oh, so there's no other secrets you're keeping? You've told me absolutely everything there is to know about you?"

Jackson's mouth forms a thin line. Emma sighs.

"Yeah, I thought so," I snarl. "You've just been hiding in the dark, playing your little games with me, and you call *me* the coward? You're the one who should feel guilty! I was so stupid to trust you!"

The expression on Emma's face changes from one of guilt to one of confusion. "Manee, are you talking to us right now?

"Of course I am!" I thunder. I want to slap Emma across her little pixie face. "Who else would I be talking to?" My head hurts and a sort of haze surrounds Emma and Jackson. "You're the ones who betrayed me! Face up to that, you fucks!"

Jackson's chewing on his lip now. He's bent over so far I can see the top of his head. Emma glances over at him and her eyes widen.

"Uh, I'm really sorry, but I think we should leave," Emma says in a rush. "We're just making you upset." She grabs Jackson by the arm, hoists him up, and starts for the door.

"No, you're not leaving me!" I snap. "You don't get to just go away after putting me through that!" I rush after them, reaching for Jackson's bare arm. A second before I make contact, I remember my hand is also bare now. I remember what will happen if I touch him. I freeze. And then comes Stephanie's voice: "You can't let them go away like this. You have to stop them. You promised me you would be stronger. Prove it!"

Yes. Yes. I stretch my hand forward slowly, agonizingly. Sweat trickles down my skin.

"Don't let them slip through your fingers!"

I press my lips together hard, trying to suppress my body's shuddering.

"Do it, you weakling!"

My head pounds, I can't breathe; I want to but I can't stop. I have to do this even if every part of me screams not to, I have to do this, I have to make them stay.

"What's *wrong*?"

Jackson's words break harshly through my fugue state. I blink. He's standing stock-still and shaking, looking at me like I'm some sort of specter.

"You look like you're going to pass out!" Emma squeaks, holding onto him. "Sh-should I get help?"

"No!" I sound almost inhuman now, I sway but manage not to collapse. My spasming hand drops to my side. "No! I *don't need help*! I'm fine!"

"Okay," Emma says. She looks despairingly at Jackson. "I-I'm so sorry. We'll just go." And without anything further, she drags her friend to the door.

I know I need to stop them, run after them, grab them, but I can't move anymore. I can barely even keep upright, so I just stand there, breathing heavily, drenched in cold sweat.

As the door closes behind Emma and Jackson, Dad comes out of the kitchen. "What happened? Honey, are you okay?"

"I'm fine. It's nothing," I mutter. I shoulder past him and run up to my room.

I drop to my knees once I'm inside, clutching my heart, trying to calm its beating. I shut my eyes tight.

"You couldn't do it. You couldn't keep them from leaving. You couldn't make them pay for what they did to you. You're still too weak!" Stephanie's voice booms.

"I am," I murmur, my arms limp at my sides.

"But you'll get stronger."

I open my eyes. Both my hands curl into fists. "I will."

Chapter Twenty-six

DAD IS SURPRISINGLY good about giving me space that night and the next morning, only checking in every so often. I use the time to continue to pore over Stephanie's notes. When I get tired of that, I rehearse what I'm going to say to Tony.

The rehearsals don't go so well, though. My questions for Tony always seem to deteriorate into ranting. I scream, "How could you? How *could* you? Didn't you realize how much you were hurting her? I hope this is tearing you apart!" I end up punching a pillow to calm down. I just can't stand it, the waiting. I have to talk to him *now*.

Fortunately, Mai sticks to our agreement and has a ride to Tony's ready when she comes home Friday afternoon. Unfortunately, that ride has Zack at the wheel.

I bound out the door only to stop short when I see my sister's beloved boyfriend waving at me from the driver's seat. "What's he doing here?" I hiss as Mai approaches me. "He's not involved with this."

"I told you, he's managed to get on friendly terms with Tony. He can get him to let us in."

"But I wanted to talk to Tony *alone*."

"What?" Mai says with an incredulous look. "I'm not leaving you alone with that guy. His temper is *infamous* at our school."

"But—"

"Look, without Zack here, he's not letting you in the house. Zack mentioned you to him once and he ranted for*ever*. I don't know what happened, but you guys are not on good terms. Zack can make sure you don't get the door slammed in your face."

I sigh. "I hate it when you're right."

"I know," Mai says with a hardy grin. "Let's get going."

I get into the back seat of the car, giving a muted response to Zack's cheery greeting. I wonder what he really thinks about all this. I study his face, but it's vacant of anything but a puppy-dog desire to please his girlfriend. I shouldn't worry about it. All I should focus on is getting the real deal between Tony and Stephanie. No matter what the cost.

By the time we get to Stephanie's house, it's like every nerve in my body is smoldering. I jump out of the car and take a step toward the house, but Mai grabs me by the back of my shirt, stopping me in my tracks.

"What?" I snap.

"Remember, we have to let Zack do the talking here. He's Tony's friend, and he says he knows how to reach him."

Zack nods, looking both eager and nervous. "Yeah, I mean Tony's not so bad once you get to know him. I think if I just make it clear you're really torn up about this, he'll take pity. If you tell him you're sorry for what happened and you want to apologize."

"It wasn't her fault!" Mai says sharply. I blink at my sister in surprise. It's so bizarre to see Mai glowering at the object of her undying adoration over something as trivial as *me*.

"I know that!" Zack says, putting his hands up as if fending off an attack. "I'm just saying that's what she should say to get us in. It'll make him wanna assure her he doesn't care. Also," he turned back to the car, rummaged around under his seat and pulled out a box of cookies, "these'll help."

I eye the cookies skeptically. "You're going to bribe him with food?"

"He's got a sweet tooth."

I suddenly remember Stephanie standing at my door, holding out cookies as a peace offering. Was that something she learned from dealing with Tony? I mean, it worked. Stephanie lowered my defenses and wormed her way into my heart. Now it's my turn to do an infiltration, to crack open a part of Stephanie's world.

Mai and I stay behind Zack as he rings the bell. When Tony answers the door, it's all I can do not to scream at him. I'm run ragged by Stephanie's suicide attempt, but he appears more energized than ever. There's no dark circles under his eyes; he's flush with health. He leans casually against the doorframe, a beer dangling lazily from his hand. He grins lopsidedly when he sees it's Zack at the door. But the grin fades when he notices me and Mai behind him.

"What the hell is this, man?" he snaps.

"Sorry," Zack says with a sheepish shrug. "I know you and Manee here have problems, but she's actually my girlfriend's sister. And well, she's been super torn up about what happened to Stephanie, y'know? She feels like it's all her fault. She's been begging me to let her see you. She wants to apologize and make it right."

I force a nod, though I have to grit my teeth and dig my fingers into my thighs as I do it.

"This is not cool!" Tony snarls. "I thought we were friends.

Now you're making me deal with this kinda shit?"

"We are friends!" Zack says quickly, looking like a deer in headlights.

"Like he said, he did it for me," Mai cuts in. "I'm just so worried about Manee. I was, uh, crying and everything."

"Yeah," Zack says, catching on. "I mean, I've gotta keep my girlfriend happy. You'd do the same for Sage, right?"

The corner of Tony's mouth twitches at this, and he clears his throat awkwardly. "Uh, yeah, I totally would."

Zack starts to smile. He holds out the box of cookies. "I brought a peace offering too."

Tony's shoulders slump in surrender. "Fine, fine. Come in then. Jesus."

Zack and Mai march into the house. I follow them, trying to keep my breathing steady.

Mai, Zack, and I take over some scattered rocking chairs in the living room, while Tony got the wide couch to himself. Zack was still chattering at Tony. I can't focus on what he's saying. Being in Stephanie's house without her is overwhelming. My breath catches when I see the elegant staircase that must lead to Stephanie's room. Stephanie should be here, but she isn't.

"Hey," Tony says. He's squinting at me suspiciously. "I thought she was here to beg my forgiveness because she was all torn up with guilt or whatever. But she isn't even looking at me."

I swallow hard. I have to remember why I'm here. I can barely bring myself to look at him; a scream of rage keeps trying to claw its way out of me.

"What happened to Stephanie was my fault. I f-feel like *I* deserve to be the person in the hospital right now. I just want to make things okay again for her." I stare down at my lap as I talk. This is all the truth, at least.

Tony throws his head back and laughs. "Don't play dumb with me. If it was your fault she jumped, then you did me a favor and you know it."

Mai reels back in her seat as if the comment smacked her in the face. "How could you say something like that?" she gasps.

I raise my head slowly and look directly at Tony. In the past, I always thought loathing was a burning feeling, but now I know better. It doesn't burn at all, it pierces like a dagger of ice, killing every other emotion. My voice is flat and calm when I speak. "Why do you hate her so much?"

"She never told you?" Tony snorts. "Of course she didn't."

"She told me that she warned your friends not to play on the stairs, but they did anyway, and one fell. She was there and she couldn't save him so she blamed herself. And you thought that meant she did it," I say, watching him carefully. His eyes narrow.

"So that's her story. Of course. Even you wouldn't have wanted anything to do with her if you knew what she *really* is."

He *does* know. I clamp down on this scrap of information. "So she told you guys she had a vision of his death?"

Mai and Tony jerk in surprise simultaneously. Zack just looks confused.

"She told me right before she jumped that when she looks straight into people's eyes, she sees all the deaths that person will ever see." I continue to stare unwaveringly at Tony.

"But that's—" Mai whispers, only to be interrupted by a scoffing sound from Tony.

"So you know and you're *still* wondering why I hate her? Some people really need everything spelled out for them." He throws his beer bottle to the floor with a groan. "Fine. I'll tell you the whole story if you want. So you'll know to stay away from her if she wakes up." He nods at Zack. "You don't want your girl around someone like that, y'know."

I cross my arms and wait. Tony leans back in his chair and lets the words out like a sigh. "I never liked her. It wasn't anything I could put my finger on, but there was something wrong with her, like something was gonna burst out of her skin."

My gut clenches. I feel dirty to know that this man and I once shared the same thought when looking at Stephanie.

"But I had to put up with her, even though we were *barely* family. Mom and Chris always cared so much about our "image," y'know." Tony does sarcastic air quotes. "How would it *look* if I didn't get along with her? That's why they freaked out when she started talking about seeing dead people and wouldn't look people in the eye." He chuckes. "Mom was especially humiliated. So they did all kinds of experiments and uh, what did her dad call them, *"discipline programs,"* to try to cure her. Not sure exactly what they were, but she would cry all night, so they felt bad and stopped after a while."

Mai has her hands up over her mouth. Zack looks extremely uncomfortable, his eyes darting around the room. There's pain in my legs and I glance down and realize I'm digging my fingers into my thighs so much they threaten to rip right through the fabric of my jeans. Now I understand why Stephanie would put on that eery demure mask around adults she didn't know well, why she would look at them with an unwavering, unbroken gaze.

"Seems like it worked," I mutter.

"Yeah, but she started *staring* at people. Became even creepier." Tony shudders. "Like she was *into* whatever it is she was seeing. I didn't believe in it at first, of course. I thought she was just a little goth weirdo making shit up. But I couldn't ignore how she made me feel. When she looked at me it was like death was crawling around inside me, like she'd infected me with something." His expression grows stormy. "I kept as far away from her as I could. But then, my friends Matt and Andrew," Tony stops here, his mouth tightening. "Matt was a good guy. Really good. I wish every day they'd never met. She took one look, and the next thing you know she's all over him about how he was gonna die and it was gonna be Andrew's fault. God, I was humiliated. It pissed Andrew off so bad I thought he was gonna beat her up. But Matt was a chill little guy. He calmed Andrew down and made her promise to stop saying it. I could tell that made her angry."

Tony puts his hand over his eyes. "She was such a freak show, but he was always *so* nice to her, to everyone. He never blamed me or made fun of me for having a weird half-sister. He was —" His voice breaks and he stops to take shaky breath.

I'm surprised to see him so vulnerable but I refuse to feel sorry for him. The ice in my veins will not thaw. My glare will not waver.

Tony pulls himself together enough to talk again. "And then the crazy bitch *killed* him!" He brings his fists down on his knees, his eyes shining. "I don't know what exactly happened. Whether she pushed him or did *something* freaky. But either way, it was *her*. It had nothing to do with Andrew. She claims she just sees the future or whatever the shit, but I know the truth. Whenever I look into her eyes, I can feel it. She's like a demon. A demon who spreads death."

I open my mouth to yell at him to shut up, that he's wrong, that he's being ridiculous. But I can't say it. Tony's voicing the suspicions and fears I've had about my own powers all along, that I'm cursed, that I'm the one causing every tragedy.

"You know exactly where he's coming from, right? If you believe it about yourself, why shouldn't you believe it about me? We have the same kind of powers, after all!" the Stephanie in my head taunts.

I hunch over, shaking my head like I can just fling the voice away. I have to stand up for Stephanie. I *have* to, but everthing's so tangled up and confused right now. Mai has no trouble speaking up. "A *demon*?" She scoffs with a horrified little laugh. "You can't really think that."

"I *know* how it sounds!" Tony reddens. "That's why I try not to talk about her! But you know, it's not just me! Andrew will tell you the same thing. My mom and her dad knew she was the one who killed Matt too! They just didn't want to admit it. They stopped wanting anything to do with her after that. Ava kept being nice to her though. And look where *that* got her."

I force myself to snap out of my confusion. I can think about all this later. Right now only one thing is important. Why I hate this man. "Th-that's right. When Ms. Carnahan got depressed you blamed Stephanie for *that* too. You started terrorizing her. You scared her. You *hurt* her." My vision blurs when I look at Tony, like I want to blot him out of existence.

Tony straightens up, his eyes burning. "I did what I had to do. All of it was to protect everyone from her. Can't you see the pattern? Matt, Ava, even your little friend from back then! What was her name, Cassie? They got involved with her and *look what happened*. God, she even *attacked* Ava, trying to get into her eyes! She was so close to being the next death! Once that *thing* gets to someone, it's too late and *nothing* can stop it. So yeah, I did my best to cage the monster. I just wish I could have kept her locked away forever."

His eyes flick toward the living room closet as he says this, and I instantly picture the scene. He shoved Stephanie in there while she fought and flailed. He pressed his body against the door, locking it with a click like a gunshot. He mocked her, told her she'd never escape. His mouth curled into a smile as she sobbed and begged, pounding on the door. She pounded and pounded until her arms grew tired and her legs gave out. She slumped to the floor alongside the scattered shoes, wishing for someone to come save her.

I leap to my feet, rage coursing through me.

"What's the matter?" The Stephanie in my head chuckles. "It was no big deal. He was just doing to me what you tried to do to yourself. Lock it away! Keep it from hurting anyone! You and him really are a lot alike".

"Shut up, *shut up,* I'm nothing like him," I mutter frantically.

Tony raises his eyebrows. "Uh, what was that?"

"I said," I growl. "You're wrong. *You're* the one who should be locked up."

Mai makes a noise of agreement. She's goggling at Tony, apparently too shocked by him to even form words. Zack looks at the door longingly.

Tony snorts. "Man, she's got you all wrapped around her little finger! Well, every serial killer has their deluded little followers." He stands up as well, his expression suddenly calm as he looks directly at me. "That's all you ever were to her, you know, a follower. I mean, did she *tell* you any of this? About her so-called visions? About why I really hated her?"

My chest starts to throb. "W-well, She did tell me! When we were, you know, on the roof."

"Just before she jumped, huh? So she lies to you this whole time and then dumps it all on you when it'd torture you the most. She makes it so you feel guilty. So you can't question her, can't argue it out with her, can't dig any deeper and see what she really is. Doesn't sound like a friend to me."

I can't find any words to answer, everything is hot and muggy inside my head. Little black stars burst in my eyes. I just want Tony to stop talking, I want him to stop making me feel this way.

Tony twirls his forelock around his finger mournfully. "I tried to warn you, remember? I told you what she was like. But now look at you. You're a wreck because of her. It's Ava all over again. This is what she *does* to people."

"No! You're wrong!" I choke. My chest is tight, so tight I can barely speak. I hear Mai get to her feet beside me. She's finally snapped out of her shocked stupor.

"Tony, I've had enough of this bullshit. Stop talking to my sister that way. In fact, *never* talk her *or* me ever again. You're *sick*. Manee, come on, let's just leave."

Tony gives us both a sad, almost pitying look. "I'm just telling her this for her own good. That girl doesn't love anyone. She doesn't trust anyone. I don't know whether she's a demon or human, but I know she's out to screw with people and spread death. And you better watch it, little girl, cuz I think you're her new target."

The whole world turns white hot for a second. "*You!*"

I feel Mai's hands on my shoulders, hear her pleas that we go, that this isn't worth it, but I don't care. I shove Mai aside and stride toward Tony.

"You don't know what you're talking about!" I snarl, my face inches away from his. "She *cared* about me. I *know* she did. *You're* the reason she jumped, you're the reason she couldn't trust anyone, if it wasn't for *you* she wouldn't have hated herself so much!"

Stephanie's words come back to me. *You hated your powers so much. If you knew I was the same, I thought you'd push me away! You'd be like him!*

Be like him.

Be like him.

You're just like him.

"Shut UP!" I scream, spraying spit on Tony's face. He doesn't even flinch. The angrier I get, the calmer it makes him. His hooded eyes are heavy with disdain.

"God, it's sad looking at you. You're really just another one of her victims. Here's hoping she never wakes up to make more."

I punch him as hard as I can. My bare knuckles smash against his cheekbone and both my hand and head explode with pain.

I'm sucked through Tony's "soul" so fast I barely have time to feel the jagged edges and hot liquid it's made of. I'm quickly thrown into the gray cityscape that is Tony's future. A haggard-looking man in his early sixties is before me, keeling over on a dirty sidewalk and convulsing with wet, hacking coughs.

No! No! I don't want to be here! I want to hurt him! I need to hurt him!

The gray cityscape around me shudders with an explosion of agony. The present Tony just punched me in the face and my nose is gushing blood. Now a fault line runs through the vision. Even though I still can't see what's going on in the living room, the pain is keeping my mind connected to my body there. I can feel my throbbing bruised fists and I swing them blindly, hitting solid flesh again and again.

It's the Tony that exists *now* I want to see writhing on the ground before me, not some pathetic old man. Knowing he'll suffer in the future is not enough, I want to make him suffer by my own hand. I want him to suffer as much as he made Stephanie suffer. Dying from disease as an old man is too good for him.

The world where Tony is a sixty-year-old hacking up a lung on the sidewalk splinters as I swing harder and harder. The concrete melts into the Pierces' patchy carpet, old man Tony shrinks and smooths out into his eighteen-year-old self and I can see my fists now, I can see them pounding mercilessly into his face and there's blood everywhere, gushing out of his nose and mouth.

Then everything shifts and I'm sucked through Tony's soul once more. I return to being a disembodied witness, but this time I'm watching a small girl with ragged black hair straddle a boy much bigger than her on a carpeted floor. She pummels him over and over again as tears stream down her beet-red face.

The girl is me. I'm watching myself punch Tony. I can still distantly feel my aching fists connecting with his face, but at the same time I'm somewhere outside myself, watching this new vision unfold. I see Tony flail under the girl, under *me*. He tries to hit her again but is clearly too disoriented to aim well. He manages to catch her chin with his elbow and I both taste the blood and watch it spurt from her mouth.

I'm shifting back and forth now. One second I look into his bloody, stricken face and my hands travel toward his throat as I scream, "You're lying, you're lying, I'm not like you, I'm not." The next second I see the girl who is me dig her fingers into Tony's neck. She starts to choke him. I just watch. I watch everything. I watch Tony as he struggles and writhes. I watch Zack run to a far corner of the room. I watch Mai as she squats behind that girl, as she shakes her shoulders and screams something.

Then I'm back inside myself again and her screams are directly and painfully in my ear. "Manee, stop it. Stop it! You're going to kill him!"

The words reverberate in my skull and something snaps. Suddenly it's no longer Tony I'm choking but *Stephanie*! Her eyes, the same rich brown color as his, have nothing but dull resignation in them as I drain her life away.

A cry escapes my lips. I wrench back, letting go of Tony's throat.

I'm instantly returned to that gloomy gray day in the far future. I numbly watch a sixty-year-old man cough up blood on a wet city sidewalk, hack and hack until he runs out of air.

And I'm back. Back just in time to see Tony's fist flying toward my face.

Mai shoves me roughly out of the way before it can connect. Tony's punch catches her on the shoulder instead. Mai yowls in pain but grabs him by his wrist before he can pull his hand away. She bends his pinky finger back, and now he's the one yowling.

"*We're leaving now!*" Mai says through gritted teeth. "But try to hit my little sister again and I'll make sure you *stay* down."

Tony doesn't respond. His eyes are completely unfocused, and he doesn't even look like he's hearing a word Mai says. He just lies there.

Mai lets him go and hauls me upright. My legs are weak, and there's still a hollow ringing in my skull. I'm sure both my hands are broken and possibly my whole face too. Blood drips from my nose and pools inside of my mouth.

Mai supports me out the door, jerking her head at Zack to follow. He does, looking almost as dazed as Tony.

As soon as we're outside, Mai exhales loudly. "Everyone okay?"

"Yeah," Zack mutters, though he's whey-faced. I can't find the words to respond. Everything feels floaty and disconnected. I can't even tell if I'm in my body anymore.

"Well, I don't need an answer to know *you* aren't," Mai sighs, taking some Kleenex out of her purse and dabbing gently at my bloody nose. She grimaces. "This needs serious first aid."

Her eyes flick over to Zack "You okay to drive, or should I?"

"I'm *fine*," Zack says curtly. He stomps over to the car.

Mai follows him and helps me into the backseat before sitting down beside me. She looks at me beseechingly as Zack started the car.

"Manee?" she whispers. "Can you just say something? So I know you're still in there?"

I open my mouth, but bile rises in my throat instead of speech. I have to choke it back, and as I do, tears begin to leak out of my eyes.

"Hey, hey," Mai murmurs, rubbing my back in soothing circles.

"I don't know anything anymore! I don't understand myself. What's happening?" The words come out in garbled sobs. "I almost killed him! I saw it!"

"Oh, you didn't really. I just said that in the heat of the moment to get you to stop. I don't *really* think you could," Mai says quickly, looking panicked.

"No!" Tears sting as they slide over my cuts and mix with the streaming blood on my face. "I saw it."

For the first time, a vision changed, and *I* changed it. Tony's fated death was about forty years from now, but the instant I put my hands around his throat, I saw a new fate for him, one I created. And it was only remembering Stephanie that prevented that from coming to pass.

Did that mean Stephanie was right? The visions weren't set in stone? They were only possibilities based on whatever? And I actually interrupted the vision by thinking about Stephanie. I overpowered it with my own guilty thoughts. Does this mean I have more control over the visions than I thought? That I can actually suppress them somehow? I want to feel something about this, joy, relief, anything, but I just felt empty. All I can think about was how it really did feel like my hands were around Stephanie's neck.

Mai's rubbing my back now. I remember she comforted me like this all the time when we were little.

"Manee, it's not your fault, okay? You've just been through so much. Anyone would snap. I wanted to hurt him too, hearing him talk like that."

I look down at my hands, bruised and spotted with blood. It didn't feel like they even belong to me anymore.

"Don't listen to what he said about Stephanie either. Tony's just, ugh, I don't even know. I had no idea that house was so unsafe for Stephanie. We'll talk to Dad and figure out a way to get her out of there when she wakes up."

Mai's voice is firm. Her face is alight with real determination.

"Really? You'll help?"

"Of course."

"Thanks," I say hoarsely. Mai tries to shrug casually in response, but her mouth tightens slightly in pain. Her shoulder. Guilt stabs into me.

"Thanks. Really. I'm glad you're my family, Mai."

Mai snorts. "What, because I'm not someone like Tony? Kinda damning me with faint praise there."

"No," I mumble, flushing. "I mean it. You're a good sister. Thanks for being there for me."

Mai blinks. A smile slowly spreads across her face and she squeezes my shoulder. "Hey, no problem."

When we get home, we find a note from Dad saying he's off running some errands. Mai helps wipe the blood off my face, applies medicine and bandages to my chin, nose, and hands, and even gives me an ice pack to nurse my wounds. Zack just stands there awkwardly, jumping at the slightest noise. He reminds me of a newborn colt with his knees about to buckle. I've got a sick feeling about the way his eyes keep darting to Mai. Finally, he comes up to her and tugs on her sleeve.

"Can I talk to you?"

"In a minute," Mai says distractedly, still examining one of my cuts. "I've gotta call Dad and warn him about this. How am I gonna break it to him?"

"It needs to be now."

"Zack, I just need a minute."

"Zack," I interject in a trembling voice, "please don't."

"*Now*," Zack says harshly, not even glancing at me.

Mai turns slowly and stares into Zack's eyes for a moment.

He stares stonily back. "Okay."

I watch them descend downstairs and listen as they open the front door and step outside, feeling like something's lodged in my throat the whole time. I soon hear the faint sounds of shouting.

Fifteen minutes later, Mai stomps up the stairs alone, rubbing at her eyes.

"What happened?" I ask with trepidation.

Mai tips her head back, inhaling deeply, and blinking furiously. "We broke up."

"It was my fault, wasn't it?" I put my hand to my forehead and grind my palm into it as hard as I can. "Great. I've graduated from ruining my own relationships to ruining yours."

Mai strides over and grabs me by the shoulders. "Manee, no. *Zack* ruined our relationship. He's just freaking out for no reason. You had nothing to do with it."

"Look, I can talk to him. I'll do anything to fix it, I swear," I plead.

"I don't *want* you to fix it!" Mai snaps, her fingers digging into my shoulders. "If Zack's going to just be all 'I didn't sign up for this' and bail out as soon as things get a little hard, then I don't need him! It's clear now we were never going to work."

"Really?"

"Absolutely." Mai lets go of me and puts her hands on her hips. "What a wuss, seriously! I was starting to get fed up with him even before this. Don't you think I deserve better?"

I grin weakly. "Yeah, you need someone at least half as tough as you."

"Damn straight!" Mai harrumphs. "I think he wanted a mom and not a girlfriend, honestly. The second I don't baby him, off he goes."

"Well, you would make a pretty great mom."

"Yeah?" Mai's expression turns wistful. "I do want to be one someday. I guess I want to give some kid the mom we didn't have. I want to be the opposite of what we got."

"You already are," I say softly. "Can you imagine how Mom would have acted in a situation like this? You stood by me and took care of me even though I was so crazy I scared your boyfriend away." I break off.

Mai sits down beside me, placing a gentle hand on my back. "You're not crazy."

My laugh is horribly mangled thanks to my nose. "That's not what you said before."

Mai falls silent for a minute.

"Look, I'm still not sure what to make of all I heard. Stephanie, the visions, and all that." She sighs heavily. "But the way Tony treated her was so awful. *He* was so awful." Her eyes glisten. "I'm kinda scared to hear the answer, but why were you screaming about not being like him?"

Mai may not want to hear the answer, but I don't want to give it even more. But I force myself. "A lot of what he said about Stephanie is stuff I thought about myself."

Tears spring into Mai's eyes. "Manee, no. No! You can't believe that."

"I don't. Not anymore." As I say it, I feel the truth of it, down to my bones. Hearing it said about Stephanie, about someone I love, made me realize how wrong it all was.

"Good," Mai takes off her glasses and wipes her eyes. "Because it's not true. None of it is your fault. And I should have been there for you to tell you that instead of calling you a liar."

I goggle at Mai. "Wait, are you saying you believe me about my visions now?"

Mai stares at the glasses in her hand. "Well, something Tony said reminded me of this one day when I was thirteen. I was braiding your hair, remember? My hand brushed against your neck and I felt *something*. It was like he said, sort of like someone was crawling around inside me. And I saw the faintest flash of a *thing*. Something white. I don't know. And you suddenly started crying. You were sick all that day, remember? You saw something, didn't you?"

My heart pounds hard in my chest. I can remember the day clearly. The day I saw my sister, shriveled and old and dying in that stark white hospital room, her family surrounding her. "Yeah," I mutter.

Mai shrugs helplessly. "I don't know what to think anymore, honestly. I need some time to process."

"Sure," I tell her. I can't help but add, "You will have kids, by the way. Who love you. I saw them."

"Okay, like I said, time to process!" Mai shoves her glasses back on. "Let's change the subject! Uh, what about you? Do you think you'll ever have kids? Like, uh, adopt or you know, the other things you can do?"

I scoff. "I'd just screw them up, honestly. I can barely take care of myself."

"C'mon, you're young, of course you can't. I'm talking like years from now."

"Honestly?" I lean back, closing her eyes. I try to picture the future I want. A little house with a garden, an art studio with my paintings all over, sunbeams coming through the window and... "Stephanie. She's enough for me. If she's safe and whole and happy, that's all I want out of my future."

I open my eyes to find Mai looking pensive.

"Is Stephanie really *all* you want? I mean, don't you want other people in your life too?"

"I," I start and stop, unsure how to respond.

"Just a thought," Mai shrugs. "Well, I gotta go call Dad. Keep the ice on that, okay?"

And with that, she walks out of the room, leaving me to my confused thoughts.

Chapter Twenty-seven

MY DAD DOESN'T react to my face with the storm of panic I expect. After initial questioning and examination, he gets very quiet. Then he mutters, "I'll do something about this. Don't worry," and leaves to have a long talk with Mai. This unnerves me more than him panicking would. I have no idea what to expect next. I sleep fitfully that night, my dreams once again bloodstained and slimy. In them, I'm a killer, roaming the streets restlessly. My hands itch for windpipes to crush.

There's Ava Carnahan, warm and tender, a halo of healing light around her. I snuff out that light, my fingers forming a noose around her neck that cinches tighter and tighter until she dies with a wet squelching sound. I look at the road of corpses behind me. There's my grandmother, Callie, Stephanie, and before me are my victims. Tony cowers and weeps, bruises in the shape of my fingerprints visible on his neck as I advance upon him. My sister crawls up to me, begging me to stop, her arm half severed at her shoulder and dangling uselessly. Dad grabs my leg, though he's so tired and frail that he can barely move. I kick them both aside and move, ceaselessly, toward my prey.

I wake from the nightmare, chest heaving. I just told Mai that I am over thinking of myaelf as some kind of death demon, but my subconscious clearly disagrees. I can't go back to sleep, so I lie there and try to sort it all out.

My vision of Tony's death changed based on my actions. That must mean Stephanie was right and the visions are just the most likely possibilities based on the current state of the person being touched. And the visions being possibilities means Stephanie definitely has a chance to survive. That's wonderful! So why do I keep rejecting this idea? Why do I keep wondering if it is just my emotional state messing up my visions or some sort of weird feedback thing? Why can't I just accept that maybe my visions *aren't* some unavoidable fate?

"Because it would be admitting that you could have saved all the others too."

I look mournfully out my bedroom window. Night has faded into the weak light of early morning. Maybe Imaginary Stephanie is right. Maybe I'm just overwhelmed by the idea I can change things. Because now if I fail I can't blame fate.

"So don't fail."

I roll over, massaging my head. Yeah, that's easy for an auditory hallucination to say. But I don't actually know how to make Stephanie wake up. I don't know how to help her at all. I said I would, but looking back on these past few days, all I've accomplished is nearly killing Tony and screaming at Emma and Jackson.

Emma and Jackson. It hurts to think of them. I didn't really give them a chance to explain themselves. I just used them as punching bags to work out my angst over Stephanie. Now that I've used Tony as a *real* punching bag, I can see that. I should have heard them out, but instead, I probably drove them away for good. We'll never make that comic book together.

Suddenly Mai's words echo in my head: Is Stephanie really *all* you want?

I do want more. I don't want Emma and Jackson to disappear from my life. I said I wouldn't be the kind of person who gave up anymore, so I can't just give up on them. It won't hurt, at least, to text Emma an apology. I get up and grab my cracked, barely usable phone.

I'm sorry, to both you and Jackson, about when you came over. I've been going thru a lot and I just sort of lost it. If you ever want to see me again, feel free to come anytime. I'll try and make it up to you.

I sit there with the phone in my hand for a while. No reply comes. I flop back on my bed. Well, can't exactly blame them.

I DON'T QUITE know what to do with myself the next day. I know I need to move forward somehow, so I sit on the living room couch with a notebook in hand. I start making a list of all the things I've learned in the last few days, hoping something will come to me. Halfway through, I'm interrupted by the doorbell ringing. When I go to answer the door, I find Emma and Jackson standing there.

Emma gasps when she sees me, eyes wide. "What happened to your face?"

"Also, hi," Jackson says, though he looks equally alarmed.

"What are you doing here?" I ask, gobsmacked.

"I got your text and we just happened to be in the area

today," Emma says, fidgeting nervously. "Um, we need to get Jackson's phone back, so we thought we'd check if you were home."

"Oh!" I say. "Right! I'll get the phone for you. Um, just take your shoes off and take a seat, please." I run up to my room and grab it. When I come back, Emma and Jackson are seated on the couch again. I sit opposite, placing the phone on the coffee table and shoving it toward Jackson. "Here."

"Thanks," he says quietly. I nod. Now that they're here, I'm not sure what to say to them. Apologize again? Explain about my banged-up face? I tap my fingers against my knee, the words stuck in my throat.

Emma breaks the silence before I can. "Thanks for texting. Me and Jackson decided we should give you some space, but we really are so sorry that we went behind your back and hurt you."

"It's okay," I say, aware that I sound shaky and unconvincing. "I know you were just trying to help. I shouldn't have yelled at you like I did. You were right, it wasn't really you I was mad at."

"It was Stephanie," Jackson cuts in bluntly "Yeah, we got that. But maybe we can help with that."

"Help with what?"

"We can't undo what we did, but we were hoping maybe these would help you somehow. I think they show a little of what Stephanie was thinking when she did what she did." Emma pulls out some papers from her purse. "I'm kind of a packrat, so I still had these."

"Packrat doesn't even cover it, she's a hoarder," Jackson says, rolling his eyes. "We really had to dig through her garbage heap of a room to even find these."

I look suspiciously at the offering. It's regular notebook paper that looks like it's been crumpled up and then carefully smoothed flat again. "What are they?"

"They're the notes Stephanie passed to me during class when we were coming up with the plan," Emma tells me timidly. "She talks about you. You don't have to read them if you don't want to."

"We thought we'd make the offer," Jackson says. "Figured you deserved to know."

My heartbeat speeds up. I almost don't want to read it, but I know I have to. If there's even the tiniest part of Stephanie I can hold, I've got to hold it, I've got to know it. I take the papers with trembling fingers. I lay it on my lap and pore over every word.

I quickly see what Emma and Jackson mean. A lot of the written-down conversation is scheming and logistics, but occasionally Stephanie writes something that hits me like a right hook to the jaw.

The first few exchanges are mostly Emma and Stephanie still working on making nice after their previous tension. You've been there for Manee and that means a lot to me, Stephanie wrote. Let's just start again.

A few sheets later, she started describing her plan to Emma and why she needed so desperately for it to work. I just want to tell her one thing. It's something I've kept from her so long because I was stupid and scared, but she deserves to know. I don't care what happens after that, I just need her to listen to this one thing, then I'll go.

Another time she wrote, Manee seems happy with you guys, in her careful, semi-cursive script. I saw her smiling at something you said.

Really? Emma wrote in round, bloated letters. I don't remember that.

She only does it when you look away. I don't think she wants to admit she can be so happy without me.

There's NO WAY she's happy without you. Emma's text is dark, firm, and double underlined. She'd be a lot happier WITH you. Don't get all pessimistic on me! This is going to work.

I'm not giving up on telling her, don't worry. I just like to plan for everything. So, if things don't work out, just promise you'll take care of her. Don't let her punish herself over me or any of that shit.

I can't read any more.

"Maybe I should have seen what she was really planning," Emma says, her voice choked up, "Looking back on it, it was so obvious. But I hope you understand from this that she did trust you and she cared about you. She cared about you and she thought a lot about you."

"Y-yeah." I wipe my eyes. "I knew that. Deep down. This just helped me remember. Thanks for showing it to me."

We all sit in silence for a few minutes. Then Jackson says, "You know, I think Stephanie had the right idea. How about we start over?"

I give him a watery smile. "That sounds good to me."

"Yeah!" Emma says eagerly. "We can meet each other all over again, and this time we'll just be totally open! There'll be no secrets between us!"

I falter at this. "No secrets, huh?"

"Yeah!" Emma jumps to her feet, eyes sparkling. "I'll go first." She clears her throat. "Hi, I'm Emma Price and I have ADHD."

"You sound like you're at an AA meeting," Jackson snorts. "Also, that's not a secret, you talk about it all time."

"Shut up, it was all I could think of. You do better." Emma scowls.

"Fine, Fine. Uh, I'm Jackson." He rubs the back of his neck. "And, uh, don't tell anyone this, but I guess I've got some anxiety issues? I get overwhelmed easily and kinda shut down. Also I'm real scared of spiders. And dogs. And a bunch of random things. Big mess of phobias basically." A flush spreads across his face, and he ducks his head.

"I keep telling him not to be so embarrassed about it," Emma says conversationally as she sits back down. "We met in first grade 'cuz I rescued him from a spider! Anyway, care to tell us your thing, Manee?"

"You don't have to say anything if you don't want to," Jackson mumbles. The flush has spread to his neck now and shows no signs of stopping.

I swallow hard. No more secrets between us. That couldn't be true as long as I'm holding back. Jackson went all out and told me his deepest secrets. Shouldn't I do the same?

"No, because it's not the same! Your secret is bigger than some stupid bug fear! They'll just use it to hurt you! You can't tell them!"

Stephanie's voice rings in my head. Except it isn't Stephanie's voice. I know that because I have Stephanie right here, in my hands.

It's something I've kept from her so long because I was stupid and scared.

If Emma and Jackson can't accept this part of me, our friendship will never work out.

But she deserves to know.

It's now or never.

I lick my dry lips. I grip the arms of my chair. I breathe in and out.

"I'm Manee and I see visions of people's deaths when I touch them." I forced the confession out at breakneck speed. "That's why I used to wear gloves."

Jackson and Emma remain completely silent, their

expressions unreadable. It's the first time I've ever seen Emma at a loss for words.

"Look, I know, it sounds like a lie," I croak. I grip the chair even harder to keep my hands from shaking. "If you believe me, that's fine. If you don't, it's not like I'm gonna make a big deal about it or anything. They're probably just possibilities anyway. I still really don't understand it myself."

Another silence. Emma's eyes are glazed over. I can't tell what she's imagining. Jackson's brow is furrowed.

"That's a really cool idea for a comic," Jackson declares suddenly.

"Oooh, yeah it is," Emma agrees, breaking out of her reverie.

"We should use that," Jackson says. "Manee, you could totally write it; we can take turns drawing."

"Uh, hello?" I say, squinting at them suspiciously. "You aren't weirded out?"

"Well, I dunno if I believe you," Jackson says, putting his hands behind his head and leaning back. "I guess I don't know you well enough to say for sure. But it's your business either way. And if you're gonna choose a delusion, that's a pretty dope one."

"Well, *I* have an open mind," Emma says haughtily. "Anything's possible. Don't be a butt, Jackson."

I go limp from relief. I hadn't realized how much I want to stay friends with them. "Thanks."

"What for?" Jackson replies with a shrug.

"So, are you gonna tell us what happened to your face too?" Emma leans forward eagerly.

I do tell them. I tell them almost everything that's happening, though I leave out some of the stuff I feel is too personal about Stephanie. We talk for hours, and the two of them end up staying for dinner again. They don't really have any advice about how to help Stephanie, but they listen and promise they'll keep thinking until they come up with something, and somehow, that's enough. We say our goodbyes at the front door as Dad goes to get the car ready to drive the two of them home.

"Take care, okay?" Jackson tells me. "If you need anything, just text us."

"It'll all work out," Emma says fervently. "You just wait. Stephanie will wake up and you'll both be happy again."

"I hope so."

Emma gives a sad little smile. "I wish I could touch you, cuz I really want to give you a hug."

I smile back at her. "I don't think I'm really ready right now, but maybe someday. I'll work on it and someday we can hug all we want."

I wave goodbye to Emma and Jackson as Dad drives them away. I look down at my bare hand. "Someday," I repeat to myself.

THAT NIGHT IN my room, I glance at my reflection in the mirror for the first time since the day after I got back from the hospital. I could just be imagining it, but my face looks slightly less gaunt. There's a big ugly bruise on my jaw like the rotten spot on a banana, but my nose isn't too swollen. I tug at my uneven tufts of hair. It looks like partially dying grass, some bits sticking up, others wilting. My vow not to cut it until Stephanie wakes up seems like a childish, empty gesture now.

"Hey, Mai?" I call, poking my head out of my bedroom. "Do you think you could take me to get a haircut?"

"Thank God, finally!" Mai calls back from down the hall. "You'll look great with a pageboy cut."

"Nah, I just want to even up the back," I say, tugging on one of my shoulder-length forelocks. "I like how it's longer in the front."

"Are you sure? It's kinda messy looking that way."

I smile at the mirror. "It's okay for things to be messy sometimes."

Chapter Twenty-eight

THE NEXT DAY, Mai takes me to get my haircut. She's her usual cheerful self when she brings me into the salon, but when I come out, it's different. Mai is hunched over, on the phone, her mouth thin with worry as she talks hurriedly into the receiver. She stiffens when I approach and covers the receiver with her hand, but I can still hear the broken sobs of the voice piping through. Muffled as it is, I get a sick shock of recognition at this voice.

"*I never even noticed – what kind of –* "

"Sorry, I'll get right back to you in a few minutes," Mai says quickly into the phone and hangs up.

"Who was that?" I ask as I follow Mai to her car.

"What? Nothing," Mai replies. She ducks inside the car hurriedly and avoids my gaze in the pretense of fumbling with her seatbelt.

I slide in beside her and stare straight at her, arms crossed. "You are the world's worst liar. Give it up."

"I don't want you to worry about this," Mai whines.

"Well, I'm already worried, so it's too late. And I think I know who it is too. It'll be easier if you just tell me."

"Fine," Mai groans. She inhales deeply. "Ms. Carnahan found out about Stephanie, finally. I guess being shut up kept her from knowing until now." Mai shakes her head and turns the key, starting the car. "Anyway, she's not taking it well, as you can imagine. But you don't need to worry about it, you've got enough to deal with right now. Focus on your own stuff; I'll help out with this."

Mai's words grow distant as a rushing sound fills my head. A burning sense of purpose has been welling up inside me ever since I heard that voice from the phone. I've been so focused on Stephanie, I forgot there was someone else who needs help right here, right now. Someone who's going through the same struggle as me.

"No. I want to talk to her. Could you take me to her place?"

Mai snaps her head toward me in surprise. "What? No, Manee, I'm not sure that's a good idea. You're both hurting so much right now."

"That's why I'm the one person who can understand," I say

quietly. "Please. I think I can help her."

Mai stares at me for a long moment. I look back at her, gaze steady. Then suddenly a honk pierces the silence and we both jump. A little black car has pulled up close to us, and the driver is clearly impatient for us to vacate our spot. Mai growls and flips them off.

"Give us a minute!" She turns back and looks at me searchingly. "Fine," she finally says, her expression severe. "But if you show any signs of freaking, I'll drag you out by the ear."

"Deal."

As we drive to Ms. Carnahan's house, the last bit of light is choked from the sky. As the darkness settles in, so does a heavy chill. Even inside the car, the cold bites deep. I hunch up, trying to warm myself. Mai turns up the heat, but the frigid air still seeps in.

When we arrive, it doesn't look like the welcoming place I remember. The windows are dark and it's eerily quiet. It feels like a haunted house. Everything in me wants to run screaming.

But if I'm brave enough to help her, I might be able to save other people too.

"Are you sure you're up for this?" Mai's voice is gentle.

I draw myself up and force myself forward. "Yeah, mostly."

I knock on the door as loudly as I can. I wait for a few minutes, but nobody answers. I try the handle. The door's unlocked.

"She's been pretty careless lately," Mai sighs. "She might be asleep."

"Well, it's time to wake up," I say and I burst into the house.

Much like my dramatic knock, my dramatic entrance is completely unheeded. Only silence greets me, and a powerful smell. The stench is a solid, scorching thing. My nose feels like it's going to melt from its intensity. I cough and sputter, clamping my hands to my face. I scan the dark living room. A crumpled heap of a woman is splayed limply on the floor. Discarded bottles litter the ground around her and her stringy brown hair covers her face like a shroud.

My throat closes up. No, no, not another suicide! I can't be too late again, I can't take this!

Half-stumbling, I run over and grab the prone woman by the shoulders. Ms. Carnahan groans faintly and weakly opens her eyes.

My knees buckle. I fall to the floor beside Ms. Carnahan in a heap of relief.

"Don't scare us like that!" My sister squawks behind me.

Ms. Carnahan sits up, her eyes unfocused. It's hard to connect her to the woman I remember: her face is waxy and bony, her very skin looks ready to peel away, and everything about her seems absent. It takes her a second to recognize us, but when she does, she droops and tears well up.

"Manee?"

"Yeah." I wipe my sweaty brow. "Sorry I took so long to come here."

"No, *I'm* sorry, about Stephanie." Ms. Carnahan's shoulders shake. "She tried so hard to help me and I never could help her. Another child I failed."

"It's not your fault," I say automatically, realizing too late that I'm parroting what everyone's been saying to me. Ms. Carnahan turns away; she doesn't want to hear those empty words.

Mai's eyes are watering from the smell. "I'm gonna go around the house and clean up while you guys talk." She heads for the kitchen where a lot of the stench seems to be coming from.

Ms. Carnahan watches her go with dead eyes. "It's so pathetic, really. I'm a teacher and my students are taking care of me." She looks despondently at the floor. "I haven't changed at all."

I look at the floor too. There's a framed photo there, though the glass is shattered and the wood is splintered. It appears Ms. Carnahan collapsed on top of it. I pick it up delicately.

It's instantly clear that the woman in the photo is related to Ms. Carnahan. She has her high cheekbones and warm brown eyes. She's maybe around sixteen, leaning against a wall and laughing, flashing a peace sign.

"Who is this?" I ask gently.

Ms. Carnahan hesitates, but then apparently decides she doesn't have the energy to avoid the question. "My sister."

Now I'm the one hesitating. "She's gone?"

"Yeah, she's dead." Ms. Carnahan's voice is flat and harsh. "Car wreck. I was the only survivor."

Wham. Everything falls into place. Finally, I feel like I see the full picture of what exactly makes Ava Carnahan tick.

"I know what you're thinking," Ms. Carnahan says, rubbing her eyes. "I know Callie isn't, *wasn't*, my sister, okay? I know Stephanie has nothing to do with her either. But at this point, I feel like I'm a curse."

"Yeah, I get it." I say softly.

"You do, huh?" Ms. Carnahan says dully. "My sister, she helped me so much when I was struggling in school. I wanted to be like her, I wanted to help people so badly but I just keep hurting them. I just keep losing."

I don't know what to say to that. I know that feeling far too well. I look around and for the first time, I notice all the papers scattered across the little table. With a jolt, I recognize the handwriting. *Callie.*

Callie's messy scrawl contrasts heavily with Ms. Carnahan's neat looping handwriting. All her words are in red pen. She made so many corrections, but at the bottom, she wrote, *You're getting so much better. Don't give up! Even if it's hard, you're moving forward, little by little.*

These motivational words apply conveniently to this situation. But I doubt pointing that out will do much for Ms. Carnahan. It's hard to take your own advice.

Still, I can't stop looking at these papers. They're smudged, they're messy, and you can see Callie's frustration and anger in the jagged way she wrote her 'M's sometimes. There's something kind of beautiful about it. Her effort, her raw emotion, her struggle.

A golf ball-sized lump forms in my throat.

Looking at this, I feel like Callie could have done amazing things with her life. Maybe she had. Maybe Callie's life was something amazing all on its own. The girl who opened up to us little by little, the girl filled with so much fear and doubt and anger, who still reached out her hand to me when I fell, the girl who wanted to read even though it strained her so much.

My eyes burn in that familiar way. I take a deep breath, close them, then open them. "Y'know, Ava, I don't think we've been fair to Callie, here."

Ava has her legs drawn up to her chest and her face is buried in her arms. "What do you mean?"

"I mean, Callie was so much more than a person we failed to save. She was more than that. We've spent so much time focused on her death. She deserves better."

I scoot up next to Ava, laying out the papers before us. "Look at all this. You were helping Callie. You listened to her and helped her learn and made her feel better."

Ava lifts her head and looks at me with empty eyes. "But none of that mattered in the end."

"Yes, it did!" I say fiercely. "Callie's *life* mattered. The feelings she had, the things she went through, all the different sides of her we saw that nobody else did, her death doesn't change that. They matter." I smooth out the paper. "I remember her hunched over this, sweating, grinding her pencil down. I remember how she and Steph would bicker over the stupidest things, and I remember how she'd look over at you and just smile sometimes. These things are pieces of her we saw that no one else did."

Ms. Carnahan lifts her head a little more. As I speak, her expression softens. I scrub at my eyes and continue.

"You know, for so long I've been thinking it would have been better for Callie if I never interfered in her life. But if I hadn't, I wouldn't have really seen who she was. I can't ever know for sure what would have happened to Callie if we'd never met. I can't say whether she would have lived longer or if things would have been better for her." I pause for a second, my lips trembling. "Maybe they would have. I wish I could have helped her more. I wish I could have known exactly what to do and what she needed. But I think, in the end, it was still okay that I tried b- because it meant I got to know her. I don't want to think of her just as 'someone I couldn't help' anymore. I want to think of her as someone I was lucky to know, who I want to keep knowing." I smile weakly. "I think deep down you feel the same way, Ava."

Ava Carnahan has fully lifted her head now, but her eyes are still hollow and hopeless. "That's a nice way to think about it, I suppose. Do you feel the same way about Stephanie?"

This question should be a punch to the gut, but instead it makes my smile grow. I reach into my jeans pocket, where Stephanie's note is neatly folded and tucked away, and pull it out. I smooth it out right next to Callie's papers.

"You know what Steph wrote in a note to my friend? She wrote that she didn't want me to punish myself over her." I snort. "It's freakin' hilarious because she's more into punishing herself than *anyone*! She always felt like she hurt people and that she had to make up for it. I hated seeing what it did to her, but it didn't stop me from doing the same thing." I trace Stephanie's words with my finger, one by one. "Stephanie jumped partly because she felt like she'd done bad things and deserved to die. Seeing her jump made me feel like I was bad and deserved to die too. And you're feeling the same way, because of the people you've lost."

It's all so clear suddenly. Even with my blurry vision, I can see the path ahead. "Don't you see? Someone has to break this cycle of pain or it'll just continue forever, spreading to everyone. It has to be us; we have to stop this here. We owe it to both of them to not give in. There's still so much more we can do."

I look at Ava. She's still listening, and it looks like she's even trying to smile, but her eyes remain the same.

"That's a very wonderful thing to say, Manee. And I—I know you're right. But even if I know that," she looks down at her hands, "I can't *feel* it. No matter how I hard I try. I can't see any way I can move forward. I can't see anything else I can do. I can't see a future for myself that isn't just *pain*."

I study the woman hunched over beside me and realize something's changed somehow. The outline of Ava Carnahan is shimmering. There's a strange humming in my ears, getting louder and louder. All the colors brighten and blur.

"I can see it!" I whisper.

Ava reels back, alarmed. "What?"

"I can see it." The humming is so loud now my brain is vibrating. My vision shakes slightly. "I can see your future, a possible one. There's so much more for you, waiting. Let me show you."

Sweat stings my eyes and something blocks my throat. It's stealing the air from my lungs. But this white-hot certainty burns under my skin, even as the rest of my body protests it.

I lean close to Ava. I can smell the sweat on her face, the alcohol on her breath. It's like I can see down to her pores. I can do this. *I can do this.*

I raise my hand. My flesh quivers on my bones.

"What are you doing?" Ava looks slightly frightened.

I can—Okay, just freakin' *do it*, already.

I squeeze my eyes shut. In the darkness, it's like Ava's not even here. It makes it easier. I reach out blindly and feel something soft, warm, and faintly hairy. And I'm off.

I slip through a soul that's both overwhelming and indistinct. It's like inhaling car exhaust.

The bedroom is wide and spacious. There's Ava, old and gray and peaceful looking as she sleeps on the king-sized bed. Someone's sleeping beside her, huddled under the covers. I'm trying to figure out who it is when I hear a faint noise. I focus on Ava again and see her chest has stopped its steady rise and fall.

A young woman with dark hair and light brown skin slips through the door. Her expression is unsettled and becomes even more so when she sees Ava. She nudges her and says her name softly. Then she says, much louder, "Mom!"

The person next to Ava wakes up. It's an old, pale man. He puts together what's happening before the woman even has a chance to speak. He puts two fingers to Ava's neck. Then he lets out a long sigh, closes his eyes, and shakes his head.

The woman's eyes well up with tears and she puts her hand to her mouth.

"I've got to go."

She runs out of the room, though the man calls after her. With another sigh, he takes Ava's hand and squeezes it. His shoulders shake slightly, and he turns away from her abruptly. He gets out of bed so quickly he stumbles and has to lean against the wall. Slowly, he hobbles over to a bulletin board above the dresser. It's covered with pictures of Ava with young children, high schoolers, and middle schoolers. Some are in groups, some are on their own. Essays and drawings and poems and thank-you cards are up there too, so many little bits and pieces. I recognize Callie's worksheet, pinned neatly in the corner.

The man looks at it and a faint smile flickers across his face.

At that, Ava finally lets go. And so do I.

I fall back to reality with a sharp gasp and collapse on the floor in a shivering nauseous heap. I groan and rolled over. Ava is also in a pile. Her face is paper white.

My chest heaves, but I grit my teeth and force the bile back down where it belongs. It's not pleasant but it beats actually puking. I struggle into a sitting position, fastening my eyes fiercely on Ava. "You felt that, right?"

"I felt *something*." Ava's hand clenches tighter around her heart, wadding up her shirt. Her eyes are wild and unfocused. "What was that?"

"That was your future. Well, a possible one. And it looks like a future worth fighting for."

Ava says nothing. I reach over and grab Callie's worksheet. I look around, hoping to find the props I need to illustrate my point. No such luck. I clear my throat. "Um. Okay. Well, pretend I have a bulletin board and like thumbtacks, or actually it looked kind of like you used some sort of putty." I crawl over to a blank piece of wall and slap the paper onto it. I mime putting the putty on and instantly feel stupid. I hear a faint snicker from Ava. I turn around and she's smiling slightly, though it fades almost immediately. It still makes my heart leap with joy.

"Ava," I say. "I want to put Stephanie on our board next." I take Callie's paper and lay it on the floor again, on top of Stephanie's note. "But I won't put it there until I know we've done everything we can for her." I lock eyes with Ava. "There's still a lot for us to do."

Ava's face quivers and I can tell she wants to look away. But she doesn't. Instead, she asks in a trembling voice, "What are you talking about? What can we do?"

"Stephanie could still wake up. And I want to give her a life she'll actually want to wake up to. I can't do that without you, though."

Ava looks dubious. "Why would you need me?"

"Because you're the only one who can get through to Tony."

"What?"

I scoot closer to Ava and slowly and carefully, I explain about Tony's abuse of Stephanie. As I do, Ava's mouth slowly falls open. "No," she says faintly, wadding her shirt more tightly. "No, Tony wouldn't, he's a nice kid."

"Even around Stephanie?"

Ava winces. I see doubt now.

"I wouldn't lie about this, Ava."

Ava sucks air in through her teeth. Slowly, she lets go of her shirt and her hand falls to her lap. She allows her eyes to drift down. "If it's true and I didn't see it." She looks up at me again and somehow her face looks a little fuller, a little more flush. She's just the tiniest bit less like a walking skeleton. "Well, I can't just let that go, can I?"

My heart soars. "You'll help me?"

"I'll try." Ava clasps her hands in her lap. A sweaty lock of hair falls onto her face. "I don't really know what just happened. There are these images and feelings crawling around the corner of my mind and I don't even want to know how they got there." She presses her lips together into something that's almost another smile. "I think I want whatever it was I got a glimpse of. And I want Stephanie to have it too. A future worth fighting for."

"Good," I say, crossing my arms. I've never felt stronger than in this moment. "Because it starts today."

Chapter Twenty-nine

I GET MAI to bring me over every afternoon for the next few days. It's admittedly pretty hard to work on a big scheme with someone who's still drowning in depression. Ava puts on a brave face, but it doesn't take much to turn her into a lethargic heap or to send her on a random crying jag.

Still, she's undeniably doing better. Her color's improved since Mai's started cooking her good food every day. And moderating her alcohol intake. A lot. When I point out how much Mai has helped, she refuses to take credit for anything. "I don't know how you did it, but you got through to her when I couldn't," she insists. "This is all you."

I don't know about that, but I know I'm glad for Ava's help with the planning of "Operation: Get Tony," even if it's a struggle. Coming up with elaborate schemes is still way more Stephanie's area than mine. There's so many little things to find out and so much to practice. Not only do we have to figure out when Tony will be home, we have to figure out how to get Mai to leave us alone during that time.

Fortunately, luck comes our way on that front. Dad calls Mai during one visit, reporting that he has a flat tire and needs her to come get him.

"I want to stay longer with Ava," I tell her.

"Okay, I'll go get Dad, and then we can swing back and pick you up. Should be twenty minutes, tops." Mai leaves.

I peek out Ava's window. Tony's little red car is still in the driveway. "I think we've gotta do it now.'

"I—I guess," Ava says, looking unsure. I run over to the closet and pull out a pretty blouse and some clean jeans for her to wear. Then we go over everything one more time.

"I know you can do this." I take her by the shoulders and look her dead in the eye. "We can do this. For Stephanie."

Ava nods and I see a little of the sharp-eyed and sure teacher she was before.

"For Stephanie." Her eyes flick over to the bulletin board I brought, where Callie's worksheet is now pinned up. The photograph of her sister is on the wall next to it—I cleaned it up and got it repaired for her. "And everyone else."

We go outside and face north. There's Stephanie's house, its windows glowing with a warm, yellow light. The little hill it's perched on is like the last in a series of mountains I have to scale. And scale it we do, ignoring the chill of the night as the gravel of the driveway crunches beneath our feet.

Once we're near the house, Ava and I exchange a nod. I drop to my knees and elbows and crawl under the porch. It's damp and tight and uncomfortable, just as I expected. My face is so close to the ground that I'm in danger of inhaling dirt. I try to ignore it and press record on my phone. My heart pounds in my ears.

I hear Ava's footsteps above me and then a knock on the door. There's a creak as it opens.

"Ava?" Tony's surprised voice echoes, a joyful lilt to it. "You're out of the house? And you look great! Come in, Mom and Chris are here for once."

"I'd rather talk out here, actually," Ava says quietly.

Are Stephanie's parents really home? That sure is a first. I didn't even think about that possibility. Maybe after this is all over I'll go in and scream at them. That'd feel nice.

"Sure." I hear Tony close the door behind him. The wood above me shakes as they both cross the porch and go down the steps. I can see Ava's frayed slippers and Tony's untied sneakers. They stop in front of me.

"I heard about Stephanie," Ava's voice floats down.

"Oh," Tony says, irritated.

"It's like a weight has been lifted."

A long pause. "It is?"

"Of course. Now I can get better, can't I?" Ava's voice squeaks. It sounds way too over-the-top cheerful. It wouldn't convince most people.

I hear a long shuddering gasp of joy and smile to myself.

"That's right! You're going to get better!"

Like I told Ava, the acting doesn't matter. It's all about what Tony wants to hear.

"I understand now that you've always been trying to protect me. From her."

"Yes! Yes, I was!" Tony's voice trembles. He sounds near tears.

"That's amazing. I want to hear about everything you did for me."

"I did whatever I could." Tony moved forward slightly. I can tell he just grabbed some part of Ava, probably her hands. "I locked her away so she couldn't hurt you."

"When you say 'locked away,' where do you mean? In her

room? The closet?"

Tony hesitates. "Her room doesn't have a lock, so the closet, yeah."

"I can't imagine it was easy, forcing her in there. She was always so spirited."

"I mean, yeah, she struggled, but obviously I can take a little girl," Tony laughs.

My experience says otherwise, asshole.

I dig my nails into the dirt. It's all I can do not to burst out from under the porch.

"Sometimes I had to tie her up though. That was an *ordeal.*"

I remember the angry red marks I saw on Stephanie's wrist and bile rises.

"A-and how many times did you do this? For how long?"

"A few times." I can tell Tony's noticing the strain in Ava's voice now. "And I mean, my parents would come home eventually and let her go."

"They *knew* you were doing this? They didn't try to stop you?" Ava says sharply, all her feigned calm falling away.

"Of course not! They know she's dangerous!" Tony shifts. "They used to do stuff way harsher than that to keep her in line. As long as no one finds out, they don't care. They get it, like we do!"

Ava's legs are trembling now. I sigh.

"It's okay, Ava!" I call. "That's all we need." I crawl out from under the porch and stand up, brushing dirt off my t-shirt and pants.

Tony jumps back, a dark shadow falling over his face. "You!"

"Me," I say, allowing myself a moment of smugness.

Tony's head snaps back to Ava. "What's *she* doing here?"

Ava lowers her eyes and clutches her elbow. "I didn't want to believe it. I really didn't." Her voice is heavy.

"Ava, this was a trick? You *lied* to me?" Tony says this in a high whine, not unlike a whimper. It should be pathetic, but there's something slightly unnerving about it. "Ava, you can't trust her! Whatever she told you, it isn't true"

Ava shakes her head wearily. "*You're* the one who just told me everything. How could you do this?"

"I did it for you!" Tony reaches out and grabs Ava's arm. "Ava, I love you!"

She jerks away sharply. Tony reels back like he'd been slapped.

"Don't you *dare* say that! I never wanted *this*!" She draws herself up to her full height, her gaze cold and severe, a teacher facing down an unruly student. "You're going to face the consequences for what you've done, Tony. And after that, I want nothing more to do with you."

Tony just stands there, his hand still hovering in the air. Slowly, he lowers it. Then he turns on me, rage painting every corner of his face. "*You* did this! You took her from me!"

The triumph tastes bitter but still delicious. "She was never yours."

Before I can even blink, he grabs the front of my hoodie, jerking me toward him. Ava yelps as Tony lifts me in the air as easily as if he was lifting a puppy. My collar strains against my neck like a noose.

He looks at me with eyes that are nothing more than dark, blank marble. For the first time in a while, he's genuinely frightening to me. This is not the person from the living room who considers me a mere annoyance, who only fought back against my blows half-heartedly. In fact, he doesn't even seem like a *person* anymore, but a hollow, twisted imitation of one that's only composed of rage and hate.

"I know what you are. I felt it when you hit me. You're like *her*."

My heart bangs in my ears. I can't breathe.

"Stop it!" Ava runs up to him and tugs frantically at his arm. But he will not be moved.

"I know what I have to do," he whispers.

Then a bright light flashes and blinds us all. Tony yells and drops me. I land painfully on my tailbone. Ignoring the ache, I squint toward the brightness, shielding my eyes from the glare. Finally, the light dims. Though my vision is still fuzzy, I can now make out Mai's car and my father and sister jumping out of it.

My father strides toward us, his glasses shining like eerie glowing orbs in the headlights. He's giving off an aura of intimidation I've never felt from him before; he even seems taller. He walks straight up to Tony and grabs him by the shirt.

"What are you doing to my daughter?!" he growls.

"Are you okay?" Mai asks me. I nod mutely. Mai makes a weary noise. "I leave for *twenty minutes*, honestly!"

"Answer me!" Dad snarls at Tony, shaking him. Tony simply looks at him, his face still that mask of rage. I'm seized with a fear Tony's going to attack him, so I scramble to my feet.

The front door of the house bursts open. "What is all this noise?"

For the first time, I lay eyes on Stephanie's parents.

Chris Pierce is a tall, thin man in a business suit. His thick eyebrows are drawn together in anger, but nothing else about his face really stands out to me. But Stephanie's mother, Jaidee, behind him, makes my heart skip a beat. She's a beautiful woman, with Steph's high cheekbones and full, perfectly shaped lips. Both Tony and Stephanie inherited the color and shape of her eyes. But the piercing look that creeps inside you, that's something reminiscent of her daughter alone.

"Who are you?" Chris rasps at my dad. "Take your hands off my son!" He stomps down the porch steps, his wife following him.

"I'll put my hands on your son when he puts his hands on my daughter!" Dad pushes Tony away with a disgusted look. Chris pulls Tony to him. Tony shakes him off quickly and walks over to his mother. Hurt flickers across Chris's face for a second, but he quickly smooths it over and becomes stern once more.

"Your daughter?" Jaidee's eyes bore into me. I instinctively duck my head. "Who is she? What's she doing here?"

"I," The scathing replies I want to make trip over my tongue. I can still feel the woman's stare burning me, branding me like a tattoo, even without looking at her.

Ava speaks up. "Manee's your daughter's best friend. It's surprising you don't know that." She's returned to being severe as she faces down her former employers.

Jaidee squints at her. "Ava, is that you? You look different." Her tone carries an unmistakable note of disgust.

Ava sighs. "While you certainly haven't changed at all."

"Wait. *Manee.*" Chris's eyes narrow. "Wasn't she the one who was there when Stephanie jumped? The one who egged her on?"

Those words slice into me, so much so that it wouldn't have surprised me if my stomach opened and spilled guts all over the ground. But I won't let him see that. I have to hold on. I hold on so hard I'm in danger of breaking the phone I'm clutching in half. I begin punching buttons with fierce jabs.

"How *dare* you!" Dad erupts, but Ava cuts him off. "Manee, don't we have something for them to listen to?"

"Yeah. We do." I press play:

"I mean, yeah, she struggled, but obviously I can take a little girl. Sometimes I had to tie her up though. That was an ordeal.*"*

"And how long would you do this? How many times?"

"A few times. And I mean, my parents would come home eventually and let her out."

"*They* knew *you were doing this? They didn't try to stop you?*"

"*Of course not! They know she's dangerous! They used to do stuff way harsher than that to keep her in line. As long as no one finds out, they don't care.*"

I stop the recording there.

The blood has drained from Jaidee's face. Chris is wincing.

"I think it's pretty clear who drove her to jump," I say, looking directly at them. Suddenly, Jaidee's gaze isn't so intimidating.

"You let your son get away with that?" Sparks shoot from my father's eyes.

"We didn't really know," Chris mutters unconvincingly.

"Funny, because it really sounds like you did," Mai snaps.

"No, we just thought, we thought she'd just had an episode and Tony was restraining her for her own safety and the safety of others." Chris's voice wobbles. "Our daughter can be delusional and violent, you see. There have been incidents."

My stomach churns. I know they must be talking about that boy who fell down the stairs. Is Tony right? Do they *really* think Stephanie killed him?

Jaidee nods fervently. "I mean, she's got some sort of psychosis."

That's it. I can't stand it anymore. "Stephanie isn't violent. And those aren't delusions!" Everyone turns and stares at me, and suddenly it's as if the inside of my mouth and throat is covered in crusty dried glue. I force the words out anyway. "I know they're not."

"Manee?" Dad asks. "What are you talking about?"

My bones have turned to water and I'm nothing more than a weak and wobbly sack of flesh. As I open my mouth, I feel a second away from collapsing into a puddle. I can't shake the fear that once I say it, Dad will put me back in an institution. And that despite all we've been through together the past few days, Mai might let him. But right now they're here, by my side. They backed me up, helped me, comforted me. I trusted Emma and Jackson. It's time to trust them too.

Besides, the institution wasn't really *that* bad aside from the touching thing. They did help me with my anxiety stuff. The prison Stephanie was trapped in was so much worse and she still tried to help me. So I can risk this for her. I take a labored breath through chattering teeth.

"Stephanie said she saw people's future deaths right? Well, it's not just her. I see them too and I have since before I met her. I couldn't deal with it before. Dad even had to send me to a hospital. But Steph helped me start to understand it." I take another breath. "I know what she and I see is real. Stephanie's not some monster and she's fine the way she is."

There's a long silence. I squeeze my eyes shut, bracing myself for whatever's coming.

I did it, Stephanie. I did it for you.

"Well, you heard my daughter," Dad's voice finally cuts through the darkness. "If she vouches for Stephanie, I support her too."

My eyes fly open. My father's staring down the Pierces, his arms crossed. Mai's nodding along with him.

Stephanie's mother lets out a shrieking laugh as Chris gapes at them. "You *believe* that? What kind of parent are you?"

"I don't think the authorities would have any problem with my parenting!" Dad snaps. "*You*, on the other hand!"

"Between my testimony and that recording, I think we could get child services over here for an investigation pretty easily," Ava finishes for him.

The Pierces cringe.

"What do you want?" Jaidee spits.

Dad draws himself up, his chest puffed out. "I want Stephanie to live with us when she wakes up. You are to have nothing to do with her. In fact, we can go through the legal channels and emancipate her from you. She'll be part of our family."

My heart does a somersault. I gaze up at Dad, unable to believe what I'm hearing.

Jaidee draws her eyebrows together. "That's it? That's all you want?"

"Yes."

The Pierces exchange an inscrutable look. "Fine then," Chris says. "If my daughter ever wakes up, she's yours. You can be nutty together. Are we *done* here?"

"I guess we are. I'll be holding you to that." Dad jerks his head at me and Mai, indicating we should go.

A sudden shiver runs up my spine though, cutting through my shock and euphoria. I glance at Tony and realize he's been staring at me this whole time. And the look on his face tells me emphatically, "*No. We're not done.*"

The car ride down the hill is completely silent. Dad is fuming. I'm having a hard time making myself even believe what just happened. Ava invites us into her house to talk, and Dad gives a short thanks. We all sit around the coffee table, except Dad, who paces around Ava's living room. I keep trying to form words but it's difficult. Dad's clearly having the same issue.

We finally both burst into speech at the same time.

"That was *incredibly* reckless, you should have *trusted* me to take care of it!"

"Did you really mean it, Dad?"

Dad stops his pacing, an eyebrow arched.

"Mean what?"

"All of it!" I rasp. My mouth is still desert-dry. "Stephanie living with us! Believing me about my visions!" I half-expect Dad to respond, "Oh no, I take it all back." But instead, he crosses his arms and frowns at me.

"I told you I was going to do something about Stephanie, didn't I? This was always the plan. I just wanted to work everything out before I told you." With a groan, he takes off his glasses. "And now I realize that was a bad decision. But of course I wasn't going to leave her in that house after what Mai told me. Besides, she practically lives with us already."

I gape at him. Once again, the words just won't come.

"And about your visions," he begins cleaning his glasses with his shirt agitatedly. "I don't know, honestly. Sometimes I think back to how I felt odd that one time you touched me." He stops his cleaning and looks at us with tired eyes. "Do you remember, back when you were eleven and I passed the salt? I saw a flash of something. Felt something. It was so strange."

"That happened to me too!" Mai says, nodding.

"It seems to have happened to all of us," Ava says with the barest shadow of a smile.

"Wait, what? When did she touch you?" Mai asks her.

Dad clears his throat loudly and Mai falls silent. "In the end, it doesn't matter what I believe. You believe it, and that's fine. It was because you were hurting yourself I sent you to that hospital. If you're not doing that, there's no problem."

He slides his glasses back on at the end of the statement, as if to punctuate it.

I can't really feel my body right now. Tears form in my eyes, but not the kind I'm used to. Happy tears. "This is a dream come true."

"There are conditions, though," Dad says, holding up a finger. "One, you need to stop running off on secret missions to pick fights with older boys."

"That's like half my social calendar, though."

"Manee."

"Sorry. I'm kind of in shock."

"Manee, when you get hurt, it hurts the people who love you too, don't you understand that?"

I bow my head, shame filling me. He's right. I should know that better than anyone.

"Please don't blame Manee for this, Mr. Srikwan," Ava says glumly. "It was my fault for agreeing to it. I should have been more responsible. I just really thought Tony wouldn't get violent with *me* there."

His stern face crumbles at Ava's devastated expression. "Oh no, I don't blame you, please don't be upset, I understand." Mai and I exchange smirks. Dad's soft heart will always be his downfall.

He finally manages to collect himself and attempts to look strict again. It's not very convincing, but I give him an "A" for effort. "Second, I want you to see a therapist again. I want Stephanie to try it too. You two can look around until you find someone you feel comfortable with, but you've both been through so much, and I think it would help."

"Yeah, that's fair," I mutter. "Steph really needs people besides me to talk to. Friends too. It helps to have a life outside of each other."

"Taking my advice!" Mai pats me on the shoulder.

"Three. Even though you and Stephanie will be living in the same house, I will allow no," my father clears his throat, "canoodling."

There's an awkward pause. Then both Mai and I burst into laughter. Even Ava smiles.

"*Canoodling*? Seriously?" Mai snorts.

"Don't worry, Dad," I gasp through my guffaws. "I know me and Stephanie have a lot of junk to work out. I think it'll be a good long while before we can even *consider* stuff like dating."

"Well, good," Dad huffs. "That's really all I wanted to say."

I'm so overwhelmed, so stuffed full of surprise and joy and love that I think I might burst. With a truly heroic effort, I stand up on my wobbly legs and throw myself into my father's arms, hugging him as hard as I can.

I feel Dad tense up in surprise. I'm shaking with suppressed sobs.

"What's wrong?" He says in an alarmed voice.

"Nothing," I tell him, my words muffled in his chest. "Just, wow, I love you." I look over at Mai. "I love both of you so much."

My sister gets up and joins the hug. "We love you too."

Ava stands watching us, a genuine smile still firmly in place, though it holds a hint of sadness. "C'mon, you too," I tell her.

"Oh no, I couldn't."

"Ava, I would have been nowhere without you. Don't you get it? We did it. The future is on its way." I can barely speak through my sobs.

Ava's eyes well up. She steps forward and I eagerly pull her into the group.

We all sink into each other.

Chapter Thirty

THE FOLLOWING MORNING, Dad shows me a stack of forms he got a couple days back. They're needed to begin the process of becoming Stephanie's legal guardian. He tells me that, despite the fact that Stephanie's family, and hopefully Stephanie herself, will be consenting, we'll still have to go to a hearing. "I'm sure the judge will approve, though," Dad assures us.

"It leaves a bad taste in my mouth that they'll get away with what they did to Stephanie, though," Mai harrumphs as we crowd around the dining room table to look at the papers. "Maybe we should fill out *this* form."

I've been eyeing the form about "intolerable living conditions" for the child in question, as well.

"The most important thing is getting Stephanie out of their custody as quickly as possible. Taking her from her parents by force will take longer. Even with Manee's recording and our testimonies, the police would probably have to do an investigation to confirm everything, which would take a while and even go wrong. So it's best to just play nice and have the Pierces give her up willingly for now. Once we have Stephanie officially out of there, we'll be safe to go after them."

I sigh and lean back in my chair. "Yeah, I know." Suddenly a thought occurs. "Hey, since we're all being civil with each other for now, can we get Stephanie's parents to authorize us as visitors for her at the hospital and like, put us down as contacts so we can get reports on how she's doing and stuff?"

Dad smiles. "That's a great idea. I'll make it happen as quickly as I can."

A gentle warmth fills me. I get up and hug Dad. It's not quite as momentous as the last one, but still something we both aren't used to.

I'm going to have to do something for both him and Mai. Ava too. But what? Throw a party? Bake a cake? Nothing's big enough to repay them. I think about it well into the night. It's nice to have something to think about that's warm and fuzzy, for once. Still, every so often, grim thoughts intrude. What if it's all for nothing? What if Stephanie never wakes up?

I push those thoughts down as best I can, but the fear's still there, always lurking. Stephanie *has* to wake up. There's so much waiting for her now. When we go see her in the hospital, I'll tell her that. I'll tell her everything, tell her she has a whole new life to look forward to. I'll visit again and again, as long as it takes.

THE NEXT COUPLE of days, both my father and I work feverishly, Dad on getting the Pierces to authorize the hospital stuff and me on planning the party.

I sneakily construct a guest list of my father and sister's closest friends and most admired people. I'm determined that they all come. I end up telling Ava about the whole thing when I visit her and try to get all of her preferences. Ava seems as excited about it as she's capable of, which is admittedly not very much. The combined forces of Dad, Mai, and me finally got her to seek professional help, so I'm hoping by the time the party rolls around, she'll be feeling at least a little better.

Finally, the day comes. Dad says that we just have to go to the hospital and sign a few forms to visit Stephanie. So Friday afternoon, as soon as Mai gets home from school, we drive over.

The time it takes to arrange everything and sign the forms feels like an eternity. I can't sit still in the lobby, so I stand by the reception desk and bounce impatiently on the balls of my feet.

"Why don't you go on up there?" the receptionist says kindly.

I blink. "Really? You'd let me?"

"Sure. Your father should be done in a minute." She nods at where he's sitting in the lobby, rifling through the papers.

"Great!" I bolt over to Dad. "The receptionist says I can go up early!"

Dad smiles. "Go ahead then. We'll catch up."

Mai flashes me a thumbs-up without looking up from the form she's checking for mistakes.

I head out of the lobby as fast as politeness allows, only stopping to confirm the room number with the receptionist and thank her.

"Just don't tell anyone. Oh, I should mention, there's a young man up there right now, so make sure to ask if he'll step outside. It's best for it to be one person at a time."

"Of course, thanks," I say, barely listening.

It isn't until I'm standing in front of the elevators that the receptionist's words really register. A young man? Visiting Stephanie? But the only person that can be is...

Tony.

I freeze, a heavy dread descending upon me. Why would Tony ever visit her?

His murderous eyes from a few nights ago are suddenly all I can see.

Chapter Thirty-one

I GLANCE FRANTICALLY at the little numbers at the top of the elevators. They're still both stuck on the tenth floor. I can't wait for them. I run for the stairs.

Everything else fades away. There's only the pounding of my feet, each step reverberating through my whole body as I urge myself to go faster, faster, faster. I barely feel it when I crash into someone blocking my way. I just shoulder my way through them. I reach the stairwell and leap up it three steps at a time, practically bouncing on air.

I know I must be close. Even though I've only been here once before, the path is clear in my mind. I burst onto the next floor and skid to a staggering stop in front of the room. The door's closed and there's no light coming out under the crack. I throw the door open, hoping against hope that I'm wrong, that all I'll find inside is Stephanie sleeping peacefully in a dark room.

Stephanie isn't sleeping peacefully. Tony is hunched over her bed, his hands around her throat as her body jerks wildly beneath him.

I don't stop to think. I lunge for Tony with all my might. I hit him in the side, smashing into his shoulder. We both fall to the floor in a tangle of limbs.

I hit my head on the bed and then the floor as we fall. Pain explodes and my vision goes blotchy. Something wet slides down my forehead. In the midst of it all, rough hands grab me. I squint at the big blur shaped like Tony.

"I was hoping you'd show up," he says. "Glad I timed it right."

"Wh-what?" I mumble. Goddammit, everything's fuzzy. I need to find my hands and feet, I need to push him away.

But it's too late. Tony's on top of me. I struggle to dislodge him, but he's positioned himself well. He pins my left arm down with his hand and traps my right arm under his knee. My chest threatens to cave in from his weight.

His face is clearer now. He's different from before. His eyes are just dead. Dead and black and cold. I saw this before with Stephanie. It's the look of someone with nothing to lose. He's capable of anything right now.

I don't know what to do. Everything hurts. I croak the only

thing I can think of. "Why are you doing this?"

He chuckles humorlessly. "Why? You're the one who tried to kill me first! I felt it when you hit me, you know. The demon inside you. I know you're just like her." His voice turns into a rasp. "You infected me. I have no choice. If I don't do something, it will never end. The deaths will never end."

I grunt. I want to shout that he's wrong, but I can't. It's true. I choked him and pushed him over the edge. There wasn't even a possibility of him turning into a killer before that day I attacked him; if there had been, Stephanie would have seen it in his eyes. I really did infect him. I really do spread death. And it's never going to stop.

"I'm going to end it. I'm going to set myself free of both of you."

Set free. Those words again. *The future is yours to make.*

My chest burns. What am I thinking? Haven't I learned *anything*?

I spit in Tony's face. It doesn't hit him in the eye like I hoped; instead, it just sort of lands on his cheek and drips right back onto me.

I don't care. "I infected you?" I snarl. "What a pathetic fucking excuse. I'm not taking the blame for your bullshit. You say we're demons spreading death? That's what you'll be if you kill me and Stephanie. And it won't be anyone's fault but your own!"

His mouth twists into a snarl and he slams a fist into my face. It's much harder than when he punched me before. It's agony, like my face is splintering apart. A tooth comes loose.

I spit out the blood and scream, hard and loud as I can.

Tony thrusts down his forearm, and my scream becomes a strangled squeak as he crushes my throat.

But as he shifts his weight to do it, I get my hand free.

I go for his face, aiming to gouge at his eyes. But the haze of pain bearing down on me makes me slow, and Tony grabs my wrist before I can get there. I gouge the side of his face as he forces my hand back down, carving out long red gashes. But he doesn't even wince. He merely snorts at my futile gesture and presses his arm down even harder.

I jerk around desperately, but my brain is already suffocating along with my body. Black spots pop in my vision. The pressure in my skull is too much, too much. I can't even feel the pain from my bruised throat and broken head anymore, it's all draining away.

My head fills with gray static. I try desperately to hold onto consciousness, focusing on the raw red grin of the man who's choking the life out of me. But I'm slipping. The only thought I can muster through the blank buzzing in my head is that there's nothing I can do. Tony is going to win.

I feel people watching me now. All the people whose deaths I've seen, they're now watching mine, silently. Witnessing my final moments so I don't have to die alone.

I try to move, even just a little, and Tony groans in frustration. "Would you quit fighting it? I have to do this! This is your punishment! So just accept it already!"

I force myself to look directly into his wild, frantic eyes. Even though it's like I'm tearing apart my vocal cords, I croak out a barely audible scratchy rasp.

"No...Tony...you're...in control. You can still stop...like I stopped with you."

A crease appears between Tony's eyebrows. He's listening. I struggle to speak some more.

The words scrape my throat raw, but I make them come out. "Ava...wouldn't want you to...do this...! You...c-can...choose to stop...you have...a choice!"

Something flickers behind Tony's eyes. His face twitches.

He inhales, and shudders.

"No," he says, his voice trembling slightly. "I really don't."

He leans in close to me, so close I feel his hot breath on my face. "Because you took her from me. You took everything from me. So this is all I have left."

He presses his arm down with every ounce of his might.

The gray static turns to solid white. It blocks out Tony entirely.

My eyes finally close.

Now there's nothing but blackness and those little lights that burst behind my eyelids like stars. Ah, how nice. I'll die looking at the stars. That's sort of okay. Everything's so warm and light. It's easy to let go. Accept it.

Accept that Tony will kill me, and then Stephanie.

No. *No.* I thrash against the soft blanket of warmth and light that's come to smother me.

No! *Please.* My thoughts are so slippery now.

Please!

There has to be something.

There has to be.

Somewhere off in the distance, there's a faint crash.

The pressure on my throat lifts and the white light leaks out of my brain. Slowly, the warm dreaminess drains away and is replaced with pain. So much pain. Pain like a flying brick smashing into my skull. My eyes snap open just as another crash reverberates through the room.

What I see is so incredible I wonder if I'm hallucinating. Stephanie stands over me and hits Tony on the head with an IV pole, over and over.

Stephanie's stick-thin legs wobble with each blow, the leg with the cast especially unsteady. The bed she leans on barely supports her. Her hospital gown is half-falling off and her IV is half-pulled out of her arm, but none of it seems to matter to her. She beats her brother mercilessly, her flesh drawn tight over her face and her mouth stretched in a snarl.

Blood flies from Tony's head. He screams, but Stephanie screams even louder. She brings down the IV pole so hard the metal shudders in her hands. He crumples.

Stephanie stands there, panting and swaying, as a doctor and nurse rush in, alerted by her roars. Stephanie drops the pole. Her bad leg folds under her and she falls.

With strength I didn't know I still had, I lean forward and catch her before she hits the floor. I hug her close, fearing that she will melt away and vanish at any second.

"Are you real?" I croak.

"Mmmmm," Stephanie groans weakly. "I hate my brother."

"But how?" I thought I ran out of tears, but more stream down my face. My chest aches again, but for entirely different reasons now. My heart is too big for my body.

"Woke up this morning," Stephanie says with a weak smile. "Wasn't able to move or let anyone know...but when I heard you...I somehow..."

"Thank you," I squeeze Stephanie tighter. She's soft and warm and alive.

The doctor and nurse are trying to question us but it's background noise. Stephanie's the only thing that matters.

"I love you so much, Stephanie." I almost can't say it through the lump in my throat.

"No," Stephanie croaks. "You don't have to...I don't deserve..." She winces. "I'm sorry. I'm so..."

Stephanie shudders with sobs. I stroke her face tenderly, feeling her sunken cheeks, her dry skin. She's so bony and fragile. But it's only temporary; she'll be able to eat again soon enough.

Tears mix with the blood on my face. I hurt all over, I'm so dizzy, but it's all nothing compared to how good it is to hold Stephanie in my arms.

"Shhhh," I say as Steph buries her face in my chest, soaking it in record time. "It's okay. I get it now. Stephanie, we're gonna be okay." I kiss Stephanie on the forehead, which not only hurts my split lips but gets blood all over Stephanie's face. But Steph doesn't seem to mind. "I'll always stay with you."

"Promise?" Stephanie's voice is almost a whisper. Her head drops to the side and her eyes flutter closed.

"I promise," I tell her, rubbing Stephanie's back in slow circular motions as she loses consciousness. I lean back against the wall and allow myself a smile at last. "I'm never letting you go again."

Epilogue

Three Years Later

I'M NOT GOING to survive this.

"C'mon, would you hurry up?" Stephanie sighs, tapping her foot impatiently.

"Don't push me!" I shoot back at her grumpily. "I'm preparing myself, okay?"

"Please," Steph scoffs. "You invited me on this trip because you needed me to push you. If you wanted to be babied, you would have invited Emma or Jackson."

"I just don't know if I'm ready to do this today. Maybe we should come back tomorrow."

"Nuh-uh." Stephanie shakes her head, slamming her hand on their car hood. "I've got the debate thing in two days. They're counting on me. We can't afford to put this off another day."

"You're so selfish," I grumble.

"I'm selfish? I practically camp out at your art showings! You could at least support me with my stuff."

"I do, I do," I mutter, chewing on my lip. "I'm just really nervous right now, okay? I can't help it. I'm—I'm scared."

I'm thrown off balance when Stephanie pulls me close and kisses me gently.

I relax into the kiss, nerves temporarily forgotten. I've been going out with Stephanie for three months now, but I still get butterflies in my stomach every single time we lock lips. You'd think after living with her for three years, going to therapy with her, after all the messy conversations between us, I'd be less easily dazzled, but no. All it takes is a touch and I'm gone.

My panic returns as soon as Stephanie detaches herself. I look down at my feet, but she cups my chin and forces me to look up into her eyes.

"You can do this, Manee. I know you can," she says. "You're the strongest person I know."

"I don't feel strong right now."

"Come on, look at all we've accomplished in the last year. We got your dad to let us share a room. We helped get Ava a job. We've even successfully raised Ace from an annoying puppy to a fine specimen of doghood. We can do anything."

"What if she turns me away? What if she hates me?" My

voice is thin and fragile.

"Then she's an idiot," Stephanie says firmly. "And I will personally punch her in the face for you."

"What if I can't help myself and start crying? Or yelling at her?"

"You should let her know how you feel. She deserves it."

I take a deep breath. "You really think I can do this?"

Stephanie laughs. "Remember how the power of your love woke me from a coma that one time?"

"Yeah, that wasn't what happened at all."

"Shush. Don't underestimate the power of love, baby. We've got it on our side, and it's all we need."

"Jesus." I roll my eyes. "Okay, I'm going to go in there just so I don't have to listen to you anymore."

"My plan worked, then," Stephanie says with a massive grin.

I try to find the courage to turn away from Stephanie but I can't quite do it.

"You'll stay with me, right?" I near-whisper, voice cracking.

"Till death do us part."

I groan.

And finally, after another deep breath, I face my mother's home directly. It's just a regular house, but to me it feels like a looming abyss that holds my doom in its murky depths.

I hold out my hand. Stephanie takes it and squeezes it reassuringly.

Together, we face the future.

About the Author

Caitlin Donovan is a writer, teacher, blogger, poet and, above all, a huge geek for fiction (especially fantasy). Her dream of being an author began in the third grade when she started scribbling down stories about twin detectives and murderous ghosts in stray notebooks. Her passion only grew with age. Now she has a MFA in writing from Queens University in Charlotte and she has been published in several literary journals, including *The Great Smokies Review*. She has written professionally about fantasy, sci-fi and pop culture for several online companies.

When not creating novels, Caitlin works as an online ESL teacher and does freelance writing. She currently resides in North Carolina with her trouble-making cat.

MORE REGAL CREST PUBLICATIONS

Brenda Adcock	Soiled Dove	978-1-935053-35-4
Brenda Adcock	The Sea Hawk	978-1-935053-10-1
Brenda Adcock	The Other Mrs. Champion	978-1-935053-46-0
Brenda Adcock	Picking Up the Pieces	978-1-61929-120-1
Brenda Adcock	The Game of Denial	978-1-61929-130-0
Brenda Adcock	In the Midnight Hour	978-1-61929-188-1
Brenda Adcock	Untouchable	978-1-61929-210-9
Brenda Adcock	The Heart of the Mountain	978-1-61929-330-4
Brenda Adcock	Gift of the Redeemer	978-1-61929-360-1
Brenda Adcock	Unresolved Conflicts	978-1-61929-374-8
Brenda Adcock	One Step At A Time	978-1-61929-408-0
K. Aten	The Fletcher	978-1-61929-356-4
K. Aten	Rules of the Road	978-1-61919-366-3
K. Aten	The Archer	978-1-61929-370-0
K. Aten	Waking the Dreamer	978-1-61929-382-3
K. Aten	The Sagittarius	978-1-61929-386-1
K. Aten	Running From Forever: Book One in the Blood Resonance Series	978-1-61929-398-4
K. Aten	The Sovereign of Psiere: Book One In the Mystery of the Makers series	978-1-61929-412-7
K. Aten	Burn It Down	978-1-61929-418-9
Georgia Beers	Thy Neighbor's Wife	1-932300-15-5
Georgia Beers	Turning the Page	978-1-932300-71-0
Lynnette Beers	Just Beyond the Shining River	978-1-61929-352-6
Sharon G. Clark	A Majestic Affair	978-1-61929-177-5
Tonie Chacon	Struck! A Titanic Love Story	978-1-61929-226-0
Barbara L. Clanton	Out of Left Field: Marlee's Story	978-1-935053-08-8
Barbara L. Clanton	Tools of Ignorance: Lisa's Story	978-1-935053-40-8
Barbara L. Clanton	Going, Going, Gone: Susie's Story	978-1-61929-009-9
Barbara L. Clanton	Stealing Second: Sam's Story	978-1-61929-110-2
Barbara L. Clanton	Out At Home	978-1-61929-184-3
Barbara L. Clanton	Tools of the Devil	978-1-61929-230-7
Barbara L. Clanton	Going Under	978-1-61929-390-8
Barbara L. Clanton	Stealing Hope	978-1-61929-406-6
Sky Croft	Amazonia	978-1-61929-067-9
Sky Croft	Amazonia: An Impossible Choice	978-1-61929-179-9
Sky Croft	Mountain Rescue: The Ascent	978-1-61929-099-0
Sky Croft	Mountain Rescue: On the Edge	978-1-61929-205-5
Mildred Gail Digby	Phoenix	978-1-61929-394-6
Mildred Gail Digby	Perfect Match: Book One	978-1-61929-414-4
Mildred Gail Digby	Perfect Match: Book Two	978-1-61929-416-5
Cronin and Foster	Blue Collar Lesbian Erotica	978-1-935053-01-9
Cronin and Foster	Women in Uniform	978-1-935053-31-6
Cronin and Foster	Women in Sports	978-1-61929-278-9
Anna Furtado	The Heart's Desire	978-1-935053-81-1
Anna Furtado	The Heart's Strength	978-1-935053-82-8
Anna Furtado	The Heart's Longing	978-1-935053-83-5

Anna Furtado	Tremble and Burn	978-1-61929-354-0
Melissa Good	Eye of the Storm	1-932300-13-9
Melissa Good	Hurricane Watch	978-1-935053-00-2
Melissa Good	Moving Target	978-1-61929-150-8
Melissa Good	Red Sky At Morning	978-1-932300-80-2
Melissa Good	Storm Surge: Book One	978-1-935053-28-6
Melissa Good	Storm Surge: Book Two	978-1-935053-39-2
Melissa Good	Stormy Waters	978-1-61929-082-2
Melissa Good	Thicker Than Water	1-932300-24-4
Melissa Good	Terrors of the High Seas	1-932300-45-7
Melissa Good	Tropical Storm	978-1-932300-60-4
Melissa Good	Tropical Convergence	978-1-935053-18-7
Melissa Good	Winds of Change Book One	978-1-61929-194-2
Melissa Good	Winds of Change Book Two	978-1-61929-232-1
Melissa Good	Southern Stars	978-1-61929-348-9
Jeanine Hoffman	Lights & Sirens	978-1-61929-115-7
Jeanine Hoffman	Strength in Numbers	978-1-61929-109-6
Jeanine Hoffman	Back Swing	978-1-61929-137-9
K. E. Lane	And, Playing the Role of Herself	978-1-932300-72-7
Kate McLachlan	Christmas Crush	978-1-61929-195-9
Kate McLachlan	Hearts, Dead and Alive	978-1-61929-017-4
Kate McLachlan	Murder and the Hurdy Gurdy Girl	978-1-61929-125-6
Kate McLachlan	Rescue At Inspiration Point	978-1-61929-005-1
Kate McLachlan	Return Of An Impetuous Pilot	978-1-61929-152-2
Kate McLachlan	Rip Van Dyke	978-1-935053-29-3
Kate McLachlan	Ten Little Lesbians	978-1-61929-236-9
Kate McLachlan	Alias Mrs. Jones	978-1-61929-282-6
Lynne Norris	One Promise	978-1-932300-92-5
Lynne Norris	Sanctuary	978-1-61929-248-2
Lynne Norris	The Light of Day	978-1-61929-338-0
Schramm and Dunne	Love Is In the Air	978-1-61929-362-8
Rae Theodore	Leaving Normal: Adventures in Gender	
		978-1-61929-320-5
Rae Theodore	My Mother Says Drums Are for Boys: True	
	Stories for Gender Rebels	978-1-61929-378-6
Barbara Valletto	Pulse Points	978-1-61929-254-3
Barbara Valletto	Everlong	978-1-61929-266-6
Barbara Valletto	Limbo	978-1-61929-358-8
Barbara Valletto	Diver Blues	978-1-61929-384-7
Lisa Young	Out and Proud	978-1-61929-392-2

Be sure to check out our other imprints,
Blue Beacon Books, Carnelian Books, Mystic Books, Quest Books,
Silver Dragon Books, Troubadour Books, and Young Adult Books.

VISIT US ONLINE AT
www.regalcrest.biz

At the Regal Crest Website You'll Find:

~ The latest news about forthcoming titles and new releases

~ Our complete backlist of romance, mystery, thriller and adventure titles

~ Information about your favorite authors

Regal Crest print titles are available from all progressive booksellers including numerous sources online. Our distributors are Bella Distribution and Ingram.